D0429137

Nadya Skylung

and the

Masked Kidnapper

ALSO BY JEFF SEYMOUR

Nadya Skylung and the Cloudship Rescue

NADYA SKYLUNG
and the
MASKED KIDNAPPER

JEFF SEYMOUR

Illustrated by BRETT HELQUIST

putnam

G. P. Putnam's Sons

G. P. PUTNAM'S SONS
an imprint of Penguin Random House LLC, New York

Text copyright © 2019 by Jeff Seymour. Illustrations copyright © 2019 by Brett Helquist.
Penguin supports copyright. Copyright fuels creativity, encourages diverse voices,
promotes free speech, and creates a vibrant culture. Thank you for buying an authorized edition of
this book and for complying with copyright laws by not reproducing, scanning,
or distributing any part of it in any form without permission. You are supporting writers and
allowing Penguin to continue to publish books for every reader.

G. P. Putnam's Sons is a registered trademark of Penguin Random House LLC.
Visit us online at penguinrandomhouse.com

Library of Congress Cataloging-in-Publication Data
Names: Seymour, Jeff (Fantasy fiction writer), author. | Helquist, Brett, illustrator.
Title: Nadya Skylung and the masked kidnapper / Jeff Seymour; illustrated by Brett Helquist.
Description: New York, NY: G. P. Putnam's Sons, [2019]
Summary: "A gang leader called Silvermask is kidnapping skylung and cloudling children in the port of
Far Agondy, and it is up to Nadya and her friends to rescue the missing kids and put a stop to Silvermask
once and for all"—Provided by publisher.
Identifiers: LCCN 2018025890 | ISBN 9781524738686 (hardcover) | ISBN 9781524738693 (ebook)
Subjects: | CYAC: Adventure and adventurers—Fiction. | Airships—Fiction. | Kidnapping—Fiction. |
Gangs—Fiction. | Orphans—Fiction. | Science fiction.
Classification: LCC PZ7.1.S468 Nam 2019 | DDC [Fic]—dc23
LC record available at https://lccn.loc.gov/2018025890

Printed in the United States of America.
ISBN 9781524738686
1 3 5 7 9 10 8 6 4 2

Design by Marikka Tamura.
Text set in Columbus MT Std.
This is a work of fiction. Names, characters, places, and incidents either are the product of
the author's imagination or are used fictitiously, and any resemblance to actual persons,
living or dead, businesses, companies, events, or locales is entirely coincidental.

To Cass and Oren, the rock and the sunshine

Nadya Skylung
and the
Masked Kidnapper

CHAPTER I

IN WHICH NADYA GOES FISHING, AND CATCHES MORE THAN SHE BARGAINED FOR.

"Ready, Nadya?"

My stomach rolls, and I stare at the gently swelling waves of the turquoise ocean. I'm clipped into the back seat of the Flightwing, a pedal-powered flying machine that can hover or rise and fall like a hummingbird, baking in the hot sun with the wind whistling in my ears. In front of me, Tam Ban, the kid who keeps the cloudship *Orion* fixed up, is squeezed next to Pepper Pott, our fireminder.

And we're fishing in dangerous waters.

My name's Nadya Skylung, and I keep the *Orion* afloat— pretty much all by myself now. I tend the garden that keeps her cloud balloon inflated, and without the balloon, the ship wouldn't fly.

"Everything okay back there?" Pep asks while she works the Flightwing's elevation pedals. What she really means is *Are you okay back there?* I don't like the Flightwing much anymore.

1

I got hurt on it last month, and riding in it makes me nervous. But our newest crew member, Aaron, asked me to come fishing with the others today. He had a bad feeling about the water and wanted me to make sure they'd be all right.

"Yeah," I say, balancing a silver cage on my lap. "Just getting the bait ready." I smear honey on some stale crackers between the bars. The water seems fine to me—shining in the sunlight, moving gently. The day's as gorgeous as a postcard portrait, and the *Orion*'s about four hundred feet above us, hanging in the sky like an eagle watching her chicks learn to fly.

Pep turns around. A cloud of fire-orange curls floats around her head, sailing every which way in the downdraft from the Flightwing's main propeller. Her face, which is usually pretty pale, is a little sunburned from spending too much time outside yesterday, just like mine. Next to her, Tam frowns at the Flightwing's controls. He's sunburned too, although you can't really see it on him because his skin's darker than ours. Both Pepper and Tam have on big tinted goggles to keep them from getting blinded by the sun and crashing us into the water or the *Orion* or something. I wish I had a pair, but there's only two of them on the ship.

The wind shoves the Flightwing around, and my mind races like a frightened rabbit, wondering if Tam's about to lose control or if a strut will snap and dump me into the ocean. I used to be able to handle a little wind, no problem, but I get scared easy these days. I hate it. I'd give anything to get my nerve back.

Pep holds the cage steady while I finish the bait, which I appreciate. Last month we had a run-in with some real nasty pirates, and I got shot in the shoulder and the leg. My shoulder's healing up okay, but it still clicks when I rotate it, and it's sore as heck, so working with it's hard.

My leg's another story. After I got shot, Nic had to cut off my left leg below the knee to keep an infection in my calf wound from spreading upward. Sometimes I wish he hadn't and I'd taken my chances with the infection. Sometimes I think my life's ruined, and I feel like locking my door and never going outside again. But most days I'm glad he did what he did, because if the infection had gotten worse I might've died. I can flex my knee and move around pretty good now, and I don't even have a bandage anymore.

I'm getting used to my stump, too, which Nic calls my residual limb and I call the Mighty Lady. It's new and strange, but nobody on the crew has anything like it, and I like my scar, which kinda looks like a smile if I flex my muscles a certain way and kinda looks like a frown if I flex them the other.

"Any day now, Nadya!" Tam shouts. The Flightwing bounces. Pep faces forward and bites her lip, concentrating. The wind's getting strong. It must be hard keeping us steady.

Gingerly, I slide across the seats and push the bait cage to the edge of the Flightwing. The honey crackers hang on hooks inside it, and there's a one-way gate at the front so fish can swim in and get the bait but can't swim out again. Tam and Pepper built it to help us catch fish for the baby leviathan

3

we're delivering, using spare parts for the engines and some kitchen utensils.

The Flightwing bobs and sways as I move. Partly that's the breeze, but partly it's my fault. The Flightwing's just two aluminum skids on legs welded to an aluminum rowboat with a tail and a couple rotors and seats. It's really lightweight, which helps it fly, but it's also easy to push around.

My shoulder clicks, but I manage to toss the cage overboard and get clear of the rope attached to it. The cage falls for a couple seconds, its rope unspooling, then splashes into the waves. I let it sink to the depth where the schoolers we're fishing for like to swim, then use a climbing device Tam clipped to the side of the Flightwing to brake the rope and tie it off.

After that we sit and wait. The Flightwing's main rotor is so loud we can't talk much, so I lean back and check on the *Orion*. Our first mate, Tall Thom, is at her wheel. He's a fireminder like Pep. Tian Li Chang, our starwinder and navigator, stands next to him, looking down at us. Salyeh Abande—our polymath—and Captain Nic must be in the cabin, figuring out how we're going to recover from our disaster with the pirates. Aaron's moving carefully on the catwalks outside our cloud balloon, checking on the plants there. They've been churning out a lot of crops, but we've eaten almost all the other food, so there probably won't be enough trade goods to sell to make up our losses on this trip.

The Mighty Lady barks like somebody stabbed her with a skewer, and I look down at where my calf's missing and remind myself it's gone, then rub the muscles in my residual limb until the pain goes away. Every once in a while I get these ghost pains, like my nerves think it's important to remind me that my leg got hurt.

I sigh and slump in my seat. I'm starting to sweat, and my sunburn's probably getting worse by the minute. I want to get back to the *Orion,* where it's cool and shady, so I lean over and check the cage, trying to see whether we've hooked any schoolers yet. Sure enough, there's a big cloud of silvery fish clustered around the spot where the rope disappears into the water. Won't be long now before we have enough fish to get into port.

The waves churn. The sun glints off them. It's so bright it makes the water beneath the fish look dark and shadowy, like a cloud's passing overhead.

My guts flutter, and I frown and squint, then look up. No cloud. I look back down, and the shadowy spot gets bigger. I remember Aaron's bad feeling, and then I get an icy chill down the back of my neck and feel like I've been kicked in the stomach.

"Pep!" I shriek. "Take us up! Get higher!"

"What?" she shouts back. She turns around, and the Flight-wing swings to the side and drops a few feet *lower* as she gets distracted from pedaling.

"Up!" I shout, pointing. "We need to go *up*!"

"How come?" Tam yells. "Are the fish not—"

I unclip my safety harness and throw myself across the bar between our seats. I don't have room to nudge Pep out of

5

the way, so I dive onto her lap and grab the pedals with my hands. "Something's coming!"

Pep jerks her feet away from the pedals, and I crank with my hands as fast as I can. The Flightwing's main rotor roars louder, and we start to rise. My shoulder grinds and hurts, but I ignore it. I'm staring straight down at the shadowy spot, and it's getting bigger.

"Nadya, I can do it!" Pep shouts. She elbows me in the ribs. "I get it! Let me do it!"

But I'm not willing to stop pedaling to let Pepper take over. The shadow gets as big as the *Orion*, then even bigger, and then the sea opens up. All the little silvery fish, plus enough water to flood a whole neighborhood, get sucked down with an enormous *pop*. Glistening teeth the size of people emerge from the water, and I realize I'm staring into the mouth of a full-grown, deep-sea leviathan, a sea serpent big enough to eat a ship without chewing.

Our little silver cage dangles between its jaws for a second. I crank harder, and Tam curses and pulls a lever. A bunch of machinery clunks into place next to my head, and then he starts pedaling too and the Flightwing shoots up like a cork at the bottom of a bucket of water. The cage clears the leviathan's teeth just as it gets above the waves and snaps its jaws shut with a resounding *boom*.

It keeps rising for another few feet, then twists as it starts to fall back to the ocean. Its eyes meet mine, and my heart tumbles.

They're completely black, flecked with little bits of purple, except for a few spots of gold in the corners. It looks sad and lost and lonely—an enormous, ancient creature losing a fight to something awful and shadowy, and terrified of what's going to happen when it does.

The leviathan hits the water with a crash so big it vibrates the whole Flightwing. We must be a hundred feet up now, but the spray still soaks me. I stare at the churning, angry water where the leviathan hit. Slowly, its shadow recedes as it dives.

"Wow," Tam says, still pedaling to keep us steady, wiping water out of his hair.

"Yeah. Wow," Pep echoes.

I shiver and pull myself out of the footwell where the pedals are, so Pep and I are crammed next to each other in the front seat. She scoots away. "Yeah," I say. I keep thinking about that glimpse of gold in the leviathan's eyes, and the sadness there. "Sorry about jumping over you like that."

Pep shrugs, but her smile looks like a rope that's about to snap. "It's fine," she says, but her eyes tell me, *I'm lying. Let's talk later, when Tam's not around.*

Slowly, I climb into the back seat, and Pepper takes over the pedals again. The leviathan's shadow has gone completely now, and all I see below us are the waves and the little cage, glinting silver and full of fish. My heart's still thumping, and I watch the water, wondering whether it just went deeper so it could get a bigger start on jumping toward us. "I think we caught everything we need to!" I yell over the rotors. "Ready to go home?"

"Ready!" Tam says. The Flightwing spins around to face the *Orion*, which got a little behind us as we blew in the breeze, then starts rising again.

The pivot faces me east, where I can see the coastline. In a couple days we'll reach Far Agondy, a city of shadows and silver and smoke. I heard a girl screaming there one night over the telepathic web of the Panpathia, getting kidnapped and calling for help. Nic's trying to convince me it was a dream, but I know it wasn't. She was in trouble. Something was hurting her.

The pirates we fought last month were stealing kids too, skylungs like me and cloudlings like Aaron. Maybe they were working with the people who took that girl I saw. I don't like all these kidnappings. If nobody puts a stop to them, sooner or later it'll be me or my friends getting nabbed.

We have a lot to do in Far Agondy—get the ship fixed up, tell the Cloud Navy about the pirates, deliver the baby leviathan, and more—but I want to help that girl and stop the kidnappers. And I'm going to find a way to do it, even if Nic and my fears and all the leviathans in the world try to stop me.

CHAPTER 2

IN WHICH A GAME OF BROOMBALL IS WON, AND A MYSTERY DISCOVERED.

"Nadya!"

The stretchy-band fights me, like an eel wrapped around my calf . . .

"Nadya!"

The stretchy-band stretches, like an overcooked pork chop . . .

"Come *on*, Nadya! Are you ready yet or what?"

It's the afternoon after our fishing expedition. The fish and the Flightwing are in the hold, the deck's been cleared, and I'm trying my hardest to forget about the leviathan that almost gobbled us up, because we're about to play broomball for the first time in ages. I just have to finish the Mighty Lady's exercises first. Two more knee bends, and then I pull off the stretchy-band wrapped around my calf, tug it back, and slingshot it across my cabin. "Just a sec!" I shout, and I scoot off my bed and hop across the floor to my desk, where my journal's open. I dash down a couple of my best lines so I don't forget them.

"Nadya, we'll start without you if we have to!"

I roll my eyes. If they play without me, the teams won't be even. "Okay, I'm coming!"

I shut my journal and hop to the corner of my desk, where my crutches—an old one and one Tam made after I got hurt—are leaning, waiting for me. According to Nic, I'm still supposed to be taking it easy on my leg and shoulder.

I grin. Easy, in my book, doesn't always mean what he thinks it does.

I crutch to the door and open it. Tian Li's waiting for me on the other side, her hair waving like black seaweed in the breeze. She smiles. I think she's looking forward to Far Agondy. Someday she wants to go back to the big city she's from, T'an Gaban, and change it for the better, and whenever we're in port she spends a lot of time ashore making notes about how she's gonna do it. "Ready?" she asks.

I nod and look over the deck. Salyeh and Tam have cleared away everything but the capstans—two giant winches we use sometimes when we're in port—and the ladder up to the cloud balloon in the center. Pep and Tian Li have hauled up two desk-sized goals made of spare pipes and netting and set them on opposite sides of the deck. One's right near my cabin, and the other's by the doorway to Nic's cabin all the way down the ship.

I start sweating, even though we're in the shadow of the cloud balloon and the breeze hasn't slacked off. Broomball has always been one of my favorite games, but I haven't played since I lost my leg.

The game normally has simple rules: two teams of two, with the fifth kid playing all-time offense. Every player gets a long broom with stiff bristles, and we use the brooms to bat around a heavy inflatable rubber ball the size of my head. We used to have problems losing the ball over the side, but now Tam puts up nets between the cloud balloon cables to keep that from happening. Broomball's usually a fast-paced game, with the three kids on offense trying to get around the two kids on defense to score a goal, then scrambling back on defense if they lose the ball.

But now Aaron wants to play too, so we've had to change the rules. For starters, we'll have two teams of three. That might make the deck too cramped, so Tam's drawn a semi-circle in front of each goal, and one player on each team will stay inside it as goalie, trying to keep the ball out of the net with their broom and their body. For this game, one of them'll be me. Nic said goalie oughta be easier on my leg than jostling around with the others.

The wind whistles over my shoulder, and I shiver a little. The dark thoughts I've been wrestling with since I lost my leg bubble up inside me, telling me my life's over, that I can't be who I used to be. I try to just let those thoughts float past. I'll probably like playing goalie, and someday I'll figure out how to play offense again. I'm gonna have a good time today. It doesn't matter that I can't run around anymore. Really. Not at all.

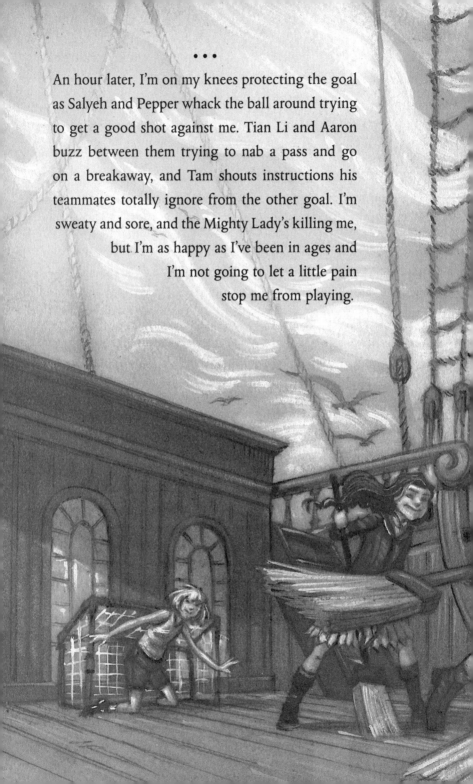

An hour later, I'm on my knees protecting the goal as Salyeh and Pepper whack the ball around trying to get a good shot against me. Tian Li and Aaron buzz between them trying to nab a pass and go on a breakaway, and Tam shouts instructions his teammates totally ignore from the other goal. I'm sweaty and sore, and the Mighty Lady's killing me, but I'm as happy as I've been in ages and I'm not going to let a little pain stop me from playing.

It took a while to get used to the new rules, but they threw everyone else for a loop too. We had to adjust on the fly. Like it was too hard to get the ball away from the other team, so we decided each person can only keep it for five seconds before passing. And nobody was scoring much, so now goalies have to stay on their knees, but don't need brooms and can use their hands. It's too hard to get a good whack at the ball with a broom from your knees.

It's a lot harder to score with both teams having a goalie all the time. Our games used to end when one team scored twenty-five points, but this time around we've decided it'll end when somebody scores five. It's all tied up right now, 4–4. Pepper got the hang of the new rules fast, and she slipped three goals past me before Tian Li, Aaron, and I figured out what to do. Since then it's been an epic comeback. Aaron scored twice, then Tian Li shot a rocket at Tam that he flubbed into the goal. After that, Pepper looked pretty mad, and she ran the ball so fast down the deck that our team stopped paying any attention to Sal. Just when we thought she was gonna let it rip, she passed it to him instead, and before I could react he slipped an easy shot into the goal behind my back. But Tam got distracted cheering, and I floated a long pass to Tian Li, who smacked it straight out of the air past him into the goal.

Now Pep and Sal are clustered right around the edge of my little chalk semicircle. Tian Li's guarding Sal as he tries to pass to Pepper, who's somewhere behind me. I can't take my eyes off him long enough to figure out where she is, because he's got a way of flicking his wrist just so and sending a shot my way when I least expect it. Tian Li's almost got the ball back when I catch a flicker of movement in the corner of my eye, and Sal loops a pass across the deck. Aaron shouts a warning, and I spin and dive blind, and *WHAM*, there's the ball all right, flying right into my face.

I catch it on the ricochet and curl it into my stomach, just to make sure it doesn't go anywhere. My nose stings, my forehead feels like it got smacked by a hammer, and I might be bleeding from my lip.

"Whoa!"

"Goshend's teeth!"

"Are you all right, Nadya?"

I open my eyes and stretch my face. It feels all rubbery and my eyes are watering, but I'm fine, and I notice two things:

First, Nic's come out of his cabin and is talking with Thom behind Tam's goal. They look pretty serious. Thom's not paying any attention to the game, which is weird because he loves watching us play, and also because I just got hurt and he seems to think it's very important that he keep us from playing too rough.

Second, Tam's left his goal to come toward me, and Pepper's right in front of me, crouching down to see if I'm all right. I've been concocting a plan for an epic dash all day, and I think now's the time to try it.

I moan theatrically. "My nose! I think it's busted! Look!"

I point to it. Tam, who's almost reached us, runs faster. Pep kneels in front of me and rummages in her pockets for a handkerchief. "Oh geez. I'm so sorry, Nadya," she says. "Here, let me—"

Quick as a fish, I tuck the ball under my arm and scramble around her, between Salyeh's legs, and straight down the deck toward Tam, who freezes. The Mighty Lady barks every time my leg hits the deck, but I keep the weight on my knees and elbows so she doesn't get bumped around too much.

"Nadya, what're you—?" Tam blubbers, and then I'm past him, and there's nothing but open deck between me and his unprotected goal.

"Nadya!" Pepper screams behind me. "That's cheating!" I hear footsteps thumping and know she and Tam are racing after me and I've only got a few seconds to score. I'm still twenty feet or so from their goal, but I roll the ball into my hand and side-arm it as hard as I can, just as Pep catches up. She dives for me with her broom, bouncing on her chin and skidding across the deck, but my shot curves out of her reach and bounces into the goal.

Tian Li and Aaron cheer, and I roll over my unhurt shoulder and come up shouting a victory whoop. Tam stares at the ball in the net like he's not sure what day it is, Salyeh laughs, Aaron jumps up and down, and Tian Li charges toward me with a grin the size of a leviathan on her face.

"That! Was! Amazing!" she shouts, and she scoops me onto her back and parades me around the deck, singing the crew's victory song, which we picked up listening to people playing spike ball on the beach in the Free City of Myrrh, where Pepper's from.

My head spins, and I have to catch my balance on Tian Li's shoulder with my bad arm, which sends a stabbing sensation up it. Now that my mega-dash is over, I'm really feeling the Lady too. I think I probably overdid it, and maybe reopened my wound, because the Lady feels sharp and stretched and there's a trickling sensation on my skin. Thinking about my leg too much makes it hurt worse though, so I just join in Tian Li's song:

"We're unstoppable! Unstoppable!
So wonderfully sweet improbable!
You can't beat us today,
because weeeeeeeeeeee're unstoppable!"

We laugh, and Tian Li parades me toward our goal, where Aaron joins the song and Sal hands me my crutches. I slide down from Tian Li's back and lean on them, hurting and happy, basking in the sun and in winning. For the first time since I lost my leg, I feel like I can do anything. I can be my old self. I can run and scramble and keep up with the others. I can score goals. I can *win*.

Grinning like a honey-drunk bee, I look for Pepper. She's my best friend. I want to celebrate with her. But all I see is a flash of her hair as she disappears down the stairs, heading belowdecks toward her room. That's weird. Usually she doesn't care who wins or loses at broomball as long as it's a good game, and this was a great game.

I start to crutch after her, but then the Lady howls like

she's been slapped with a cheese grater. I yelp and notice blood on my calf, and Nic thumps across the deck with an enormous frown and tells me he'd like to see me in the infirmary, immediately.

"Ouch!" I shout. I have to bite my lip to keep from swatting Nic's hand away from the scar on the Lady's face.

He looks up, still frowning. He's got his spectacles on, glinting gold in the afternoon light through the infirmary's porthole, and he's dabbing some iodine on a little rip that's trickling blood at the end of my scar. You'd think he could give me a break. It's my first game back at broomball after all. But he's all business. "If you don't let this heal, Nadya, it's always going to hurt."

I sigh and flex the Lady back and forth. The skin over the end of her feels swollen and maybe a little bruised, and the ripped scar stings, but it was worth it. I *won*. I was the hero for a minute, just like I used to be. "It *is* healed, Nic," I say. "You told me it was never going back like it was, to learn to live with it like this. That's what I'm doing!"

Nic straightens up, gently setting my leg on the examination table and throwing away his iodine swab. He takes off his glasses and polishes them before returning them to his shirt pocket. "It's *mostly* healed, Nadya. The wound has closed, and it looks fine from the outside. But it won't be finished healing on the inside for a long time. It will keep changing for months. Years, even. The things you do now will help set the course for that long process. If you take care

18

of it—if you're *kind* to it—it will heal well. If you abuse it, you could set yourself up for a lifetime of pain."

I huff and turn away from Nic. He may have once been a doctor, but he doesn't have a clue what he's talking about. Then what he said—*years*—sinks in, and my anger bubble pops and I start sniffling. That happens now sometimes, when I think about a whole life having to deal with my leg and how hard it might be. The month since my amputation has been so tough already.

I wipe my eyes and stay facing the wall. I don't want Nic to see me crying, but he does anyway. He never misses a thing.

He sits on the table next to me, then clears his throat. "You'll be all right in the end, Nadya," he says. "If there's one thing I've learned about you over the years, it's that you always are."

I sniffle a little more, and I stare at the corner of the infirmary. "I miss Mrs. T," I mumble. Mrs. T was our tutor and a skylung like me, but she stayed on the pirates' ship last month so the rest of us could get away. Some nights I dream she's back on board, teaching me about being a skylung and the Roof of the World where we came from, telling me about my parents, holding me and making me tea and saying she's proud of me and that I'm doing wonderfully at a hard job. She was like a mother to me. Sometimes I miss her even more than I miss my leg.

Nic takes a deep breath and sighs. "I do too," he says. "But we'll get her back. I promise."

I lean against him. His shirt smells like soap and seawater

and iodine. His arm trembles a little, like it's hard for him to hold the weight, but that's okay. He's Nic. He's always been there one way or another, ever since he and Mrs. T found me in a cloud balloon in the desert. And he's always looked out for me. If he says we'll get Mrs. T back, we will. We just have to get to Far Agondy so he can make it happen.

CHAPTER 3

IN WHICH NADYA FIGHTS WITH PEPPER, AND DISASTER STRIKES.

After I leave the infirmary, I head straight for Pepper's room. Whatever's bothering her, I want to sort it out now and not have it hanging over our heads when we get to Far Agondy. That city's got fire spirits, smoke, skyscrapers, zip lines, and enough people to cause anybody a whole mess of problems. I'll feel a lot better there if I know Pep's got my back.

I knock six times, in the *rap-a-tap-tap-tap-rap* pattern we use between the two of us.

"Come in," Pep mumbles.

I open her door and crutch in. It's edging toward evening, which is why she's here instead of working on the engines. Her room's almost exactly the same as the last time I saw it: mirror in the corner, big cargo net full of stuffed toys on the ceiling, bed up against the wall under the porthole, book-shelf full of engineering manuals and storybooks all jumbled together, desk against the wall she shares with Tam. The only

21

difference is there're some papers on her desk with a bunch of stuff scribbled out on them, like she's been writing something over and over trying to get the words right.

Pep's sitting on her bed with a book in her lap. When she sees me, she pushes her curls out of her face and takes a deep breath. "Hey," she says.

I crutch toward the chair by her desk. "Hey." Something must be wrong. Usually Pep's all fire and energy, ready with some game to play or story to tell. Usually she's got something to tease me about or wants to tell me what happened with the engines or something one of the other kids on the crew did. When she's quiet like this, it always means trouble.

Pep nods toward my leg. "Your visit with Nic go okay?"

I shrug. "He told me to take it easy, the usual stuff."

Pep fiddles with her book. "That's good."

I lean forward. "Pep, what's going on?"

She pushes her curls back, then huffs. "You . . . you keep . . ." She goes over to the shelf and starts moving books around like she's organizing, except she's not because she never organizes them. She must just be nervous. "I'm mad at you." She looks at the floor, like it's hard for her to say it.

My stomach flutters. I mean, I knew she was upset, but it always feels sorta like finding out the sky is upside down when Pep's mad at me. Things aren't supposed to be like that. "About what?"

Pep fiddles some more. *The Adventures of Spiritus in the World Beyond* changes place with *Principles of Steam Locomotion*, and *An Annotated Encyclopedia of Fire Spirits* moves to the end of the shelf. "Lots of things. Like today. You cheated. You embarrassed me in front of everybody. You took advantage of the fact we're friends, just to score a stupid goal."

I keep real quiet and still on the outside, but on the inside my mind's running a million miles an hour. This can't just be about broomball. It's lots of things, like she said. A month ago we were tight as vines and flowers, so whatever happened must've happened since then. Pep helped me get better when my leg was at its worst, but I don't think she'd be mad about that. I sat next to Tian Li instead of her at dinner a couple times, but I don't think she'd be mad about that either. She wanted to sit next to Tam.

She's been spending a lot of time with Tam, actually. Like in the Flightwing when they go fishing. And she seemed kinda frustrated after I upstaged her in front of him this morning. And then when I beat her in broomball when she was on his team.

Oh. *Ohhhhh.*

Pep stops fiddling with her books, sighs, and plonks down on the end of her bed. "Whenever you're around, people don't pay attention to me," she says. "And you always—"

I cut her off. I'm pretty sure I know what's going on. "Like Tam?" I say.

She seizes up like a cat that's just spotted a dog. "Yeah," she says slowly. "Tam too. But—"

"You've got a crush on Tam, don't you?" I grin.

Pep turns bright red. She turns away from me and looks at the wall.

"It's okay," I say. "I mean, I sorta think maybe he likes me a little, but it's not a big deal and—"

"It's not about that!" Pepper shouts. She whirls around and I realize she's not red because she's embarrassed, she's red because she's mad. Her curls fly in front of her face, and she shoves them back and snorts. "Yes, I have a crush on Tam. But that's not what—you know what? Forget it." She crosses her arms. "Just forget I said anything, okay?"

The rush of figuring out what's bothering her fades. She's still mad. "I can help," I say. "I won't show you up in front of Tam anymore, and maybe I can even talk about how great you are, kinda—"

Pep smacks her bed so hard they can probably feel it on the deck, and I stop talking. "It's. Not. About. That," she growls. "You never *listen*!" She shakes her head, and her lip quivers. "Never mind, Nadya. Just go."

I feel like she punched me in the gut. "What's it about, then, Pep? What's the problem?"

She looks up, and there are tears in her eyes. "You're supposed to be my best friend, Nadya. You figure it out."

Fighting with Pep feels like having the flu. I can't concentrate on anything else, and my stomach is queasy. It gets worse when I go down to feed the gormling, which is what we call the baby leviathan. Doing that takes me past the room we turned into a jail for the three pirates we captured last month. They always jeer at me and make fun of my missing leg, but Nic told me I couldn't retaliate anymore after I threw a bucket of fish guts and gormling muck on them. Luckily, today they're asleep when I go by.

At dinner Pep won't look at me, and even though Nic's whipped up an amazing meal out of fresh fish, dried vegetables, rice, and powdered milk he's somehow turned into a salty, savory sauce, I don't feel like eating. I sit next to Salyeh at the end of the table and watch Pep, who looks as sick to her stomach as I feel. I want to keep talking with her, but she made herself pretty clear. She wants me to figure out what's bothering her on my own, and I guess that's fair. I *am* her best friend. I oughta be able to do it.

I head up to the catwalks with Aaron after dinner, checking on the plants, carefully working my way between the bays they grow in and taking soil samples to test at my chemistry bench tomorrow. The plants out here are doing fine. They're green and vibrant, and they get plenty of water from the clouds we've been flying through as we work toward Far Agondy. There's no yellowing, no pests, no signs that anything's wrong.

With the plants doing so well, I have time to think about what Pep said. Something about people not paying attention to her when I'm around. I don't see it, though. I mean, sure, she gets less attention when I'm around, but that's normal, isn't it? Like, everybody has more people to pay attention to.

I sigh, leaning back in my harness, and give my mind a rest from Pep being mad at me. This is one of the best parts of my job these days. Even with two legs, you have to be pretty careful when you're crawling around the plant bays on the outside of the balloon, so only having one doesn't slow me down too much. The sun's just set over the ocean to the west, and the sea and the thin strip of land to our east are plunging into darkness. The stars are coming out. The deck lamps are on, and below me Tian Li's reading the stars and charting our course. Everything's normal. Everything feels good. I'm on top of the world.

Nadya, I hear in my head, *is this plant supposed to be pink?*

I frown. The voice is Aaron's. He's just a few feet above me on the catwalks, but he's talking to me over the Panpathia, a web of golden light that links everything in the world. Cloudlings and skylungs can use it to talk to each other and to other creatures, like the plants and animals in cloud gardens. All I have to do is shut my eyes, step onto it with my mind, and flow along the golden lines I see until I find whatever I need to talk to. Mrs. T said the best skylungs can talk from one side of the Cloud Sea to the other, but I can't get that far. Normally I just use the Panpathia to keep tabs on the garden and let the plants and animals inside know what's happening on the ship, but lately I like going on it because I still see myself with two legs there, the same way I do in my dreams.

Trouble is, I promised Mrs. T I wouldn't use it anymore.

There's something dangerous on it, see, called the Malumbra. It's a shadow creature that infests the mind of anybody who touches it. Aaron and I had a run-in with it last month. It got control of me for a few minutes and tried to make me let the air out of the *Orion*'s cloud balloon, but I shook it off, and then

Aaron burned it out of me completely. I still don't know how he did it.

Whatever the Malumbra is, it's real dangerous. It took over the whole Roof of the World, and Nic thinks it wants the rest of the Cloud Sea too.

Aaron, I say cautiously. *You're supposed to ask me out loud if you need something. The Panpathia's dangerous right now.*

It's always *dangerous,* Aaron huffs, but he gets off it anyway.

"I'm up h-h-here," he says, pointing at a bay with a low, leafy green plant turning pink around the edges. He's younger than the rest of us kids on board by about five years and skinny as a beanstalk. His hair's getting shaggy too, forming a curly red-brown dome around his head. With his pale skin, he could be Pepper's cousin. He's been through a lot. First he lost his family, then he got imprisoned by pirates on the cloudship *Remora,* and since we rescued him and took him aboard he's been trying to adjust to life in a new place. He's kinda latched on to me, and I try my best to be nice to him.

I sigh. "That plant's Ironbelly. He starts off green, then turns pink, and then in about a week he'll grow a big red bud. When the bud blooms, there'll be a chunk of iron the size of your fist inside, ready to harvest. Then he'll go dormant and the cycle will repeat." Ironbelly's one of the plants that grows trade goods for us. They're a big part of how we make enough money to keep flying.

"Oh," Aaron mumbles. "Sorry." He looks down, and I feel bad for sighing at him. He's got a lot to learn, and he's doing a good job of it.

I scramble over the catwalks to him, hopping up a ladder, then moving the lobster claws that keep me clipped to the ship. I sway with the balloon as the night breeze pushes it. Below me, little fire spirits dance cozily in lanterns along the *Orion*'s deck, and Thom starts chatting with Tian Li about something.

"No worries," I tell Aaron when I get to him. I smile and pat his shoulder. "You're doing great." I ruffle his hair. "Why don't you go see if you can scrounge us up a treat in the galley? We're running low on supplies, but I'm pretty sure Nic has an emergency chocolate stash behind the sink. I'll finish up here and then come find you."

Aaron grins. "Okay, Nadya," he says, and he starts the long climb down to the *Orion*.

I lean back and look at the stars as they come out, some in big streams crossing each other up high, others clustering near the horizon. The catwalks click and clack around me. I feel like everything's part of a huge machine, changing gears and moving the world along. I hang there enjoying it until a ladder clanks below me and I see Thom climbing my way. I wave to him.

"How're you doing?" he says when he reaches me. He leans back against his harness too, stretches his arms behind his head and relaxes. He doesn't usually work up here, but he knows the whole ship stem to stern, and he's comfortable everywhere.

I shrug. "Pretty good." I don't want to tell him about my fight with Pep. "My leg's a little sore."

"Well, you did give it quite a workout this afternoon." He raises his eyebrows. "The *second* my back was turned."

I roll my eyes. "I didn't stop and see what you were doing, Thom. I just wanted to win the game!"

Thom chuckles. "I guess I can't blame you for that. I used to play a pretty mean game of broomball myself, back when I was a kid." He smiles at the stars on the horizon. "Man, it's pretty up here. Y'know I used to take care of the outerplants on one of the ships I worked on between leaving Nic and coming back as his first mate? I always loved it." He peeks over my shoulder at Ironbelly. "Looks like you're doing a great job."

I flush a little. "Thanks." I've been worried about whether I'm doing well now that Mrs. T isn't around to supervise me. It's really nice to hear that Thom approves.

When I look back at him, Thom's rubbing the stubble on his jaw. He opens his mouth, closes it, then takes a deep breath. "Look," he says, "I wanted to talk to you about the Malumbra. I've been doing some reading, and I've learned a few things you should know. There are stories in some of the fireminder histories about a war between it and the fire spirits, hundreds of years ago, that raged across worlds."

Slowly, my mind shifts gears away from thinking about the plants. "Worlds?" I ask. "Like, more than one?"

"Yes," Thom says. "All the worlds in the universe—ours, the World Beyond, and probably others we don't know about—exist in parallel, sort of like sheets of paper with empty space between. This fight happened over several of them."

29

Down on the deck, Tian Li turns the ship, and I watch as the stars wheel around Thom's head. He and I brace ourselves against the plant bays as the balloon swings. I can't imagine anything so big it could fight a war over one world, let alone a bunch of them. "What *is* this thing?"

Thom looks up at the stars. "Imagine a leviathan, swimming in the space between the worlds, insatiably hungry for life and intelligence. When it sniffs out a world like ours, it sticks its head in and starts eating. That's the Malumbra."

I shiver. Back down on the ship, our little deck lamps seem awfully small and fragile.

"It consumes whole planes of existence, Nadya. The fire spirits only fought it off because there were a lot of them, and they were united, and fire's the thing it hates most." He frowns and touches the faded fabric of the cloud balloon. "I know that's a lot to swallow, but I wanted you to be aware of it. This thing got its teeth in you once, and from what I read, it doesn't let go easily. It must be tempting to explore the Panpathia, and I'm not gonna waste my time telling you not to do it at all. But be careful. If you see anything funny on there, you run first and ask questions later, okay?"

I nod, my mouth dry. I remember feeling shadow and ice on my neck, and my body moving without me telling it what to do. I don't want another run-in with the Malumbra any more than Thom does.

Thom unclips his lobster claws and gets ready to head back down. "I know you think you can do anything," he says, "and you've amazed me with what you're capable of. But the

Malumbra is bigger and more powerful than you can imagine. For now, you leave it to me and Nic."

The next day I'm sitting on the edge of the pond in the cloud garden, swirling my foot in the water and trying to ignore the ghost pain shooting up my injured leg. Pep barely said two words to me at breakfast, and Thom's warning is sticking with me like aphids on a plant stem.

But at the same time, the Panpathia calls to me. I woke up three times last night with it glowing in my mind, almost ready to jump onto it and go look for Mrs. T or that girl I saw on the Panpathia. She reached out hundreds of miles looking for help, and she found *me*. I could be her only hope of getting rescued.

Sighing, I get up to check the controls that let air in and out of the balloon to make us rise or sink. I pass a couple of tall, shady palm trees with their leaves yellowing and frown. Even though the plants outside are in good shape and I'm trying my hardest, I'm having trouble keeping everything inside the cloud balloon healthy. And I can't figure out what's bothering them without going on the Panpathia to ask.

"You guys okay?" I ask, patting the trunk of one of the yellowing palms. "Tell me what you need."

They're silent. Trees don't have ears, you know? You have to be able to talk to the spirit inside them. I grind my teeth and decide to come back and check on the palms again later. We're coming into Far Agondy, and it's my job to fine-tune the elevation as we pull up to the docks.

31

I continue to the controls and see that the levels are holding steady as a rock, so there's nothing for me to do but wait for word from Nic as we get closer.

Something thumps gently below me, like maybe the *Orion* bumped into another ship, but everything seems fine. That happens sometimes when we get into heavy ship traffic, and we have bumpers to cushion it.

I close my eyes and try to lose myself for a bit. It's warm and damp in the garden, and the sun-in-a-jar that hangs in the center is going from its day cycle to its night cycle. It feels like sunset in the sugar islands. The birds are chirping. The bees are buzzing. The plants smell damp and rustle quietly. The frogs jump in and out of the water, chattering in their language. Aaron moves around on the other side of the garden, humming to the plants.

"Nadya!" Tam shouts through a tinny speaker near my ear. His voice sounds like a trumpet, so loud I flinch. He must be up on the catwalks, which is weird because his docking station is down on the deck, where he can make sure nothing happens to the rigging.

I rub my ears. "Yes, Tam?"

"We need you on deck!" he says. "It's an emergency! Nic wants everybody right away!"

My stomach plunges faster than a cloudship with a punctured balloon. "What? Why?"

"It's the pirates," Tam says. "They're gone!"

CHAPTER 4

IN WHICH NADYA GETS IN DEEP, DEEP TROUBLE.

I crutch out of the balloon as fast as I can. It's pretty hard cranking the locking wheels in the waiting house open and shut with a bum shoulder while standing on one leg, so Aaron does it for me this time around. Then, after the *whirr* and *pop* of the garden air being pumped out and the outside air rushing in, I head for the ladder, working my safety lines with one hand.

Tam's waiting there, next to a winch and a swing we've set up to raise and lower me from the catwalks to the deck when I need to move fast. He's frowning and fidgeting, bouncing around like a squirrel with a hawk perched above it.

"What happened?" I ask while Aaron heads down the ladder. The rest of the crew's already on deck. I can see the *Orion*'s whole topside from bow to stern, and it doesn't look like anything's wrong.

Tam takes my crutches and holds the swing steady while

I sit and clip it to my harness. "I dunno," he says, handing my crutches back and heading to the winch. "We were approaching the docks. There was a lot of ship traffic around us. I had my eyes on a big liner just above and to the left of us, but there were a couple other ships around too. Then there was this big *boom*, and I thought we must've crashed into one of them, but I didn't see anything except smoke under the portside bow. I was still trying to figure out what was happening when Pepper ran out from inside the ship shouting that the pirates were gone, and Nic called everyone on deck."

Tam starts lowering me. The winch creaks a little, but it's a smooth ride through cool, salty air as I descend. I look for the smoke he's talking about, but it's not there. Whatever caused the problem, it seems like it's over.

Except that the pirates are gone.

My stomach twists. The pirates were going to be our key piece of evidence that Mrs. T got kidnapped. Our plan was to turn them over to the Cloud Navy, a fleet of armed cloudships maintained by the Six Cities around the edge of the Cloud Sea, and hope that the navy could get them to fess up about where their friends might've gone. Then the navy could track the *Remora* down, stop it from pirating any other ships, and, most important, rescue Mrs. T.

Without them, we can't do any of that.

As I swing in the breeze, I turn and watch our approach into Far Agondy. Tall Thom's at the wheel, and the ship's moving ahead real slow. We're about two hundred feet above the waves, which are deep blue and dotted with sailing boats and steam-powered coast crawlers that trade up and down the continent in the shallow water where they're safe from leviathans. Behind them, the city stretches toward cloudy mountains inland like a forest of silver knives.

Far Agondy's *tall*, see, like other cities aren't. It's built around a dagger-shaped island in the middle of a river, with the point of the dagger stabbing toward the ocean and the harbor. Nic says it got its start as a place for coast crawlers to meet and trade with river runners heading inland to the deep forests and silver mines. It grew bigger and bigger, and now the harbor at the tip of the dagger has slips for eighty water-going ships, and the cloudship spires sticking out of the shallow waters of the bay like needles have room for a hundred flying ones.

We're cruising toward our usual spot: Slip 6, Spire B. There's four spires total for cloudships. Each one's an ironwork column about fifty feet in diameter and thirty stories high, with jetties for ships to dock at sticking out in four directions every five stories. We use a slip that's owned by a supplier Nic knows. Because we buy so much, they give us a pretty good deal on the fee for tying up.

Slip 6 is on the city side of the spire, so Thom has to bring us around. The cloudship closest to us, on the ocean side of the spire, looks like a deep-sea trawler. Its deck's covered in nets and cages and has two big winches off either end. Its cloud balloon's got a design of a school of fish leaping out of the waves in a storm.

I lose sight of the spire as Tam finishes lowering me and

I unclip from the swing. Nic's standing by one of the capstans, staring worriedly at the *Orion*'s bow. The wind puffs strong scents off the city: motor oil, the hot and sweet stench of garbage, a sort of fishy funk, and—more than anything else—smoke. Far Agondy's the smokiest place in the Cloud Sea. There's a giant fire spirit living in a cavern underneath it. It burns trash, coal, oil, and a whole bunch of other stuff that the city government feeds to it in big power stations. All that heat makes steam, which turns turbines, which generate electricity, so on top of being the world's smokiest city, Far Agondy's also its most electrified. The trams run on electricity. The elevators in the skyscrapers run on electricity. The lights run on electricity. At night, it's like a firefly wonderland.

I crutch into line between Pepper and Salyeh, who's staring forward like Nic. Tian Li frowns next to him.

"What happened?" I whisper to Pep while Aaron, who's still pretty slow on the ladder, gets down behind us and falls into line. Tam clanks rapidly down the rungs above him.

Pep fidgets and wipes some soot off her nose onto her overalls. "I was keeping an eye on the engine room, making sure the fire spirits didn't get too rowdy or slack off, and I heard this real light thump from forward, near the pirate brig. I stuck my head out to investigate, and when I did, there was a huge *boom*, and a cloud of smoke poufed back at me. I grabbed a water bucket and ran forward in case it was a fire, but when I got to the brig there was nothing there—just a hole in the hull where the wall used to be—and no more pirates."

She looks up worriedly toward Nic, who's still staring silently forward. We've gotten into the flow of traffic around the spires, following a garbage scow. Thom should have us into Slip 6 anytime now, which means whatever Nic's going to say, it'll have to be quick. It takes all of us to tie up the ship.

Tam thumps to the deck and runs up, puffing hard. Nic starts talking, right on cue. "I'll keep this short," he says. "About fifteen minutes ago, there was an explosion in the room we've been using as a brig. By the time I got down to investigate, Pepper and Salyeh were already there, and the pirates were gone."

My guts churn. Hearing Nic say it makes it seem more real, somehow, and the realer it gets, the less likely it seems we'll ever get Mrs. T back. "What do you mean, 'gone'?" I ask. "Gone where?"

Nic sighs. "That, it seems, is the operative question. We're still two hundred feet off the waves, high enough that if they jumped, they almost certainly perished. We don't—"

I crutch toward the deck railing over the brig. "They're still here, then!" I blurt out. "They must be on the lines somewhere! We have to catch—"

"Nadya Skylung, freeze!" Nic shouts.

I stop moving, and a feeling like midwinter snow tumbles down my back and collects in my spine.

"Turn around," Nic says more softly, but there's still a nail-sharp edge in his voice. When I do as he says, his nostrils are flared and he's taking short, fast breaths. His arms are trembling.

"On this ship," he says, and he says it like he's talking to all of us, but I know he's talking to me especially, "we often let discipline slide. We want you to think and act for yourselves, to ask questions, to be independent. I think the benefits of that approach have spoken for themselves over the last month."

When we were on our own after the pirates kidnapped him, Thom, and Mrs. T, he means.

He takes a deep breath. "But we are nevertheless a crew. I am the captain. You are the hands. When I speak, you listen. When I give orders, you obey."

I cringe, feeling about as small as a cloud bug that's just encountered a sparrow. I didn't mean to disobey any orders. But I thought there was still a chance to catch the pirates.

"All the ports we visit are dangerous, Far Agondy more so than most. And this trip, Far Agondy may be especially dangerous, so I want to be crystal clear: This is an order. From this moment on, you will do nothing without consulting myself or Mr. Abernathy first. You will refer to us properly, by our ranks. You will maintain proper discipline, and you will toe the line, or we will reconsider our crewing arrangements. Have I made myself clear?"

My throat closes up. I can't feel my lips. My fingers tingle. He can't mean what he just said. Just yesterday he promised he'd help find Mrs. T. He *promised*!

But he looks as serious as a hurricane.

You could cut the silence by breathing on it. Pep gets tears in her eyes. Tian Li's lips tremble. Sal's hands shake. Tam's not

40

showing it, but I'm sure he's every bit as scared as the rest of us. Aaron looks confused.

And me?

I feel like Nic just pulled the ship out from under me, and now I'm falling into the sea. I'm the one who stepped out of line just now. I'm the one he's looking at. I'm the one who got in trouble, so I must be the one he's thinking about kicking off the *Orion*. I could throw up.

"Well?" he asks.

"Yes, sir!" Tam shouts, and we echo him in a tumbling shower of mumbles and mealy-mouthed whispers.

"Yes, sir," I hack, and I look at Nic and feel like he's a stranger. Yesterday he was Nic, and he was comforting me. *Captain Vega*, I'm supposed to think of him as now. *Mr. Abernathy*, instead of Thom. I feel all dry and crumbly, like clay left out to bake in the desert sun. The wind blows over the bow from Far Agondy, and it stinks of rotten fish and garbage. I wish we'd never come here. I wish the last ten minutes hadn't happened. I wish the whole last two months hadn't happened and we'd gone south to T'an Gaban, and somebody else had rescued Aaron from the pirates.

"Good," Captain Vega says. He clears his throat and takes a deep breath. "Now, as I was saying, we don't know what happened to the pirates, but searching for them would be catastrophically unsafe. They could have fallen, but they could be aboard and armed with makeshift weapons from the debris in the brig. The hull may be too damaged to safely support a search team. You could fall. You could be overpowered and thrown from the ship. You could be crushed against the docks. These pirates are not worth risking your lives over." He stares at me directly, so hard it almost hurts. "Any questions?"

Pepper sniffles. Everybody stands stock still, frozen.

Yes, I think, looking at Captain Vega and wondering where Nic went. *What about Mrs. T?*

But I don't answer. We're not allowed to answer now. We're just crew. Just here to follow orders and do what we're told. I want Mrs. T back. She never would've let him do this. I almost look up toward Thom—*Mr. Abernathy,* I remind myself—at the wheel and see what he thinks, but I don't dare break eye contact with Nic.

Because whatever else I want—and I want a whole lot—I really, really, *really* don't want to lose the *Orion.*

"Excellent," Captain Vega says. "You all know your docking stations. Go to them and await further orders. We will be reaching port shortly. Dismissed."

We scatter like a startled flock of birds. Tian Li runs to the port side of the ship's aft castle to help with the lines. Salyeh bolts toward the forward lines starboard, and Pepper toward the aft starboard. I crutch to my post at the forward part of the ship on the port side, where the pirates are probably hiding, right now, with all their information about where the *Remora* might have gone with Mrs. T about to slip out from under our noses forever.

I edge around my cabin and settle on a bench Tam and Thom built for me so I can do my duties sitting down. The crumbliness inside me melts into numbness. My missing leg starts up a symphony of burning pains, and I try to knock it against the deck railing to make it stop and nearly pitch myself off the bench.

The ship slides into the cold iron arms of the dock. The dockmen shout friendly greetings at me that soon turn into concerned questions about the hole in the ship, what happened to my leg, what in the world we ran into out there. We see them pretty often, and I think they find us interesting—a ship full of kids doing jobs meant for adults.

"Ask the captain," I mutter until they stop talking. I do my job like a machine: catch the rope they toss to me, tie it to a notch in the railing. Slide down the bench, catch another rope, tie it up. Slide, catch, tie, slide, catch, tie, until I run out of bench. The dockhands look at me like they want to help, but a whistle calls them away to do something else because they're just a crew too.

The engines cut out. The ship slides to a halt, caught in a web of ropes. The stench of Far Agondy wafts over me, and I look forward off the bow, toward the city's nest of silver towers and cabled zip lines, the billowing clouds of thick gray smoke from the power stations, the trains, the cars, the life of a million buzzing, smelly people. I try not to look at anyone on the dock, try to imagine that the pirates fell into the sea and died. But I still see three people in frayed, dirty coats hurrying into the spire below us, and they look just like the pirates we captured. I call out to Nic, but he stares at me

43

so stonily that my mouth dries up and the words stick in my throat. I don't want to hear him say it's just my imagination, so I keep it to myself and slink off back to work instead.

Usually when we get to port, I feel excited. This time, I just want to curl up in bed and cry.

I'm all done crying by the time someone knocks on my door.

It's late—well after turtlehen, most of the way to midnight. I'm in bed staring at the ceiling, trying to wait out a bunch of sparks in my ghost foot so I can fall asleep, but it's not working very well. All I can think of is Nic telling us that if anybody steps out of line, he'll kick them off the ship.

He's scared. I can see that. The only other times he's gotten really stern with us, something bad was happening or about to happen—that time we almost got stranded out on the Cloud Sea, or just before the pirates boarded us.

But I can't figure out what he's so afraid of. Far Agondy can be dangerous, sure, but so can everywhere. I don't know why he's so much more spooked by it now than he was the last time we were here. Thom mentioned the Malumbra, so maybe that has something to do with it, but if that's it, why hasn't Nic said so?

The knock, when it comes, is timid, like a cat scratching at the door to come in but not sure whether the person inside likes it. Carefully, I crutch to the door, trying to be quiet. We're all supposed to be asleep except Tian Li, who's on watch. And with Nic's new rules, who knows what kind of trouble being up after curfew might get us in?

I ease open the door to my cabin, wincing when the hinges squeak.

Outside, Aaron's fidgeting nervously, trying to stick to one side of the door where it's darker. Because we're in the slip, there's a lot more light around the ship than usual. Most nights we just have the fire spirits dancing on the deck railings, giving off a friendly orange glow but leaving it dark enough to see the stars. Here, the dockyards are lit up with big electric floodlights, to identify thieves and spies. Some of those lights are so bright I have to put two curtains over the windows in my cabin if I want to sleep. The lights are placed between the slips shining up and down, so anything in their way, like the ladder to the cloud balloon or the cables attaching it to the deck, casts a long black shadow.

I don't like being out at night in the docks. It looks like Aaron doesn't either.

"Can I come in?" he whispers urgently, looking over his shoulder toward the wheel, where Tian Li's pacing, one hand on the whistle around her neck she'll use to call for help if she spots an intruder.

"Sure," I say. He squeezes into my cabin, and I close the door behind him. "What's going on? We're supposed to be

46

asleep." I wonder what Salyeh said when he snuck out of their room, or whether Aaron was just really quiet about it. At first we gave Aaron Mrs. T's old room, but he didn't sleep very well without any company, and Salyeh offered to take him in.

He goes straight to the curtains over my window—which is open because my room got stuffy in the sun this afternoon—peeks out, then puts them back in place. "I couldn't sleep," he says. "Someth-thing's wrong."

There's a lot that's wrong, with Nic being a tyrant, the hole in the hull, and the missing pirates, but I don't think he's talking about anything so obvious. "What do you mean?"

He shrugs. "Just wh-wh-wh . . ." Sometimes when he gets agitated he has trouble finishing words. I tried to help him once and he quietly asked me not to, so I just wait for him to work through it on his own. "Like I said. Something's wrong, h-h-here in the city. Can't you feel it?"

My skin pricks up in goose bumps, like there's a spider tickling the hair on my forearms. "No," I say, but I realize he's right. There's a shadow on the Panpathia here. Even staying off the web, I can feel it, sort of like you can tell whether it's dark or light out even with your eyes closed. The Panpathia feels cold and unfriendly.

"It's not always like that here?" I mumble. I'm new to feeling the Panpathia. Last time we were here I didn't know it existed.

Aaron shakes his head. "No. It feels like my h-h-hometown did before th-the shadowy men came."

The goose bumps run down my spine and back up again

47

in little waves, like ants scrambling toward their nest when there's a storm about to break. *Quiet,* I tell my nerves. *You're just getting all spooked over nothing.* But it doesn't really work.

"Okay," I say. My leg's getting tired, so I sit on the edge of my bed. "What does that mean?"

Aaron shrugs. His attention wanders sometimes. He's hot and cold—either focused like a hunting hawk or scattered as a foraging squirrel. "I dunno," he says, and he peeks out the curtain again.

"What're you looking for out there?" I ask.

He lets the curtain fall back. "Anyth-th-thing weird. But it's all weird. So I guess I dunno about th-that too." He looks at his feet. "I miss my sister."

My stomach knots up like a rope left uncoiled in a corner. Aaron hasn't seen his sister since he got kidnapped. A group of shadowy men showed up in his village in the middle of the night with torches. They burned the houses and caught everyone they could who came out of them. Only a few cloudlings escaped. Aaron and his sister were two of them, but they got separated trying to get to Far Agondy, and he got nabbed by the pirates.

"Tell me about her," I say softly. Maybe it'll make it easier. I always used to like talking about my parents with Mrs. T when I got sad.

"Sh-she's really brave," he says. "And smart. Sh-she loves the Panpathia, and she always goes farth-ther on it than me. We did contests, to see h-how far we could reach. I wanted to beat her someday." His chin quivers. "I guess now I never will."

"Maybe we can find her in Far Agondy," I say gently. "What's she look like?"

He frowns, like he's thinking. "A little taller th-than you. Her hair's really long but she puts it in a bun to make her look older. She has brown eyes and tan skin." He blinks. "Does that h-h-help?"

The girl I saw on the Panpathia was a little taller than me, and she had a bun that was getting tugged on by one of the people kidnapping her. My heart speeds up. "Aaron," I ask slowly, "does she wear any jewelry?" The girl I saw had a metal stud in her nose, which almost nobody our age has.

"Yeah," he says, messing absentmindedly with some papers on my desk. "A gold thing in h-h-her nose. She f-fought with Mom for a year to get it."

My heart does a backflip and flies into my mouth. "I might've seen her on the Panpathia. But she was getting kid-napped."

His eyes bug out as I tell him the full story, and he starts bouncing up and down. "It was h-h-her!" he says. "It h-had to be! Can you h-h-h-h-h . . . will you rescue h-h-her?"

I listen to the ship creak against her moorings, thinking about Nic's order today. I don't want to make a promise I can't keep. Far Agondy's a big city, and Nic's not likely to let me run around it looking for a missing girl.

But this kid's been through so much. He lost his parents,

his hometown. If I can help him get his sister back, don't I have a duty to try?

"Okay," I say. I hold out my hand and we shake on it. "I will."

Aaron smiles like I'm the sun coming up after a long, cold night on deck watch. "Th-thanks, Nadya," he says. He jumps up and hugs me, and I hold on to my headboard with my good arm and wrap my bad one around his shoulders. He's so brave, so trusting.

"Come on," I say. I slide off my bed again and rummage through my drawers for a black sweater, then grab a dark blue one for Aaron and toss it to him. "Put this on." I hop toward my crutches. "Let's start by checking out the pirate brig. Those pirates were kidnapping kids, right? Maybe if we can find out where they went, we'll find your sister there."

My leg sparks up again as I open the door to my cabin, but I don't mind. I'm doing what's right, no matter what Nic says, and that's worth missing a night of sleep, risking being kicked off the ship, and a whole lot else too.

A few minutes later, Aaron and I are down on the mid-deck, staring at a gaping hole in the *Orion*'s hull lit from below by the floodlights of the docking slip. It's misty and damp because the nighttime fog that boils up off the water and mixes with the smoke in the harbor has set in, and with the hole in the hull there's nothing to stop it getting into the ship.

The combination of the electric lights and the fog makes it feel like we've fallen into the space between worlds. Every time somebody moves down below, it sends shadows skittering over me, and I'm all jumpy because I don't know what'll happen if Nic or Thom catches us sneaking around. Thom's bedroom is just down the hallway, so we have to keep really quiet. I heard him snoring as I went by, which is a good sign, but you never know when he'll wake up.

We had to sneak by Tian Li too, which I didn't like. I doubt she would have ratted us out or anything—heck, she'd probably have helped us if we asked—but I didn't want her to get in trouble if we got caught. It's bad enough risking me and Aaron getting kicked off the ship.

"Wow," Aaron whispers. He's holding on to the wreckage of one of the iron bars we used to jail the pirates, leaning into the fog and looking down. "Th-that's a long way."

I pull him back from the edge. "Yep," I whisper, trying not to think about the time I fell off the ship. I still get a little queasy looking down at big heights. "Stay back. Let's try to figure out what happened."

"Okay," he says, and he steps into the hallway.

I keep by the edge and look hard at the hole the explosion caused.

It's pretty big, maybe eight or ten feet across, although it's all jagged because some of the planks in the *Orion*'s hull held up better than others. Maybe most important, all the splinters are facing inward, and there are little slivers of wood like needles embedded in the walls all through the rest of the room and the hallway.

"The explosion happened outside the ship," says someone

51

behind me, and I flinch so hard I bang my knuckles on one of the twisted iron bars of the cage.

"Mmf!" I mutter, trying to be quiet. "Darn it, Tam!"

"Sorry," he whispers, and he sneaks up close to me. "Didn't mean to startle you."

"Sure you didn't." I bet he did. He loves being dramatic. "Anyway, I figured that part out myself. But there were no other ships around, right? So where'd the explosion come from?"

"There was one," says another voice, approaching from the forward part of the hall. "A little tug that helps ships into port. It was below and in front of us."

My stomach warms a bit. This voice I recognize right away. "You came too, Sal?"

Salyeh emerges into the light and smiles sheepishly. He shrugs. "I couldn't sleep. And I wanted to know what's going on."

"Me too," says Pepper behind me. She comes in from the hall, and then we're all standing around the hole in the brig, looking at each other while the misty shadows flicker.

"Goshend's teeth," Tam says. He runs a hand through his hair. "I didn't think we'd *all* be this dumb. Nic'll have a fit if he finds out we're down here."

I frown. "We're not *all* here. Tian Li's up on deck."

The grins that were starting up around me fade. We're supposed to be a team, all five of us—six now with Aaron—working together. That's how we beat the pirates. "I'll tell her tomorrow," I say. "It'll be fine."

52

"I'm sure she's guessed it anyway," Salyeh says, rubbing the back of his neck. "She always knows what I'm about to do before I do it."

We chuckle nervously, and then the silence settles in again and we're back to staring at the hole in the ship.

"So there was a tug . . . ," Tam prompts, and Sal continues his story.

"Right. A Far Agondy customs tug. And it got so close it nearly bumped us, and then it drifted off, and a few minutes later the explosion happened."

I scratch my head. "Why would Far Agondy customs help the pirates escape?"

Pep kneels by the edge of the hole and runs her fingers along the splinters. "Maybe they weren't helping them. Maybe they tried to blow them up."

I shake my head. "No way. They must've been helping them. I'm pretty sure I saw the pirates escaping when we docked."

Pep glares at me, and I get that stabbed-in-the-gut feeling again and remember she's mad at me. But all I did was disagree with her. Why would she get mad about that?

"I agree with Nadya," Salyeh says. "Look, in one part of the cell there's no splinters. That bomb was placed where it would leave a space for the pirates to avoid getting hurt. And remember the badge we found?"

It takes me a second to figure out what he's talking about, but I get it eventually. One of the pirates we captured had a Far Agondy customs inspector's badge with him. Sal found it after we tied them up. The two of us figured that meant the pirates had connections in the customs office. "Goshend's teeth," I mutter while Sal explains the badge to the others. "But how'd they know where the pirates were?"

That stumps us. We stand in a silent circle, thinking while the ship bumps against its moorings and the shadows flicker in the mist. I can only come up with one answer, and I really, really don't like it. "The Panpathia," I say at last. "It links everything in the world, and if you know what you're doing on it you can see where other people are, especially if they're nearby."

Tam frowns. "But I thought only skylungs could go on the Panpathia."

I try to work some spit into my mouth, which has suddenly gone dry. "As far as anybody knows, yeah. Skylungs and cloudlings."

"So," Pep says, raising an eyebrow, "that means they have a skylung helping them."

"Or a cloudling," I add quickly. "But why would a skylung or a cloudling help them? The pirates are on the same side as the Malumbra."

"The Mal-what?" Tam asks.

"Malumbra," Salyeh says, and I wonder for a second how he knows about it before I remember that he's read just about every book that's ever come in front of his nose. "It's what the skylungs and cloudlings call the thing that drove them away from the Roof of the World."

"It's real," I say. "Aaron and I saw it, or at least a part of it, on the Panpathia. And it's nasty. It hurts people, tries to take over their minds. Nic said he thinks it wants to take over the whole world. I can't imagine anybody helping it on purpose."

"Well," Pep says, "you said it takes over minds, right? So what if it took over someone's mind?"

I shiver. Maybe that's what Aaron could feel on the Panpathia. Maybe that's why it's so dangerous here in Far Agondy. Maybe someone's kidnapping skylungs and cloudlings so they can turn them over to the Malumbra. "Goshend's teeth," I mutter again, while Tam swears more creatively next to me.

"Hey," Sal says, "speaking of Aaron, where'd he go?"

I whip around. "He was right behind us a second ago." But he's not there anymore. "Aaron!" I whisper. "Hey, Aaron!" I stick my head into the hall, but I can't see him. It's too dark in here, and my night vision's all messed up from the lights. "Did anyone see him leaving?"

Pep and Sal shake their heads. So does Tam.

"Shoot," I say, and I grind my teeth. I brought him down here. I feel responsible for him. And if he wanders around until he gets caught, Nic might boot him off the ship. "I'll find him. The rest of you get back to bed. We can talk more in the morning."

Salyeh nods, but Pepper just looks down and sighs. Tam shakes his head and opens his mouth to say something.

Then there's a creak from the floorboards near Thom's room, and the sound of Thom's door opening very fast.

CHAPTER 6

IN WHICH NADYA VERY NEARLY GETS CAUGHT.

"Who's there?" Thom shouts, loud enough to wake the whole ship. He's got a whistle too, and it's probably already halfway to his lips.

Everyone freezes. I don't know what to do. We're one hundred and ten percent busted.

"Hide!" Pep hisses, and then she walks into the hallway. "It's just me, Mr. Abernathy," she says forlornly, and then she disappears, walking toward Thom and away from the brig— distracting him from the rest of us.

My heart pounds a million miles an hour, but I dive behind the tumbled-over remains of one of the pirates' beds, just in case. Salyeh looks sick to his stomach as he steps into a deep shadow in the corner. Tam's mouth hangs open like a snoring fish's, but he joins me. I feel nauseous. Pep moved so fast there was nothing we could do, and now she's going to take the heat for all of us.

"Pepper?" Thom says. He sounds half relieved, half furious. "You're supposed to be in bed unless you're on duty! Didn't you pay any attention to what Captain Vega said today? What were you even *doing* over there?"

"I couldn't sleep . . . ," Pep says, and then her voice gets so quiet I can't pick out the words anymore. But her footsteps, and Thom's, keep moving away from us down the hallway. Pepper sounds upset, like she might start crying any minute. Thom sounds less and less frustrated and more and more like he wishes he could let her off. Their sounds reach the end of the hallway, then disappear up the stairs, toward the deck and Nic's cabin.

I swallow a lump. "He's taking her to see Nic," I say. I decide I'll only call him Captain Vega to his face. He's still Nic, somewhere under there, or else the *Orion* isn't really the *Orion* anymore.

"What if he throws her off the ship tomorrow?" Salyeh asks. He sounds horrified.

I stand up. "We won't let it happen. We'll make him throw us all off if he tries to throw any of us off. Deal?" I hold out my hand. Looking a little relieved, Sal comes over and puts his palm over my knuckles. Tam gulps and then does the same.

"Deal," Tam and Sal whisper in unison.

I take a deep breath, but I only have half a second to celebrate before Salyeh speaks up again.

"We need to get back to bed," he says. "They might start doing checks once Thom tells Nic he found Pepper up."

My stomach shrivels up like a cloud vine in a storm. "What do you mean, 'checks'?"

Salyeh looks into the mists. The electric lights flash over his face. He looks older for a second. He always does when he talks about his past. "They used to do it in the pits back in Vash Abandi, when they were worried about kids trying to escape. A couple times a night, somebody would come check on you, just to make sure you were in bed. They did it at different times every night—sometimes twice in just a few minutes even—so you could never be sure when you'd be alone."

Tam curses. "We need to move, then, fast."

"What about Aaron?" I ask.

Salyeh's frown deepens. "He could be anywhere, Nadya. There isn't time. I'll try to cover for him if they check our room."

But that's not good enough for me. I already might lose Pep tonight. Aaron's my responsibility. I'm not gonna lose him too. "I'm going to look for him," I say. "You guys head back to bed."

Tam and Salyeh shake their heads. "We're a team," Tam says. "We'll help."

"Salyeh needs to be there in case Aaron comes back to their room, and Tam, I need you to let me know if they're starting bed checks. Bang on the floor, cough loudly, do something that makes a bunch of noise so I'll know I've got to get back to my cabin, okay?"

Tam grunts and stares at me for a second. Then he sighs. "Be careful, all right?" Salyeh nods in agreement.

"I will, I promise. Just go!"

Tam and Sal look at me one last time, and then they disappear into the hallway, leaving me alone in the shadowy mist, wondering where in the world Aaron might've gotten to.

I start my search in the engine room. Aaron liked it there out on the ocean because it was always warm and bright. Every once in a while we'd find him sitting next to the fireboxes in the middle of the night, watching the light play over the rods and gears that jut up out of the engine mechanism. But he's not there. The engines are cold, and there's nothing but shadows and things to bang against in the dark.

Next I check the brig again, in case he came back to it, but it's empty too. I pause for a few seconds, sweating. There's a little clock ticking in my head, and it tells me I don't have much time. Nic can't be taking long to scold Pepper and choose whether he's going to start checks. In the middle of the night, he tends to be pretty decisive.

"Aaron," I mutter, "where'd you go?" Every creak of the ship as it drifts against its moorings makes me flinch. Our all-for-one, one-for-all vow felt good when I was thinking about it protecting Pepper, but I realize now that if I get caught and Nic tries to kick me off the ship, it means Sal and Tam go down with me. I don't wanna be responsible for that.

Just as I'm starting to think there's no hope, I hear a sound below me—a little one, like somebody talking down in the hold—and I know exactly where Aaron disappeared to.

A few minutes later, after I've crutched slowly down the stairs, trying to be quiet, I find him standing in front of the

59

gormling's tank with his fingers splayed against the glass. The gormling, which looks like a giant, elongated catfish with enormous whiskers and glowing spots below its spine, circles in front of him hypnotically.

"Aaron," I whisper, "we have to get back to bed. Pepper got caught!"

"He's worried," Aaron says. The glow from the gormling lights up his face in shifting aquamarine. "Can't you f-f-feel it?"

The gormling stops swirling and looks at me. Its eyes are deep and gold, like stars condensed into tiny pools. I can feel its fear, now that Aaron mentions it, and maybe it's worth a minute to figure out why it's scared, even now. We're going to deliver it in the morning. This might be our last chance to talk to it.

"You didn't want to be in the ocean," I say, remembering my time with it last month, when it seemed terrified of being let loose in the deep water. "Are you afraid of Far Agondy too?"

It jets down to the bottom of its tank and purrs there, shivering the water with its spines, then floats back up and meets my eyes again. "Why?" I ask.

It stares at me. I can feel myself drifting into its eyes. The Panpathia calls to me. It would be so easy to let my mind trot across the little bit of glowing thread between us and find out what the gormling is worried about. Aaron just did, I think, and nothing bad happened to him. It must be safe.

Sweating, I break my promises and give in. The Panpathia

opens up in front of me in soft golden light, and I see the gormling in my mind as it sees itself—a shimmering creature of pure brightness. It doesn't speak to me—it never does. But I can feel what it feels. There's a shadow in the city, and it worries that the shadow is looking for it. It worries we're going to deliver it right into its hands.

We're delivering you to the Lord Secretary of Far Agondy, I say softly. *You'll be as safe with him as anywhere. He's a big muckety-muck, helps run the city.*

The gormling swirls in a circle. It seems unconvinced, so I press my forehead against the glass. *I'll come check on you then, okay?* I'm getting nervous being on the Panpathia, and I want to wrap this up. Shadowy things are moving in the distance. I don't think they've noticed me, but they feel like bugs crawling up my arms and legs. *I'll ask the Lord Secretary if I can visit you, before we go.*

The gormling seems to relax a little, and I realize the clock in my head has ticked way past *Safe* into *Nadya, get out of here!*

I let go of the Panpathia. "Come on," I say to Aaron, and I grab his hand. "Let's go."

Five minutes later I'm closing the door to Salyeh's room, breathing a sigh of relief. Sal was still awake, even though he was lying under his covers, and he explained the situation to Aaron. Hopefully he'll be able to keep him there through the rest of the night, and I can get up to bed, and Pep won't be in too much trouble, and we'll get away with this.

As I turn toward the stairs, I hear footsteps again. Heavy

ones, creaking the boards as they come down. Nic's footsteps. The light from a lamp, swinging as Nic moves, tumbles down the staircase.

I crutch back from it like it's poison. "Oh no," I whisper, and I look frantically for an escape route.

But there's nowhere to go. This hallway runs straight along the heart of the ship, fore to aft. Salyeh's and Tam's bedrooms come first, then Pepper's and Tian Li's, then the kitchen, galley, and storage, and then the brig and Mrs. T's old room. The galley or Mrs. T's room would be the best places to hide, but I don't think I can get to them in time. Tam's and Salyeh's rooms are a bad idea—Nic will search them first, and I might not be quick enough to hide before he gets there. Pepper's room is out too, since he might be bringing her back down after scolding her.

That leaves Tian Li's room.

I crutch into the darkness as fast as I can, which isn't nearly fast enough to make me comfortable. Every time I plant my crutches, I'm terrified they're going to make enough noise for Nic to hear me. His footsteps plod slowly down the steps, and the light from his lamp chases me down the hallway. By the time I get to Tian Li's doorway, it's right on my heels, and Nic's just about out of stairs. I shoulder the door open, hop inside, jerk my crutches after me, and ease the door shut just as the line of Nic's light reaches this part of the hallway.

For a few seconds I stand there, my heart racing, breathing hard. No shouts. No footsteps coming toward me. Just a gentle squeak on the floorboards as Nic peeks into Salyeh's room.

So I'm safe, for now. But how long will that last? It won't take Nic much time to check the rooms, and even if Tam pulls off some kind of distraction, I've got to get out of here and back up to my cabin before Nic finishes up and decides to see what I'm doing. But how?

I look around Tian Li's cabin. Her desk sits quietly in the misty electric light drifting in through her porthole. A framed painting of the harbor in T'an Gaban, where she's from, hangs above it. There's some inspirational quotes from great thinkers and the revolutionaries who founded the Free City of Myrrh written out artistically in pen and pencil on scraps of fancy paper and tacked to the walls. Her bed's rumpled and unmade, and a pile of dirty clothes slumps in the corner next to her dresser.

I have no idea how I'm going to get out of here.

There's a thump and a shout from Tam's room, followed by a quick scuffle and some harsh words. My heart races again. That's Tam's signal, meant to warn me.

My eyes keep lingering on the porthole. It opens. There's a way out there. But I have no idea how I could get from the window up to my cabin.

The conversation in Tam's room quiets down. That's it for the checks down here, so unless Nic's going to do something with Pepper or Tian Li, I'm almost out of time. Whatever I'm gonna do, I've gotta do it fast.

I hear more talking from Tam's room, and then the voices head this way. I freeze, but they pass by toward the fore of the ship. I catch a few words as they do.

"What did you hear, Tam? Quick, tell me exactly," Nic says. Tam's really pulling out the stops for me. He must've heard me dropping Aaron off and figured out the score.

The two of them go by, and I turn back to the porthole. If Tam can be brave enough to distract Nic, then I can be brave enough to at least try to get out of Tian Li's room.

I throw open the porthole. Cold, misty air flows in, and I stick out my head, looking around in the electric light. The *Orion* gets rigged a bit differently when we're in port. There are lots of lines tying her to the slip, to make sure she doesn't move in the wind and damage it. When she needs repairs like she does this trip, other lines get slung around her hull to help the work crews.

Goshend be good, one of those lines is right under the porthole, running fore to stern. In the morning, the work crews will clip onto it while they check the damage to the hull. But tonight I can probably squeeze out on top of it, then work toward my cabin. I'll still have to get up to the deck, but one of the mooring lines is drooping down near the ship's bow, and maybe I can climb it.

I look down at the Mighty Lady, hanging there in the shadows and the mist, a little sore, a little swollen after all I've put her through recently. "You're gonna help me on this one, right?" I whisper. "Don't let me forget I'm missing a foot."

I still do that sometimes, when I'm focusing real hard on something else. Usually it just means I trip and fall on my face and it's embarrassing. But if I'm going to be out on those ropes, no safety belt, nothing to tie me to the ship, it could be a whole lot worse if I fall.

I've got no other choice worth making though. There's supposed to be a net under the *Orion* in port, to keep anything that falls or gets dropped off it from hitting the ship below us. As long as it's there, it'll catch me if I fall, so all I've got at risk is getting caught out of bed, right?

I lean out Tian Li's porthole again to check the net, but I can't see it. The mist's too thick. There's a few shadows in the electric lights below that *might* be a net, but nothing I'm totally sure of.

My fears lurch up from the depths of my heart like that shadow-touched leviathan, and I hesitate. Maybe it's not worth it. Maybe I should just own up to what happened tonight and quit trying to keep things from Nic. Maybe he's got a reason for all this, and he's not going to throw anyone off the ship after all.

But that seems a worse risk. The net *has* to be there. It's always been there before.

I take a deep breath and hide my crutches under Tian Li's bed. Footsteps down the hall. Nic's voice coming closer again. No more time to think.

I squeeze through the porthole and stick my legs into the mist. Facing the dock, I gingerly let myself down until my foot finds the rope. It wiggles and sways when I put my weight on it, but not so much I can't keep my balance.

Carefully, I slip out of the porthole and sit on the rope.

I take a couple seconds there, listening to Nic lecture Tam inside the ship and getting used to the way the rope moves when I shift my weight. The mist tickles my nose. My stomach flutters. I'm pretty high up, and I'm not tied to anything. The lights scatter around me like sun coming through a crystal vase in the early morning.

Softly, I lean against the *Orion*'s side and slide toward the bow. "You've got me, right, old girl?" I whisper, and the *Orion* creaks back reassuringly. I slide a little farther, then do it again. As I get closer to the fore of the ship, I see the mooring line I was counting on more clearly, dangling toward me just this side of the hole in the hull. It runs up to a ring on the *Orion*'s rail, then down into the mists, probably hooked to one of the bigger iron rings in the dock. The angle's pretty tough, but I bet I can climb it.

Tam's door closes inside the ship. No more time to be careful. Nic'll be heading to my room next. I slide faster, working like crazy to keep my balance on the wiggly rope. After a few seconds I'm almost to the rigging I need. Two more slides. One more. I grab the hull and struggle up on my foot.

Just as I reach for the mooring line, I slip off the rope.

I try to catch my weight with my missing leg, but there's nothing there and I whiff, hard. My fingers slip, and for a second I start to fall toward the mist and what I hope to the ends of Goshend's judgment is a net.

But somehow my fingers find another inch to stretch. They get over the top of the rope and catch my weight, and even though my hurt shoulder grinds hard enough to make my eyes water, my grip holds. I dangle over the mist, breathing hard, staring down, and then I swing my body up, hook my leg over the rope, and curl the Lady across the top of it.

For a second, I just hang. I shut my eyes and try to catch my breath. My arms shake. My stomach muscles are killing me. I'm gonna be more sore tomorrow than I've been since I got hurt.

But if Nic takes a little longer, and if my body holds, I think I'm gonna make it.

Climbing ropes like this is hard. Like, wicked hard, even if you've got two unhurt arms and legs. The rope's at about a forty-degree angle, so I'll have to dig my heel into the rope to take the weight off my hands, then reach forward, then dig the Lady in and reach again. Pep and I used to practice horizontal climbing on a rope someone had set up on a beach in Myrrh to play on, but I've never done it like this. I hope the Lady's up to it.

I dig my heel in and pull myself forward. So far, so good. Now for the hard part. I press the Lady real hard into the rope to take my weight. It hurts. A lot. I'm probably going to open up my scar again, and I have no idea how I'll explain that to Nic, but that's tomorrow's problem. I reach forward and pull myself along the rope, then repeat the whole thing twice more, trying to move fast. Nic must be on his way by now, and I'm so tired that if I stop to rest I might never get started again.

My hair touches the *Orion*'s hull. I crane my head over my shoulder. Almost there. One more dig. One more reach.

And then I'm over the deck. I uncross my legs and lower myself to the little bench I sat on to tie us up this morning. My arms are so stiff I can barely open my hands. My stomach feels like I just spent all night throwing up. My legs burn, and my missing foot aches. I take a few seconds to breathe.

Big mistake. Nic's light comes up out of the stairs below-decks and moves toward my cabin. I can't chance the door now—he'll see me for sure. The only shot I have is to go through my porthole, which, Goshend be good, is still open.

Biting my lip through the pain in my leg and my shoulder, I hop toward the porthole, then jump in and wriggle through it. Nic'll be here any second. I squirm into my room and thump across my desk, realizing as I go that I'm wet as a fish after spending all that time out in the mist and rubbing against the *Orion*'s hull. If Nic spots that, I'm done for.

He knocks on the door, three times.

I freeze, leaning against my desk, breathing hard, sweat trickling over my face, covered in incriminating mist. All that work wasted. I almost made it, and I'm gonna get given away by a little bit of water! It's not fair!

Nic knocks again, and I see a pitcher of drinking water— which Nic wants me to finish every night because my body's still healing—sitting on the floor near my bed. I remember the sounds Tam made. I've got a hunch about what kind of distraction he threw, and maybe it'll work for me too.

I take a deep breath, then let out a loud gasp, like I'm waking up real fast. I toss my covers down to the foot of the bed, then throw myself on the floor and knock over the pitcher.

"Nadya?" Nic says. "What's wrong?"

The door opens, and I roll through the puddle and cross my fingers it'll fool Nic.

I look up at him from the floor and do my best to look like I just woke up from a nightmare. "Wha—?" I ask. "Where are we? I—*owwww!*" I reach for the Lady, and I start paying attention to what she's feeling, and I let all my fears break over me. I don't have to fake crying.

"Easy, Nadya," Nic says softly. He kneels next to me. "Did you fall out of bed?"

I nod, closing my eyes.

"Where does it hurt?" he asks.

"My scar," I whimper.

"Let me see," he says. He straightens and lights my lamp, and a little dolphin of fear jumps up my throat, but he doesn't pay any attention to the water on me, or the puddle on the floor. He looks down at the Lady, which is sopping wet from the puddle and weeping a little bit of blood from my scar, and frowns. "I apologize, Nadya," he says. "Pepper was out of bed, and I wanted to make sure everyone else was accounted for." He sighs. "Let me clean this for you. I shouldn't have startled you."

He helps me up to my bed and gets a bit of gauze and some tape from the infirmary, then bandages my scar as gently as he ever has. There's a chance here to ask what's going on. He must feel like he owes me something.

"Captain Vega," I ask quietly, "why are you being so hard on us?"

He stops working on my bandage and looks me in the eyes. "I have a duty," he says softly, "to keep you safe. And I will not fail in it." He looks back down.

"What about Mrs. T?" I ask. "How are we going to save her?"

Nic finishes my bandage and stands up. He closes my porthole. "We'll still report her abduction. The Cloud Navy will look for the pirates. And until they find them, she can take care of herself. She's more capable than you know."

He leaves then, and I put on a dry set of clothes and lie in bed with my heart pounding and my lamp lit. My head whirls. Nic does still have a plan to get Mrs. T back. But it seems like a bad one. The Cloud Sea is huge. I don't understand him. I don't think I can trust him anymore.

And that means it's all up to me.

CHAPTER 7

IN WHICH NADYA MEETS THE LORD SECRETARY OF FAR AGONDY, AND LEARNS SOMETHING WORRISOME.

The next morning starts with a loud knock at my door. I sit up slowly, wincing. My shoulder feels like I yanked it out of its socket, the Lady feels like she got caught in a mousetrap, and my hands and arms and stomach and legs and pretty much everything else is sore.

"Come in!" I say, starting my slide out of bed. It's a cool morning, but the sun must've burned off the mist outside the ship, judging by the light trickling in through the curtains over my porthole. I hear shouting and the rumble of cranes— it's always loud during the day in port, no matter where we are or what's going on.

I reach for my crutches against the headboard and hit nothing but air, then remember I left them under Tian Li's bed and cringe. I'm not done hiding yet if it's Nic or Thom at the door.

Luckily, it's Pepper.

71

She looks tired, and pretty grumpy. Her overalls are rumpled and sloppy with engine grease, and her curls are matted and gnarled on one side, like she's been lying on the ground working under something.

She's holding my crutches, which she sets against the foot of my bed. "Hi," she says. "Glad you're okay." Then she turns around and starts to go.

"Wait, Pep!" I say, and she stops. "Come in for a second, would you?"

She stares at me, then sighs and walks to my bed.

"What happened last night?" I ask.

Pep looks at her feet. "Nic got mad at me. Real quiet, real stern, like he does sometimes." Her lips quiver. "'I'm so disappointed in you,' he said. 'I expected this from Nadya. But not from you.'" She wipes her eyes. "And then he told me I'm not allowed to leave the ship while we're in port, and that if I break the rules again, the consequences will be worse next time." She yanks on one of her curls. "I *knew* it was a dumb idea. But I heard everybody else going and I didn't want to be left out."

I swallow. I want to hug her, but I'm not sure she'd want me to so I don't. "Thanks for taking the heat like that," I mumble. "That was really brave."

Pep shakes her head. "We shouldn't have been *down* there, Nadya! What'd we figure out that we couldn't have during the day, without breaking the rules? Nothing."

I chew my thumbnail for a second, thinking. "Well, we wouldn't have all been there at the same time, so it would've taken way longer to put our heads together. It might've been days before we figured out what happened."

"You didn't know that when you went," Pep snorts. "And so what? We've got days. *I've* sure got days, stuck here on the ship. I was really looking forward to meeting Gossner when you and Tam go ask about your prosthesis. She sounds so cool when he talks about her." She yanks her curls again and frowns.

I reach for her shoulder, thinking maybe she will let me comfort her after all. She's talking to me. Maybe I can figure out what's eating her.

Pep gives up on her curls and throws her hands up. "It's always like this. You always—"

"Nadya!" Tam shouts from the deck, and I freeze. Pep jerks her hands down and wipes her eyes real fast before Tam pokes his head in. "Nic wants you on deck and ready to go ashore in an hour. We're delivering the gormling today."

I lean forward and raise my eyebrows at him, waiting. Hoping. After a second, I jerk my head toward Pep.

Tam squints at me, then gets the hint. "Oh. Hey, Pep," he says. "Thanks for what you did last night. That was pretty cool. Have you seen Salyeh this morning?"

Pep shakes her head, and Tam smacks his hand on my doorjamb. "Darn. Thanks anyway." He turns around and runs toward the stairs that lead belowdecks.

Pep lets out a big, heavy sigh. "Good luck with the gormling, Nadya," she mutters. She leaves before I can say another word.

I stare at the door after she closes it, my stomach flip-ping and flopping like a fish trying to get back to water. It sure *seems* like she's bothered about Tam. But she told me that wasn't it. She keeps trying to say something else. That I always do something. But what? What do I always do?

I lean forward and knock my forehead against my knee. Outside, the men and women who work the dock call to one another, shout and curse and laugh. Cranes creak. Saws screech. Drills whizz. The *Orion* moves gently against the ropes holding her in place. Life goes on. I have to get up and go be a part of it.

But I really, really wish I could just take a day off and figure some things out instead.

An hour later I'm crutching carefully along the narrow, rope-lined gangway between the *Orion* and the dock, looking down. They're slinging the safety net under the *Orion* now as another ship comes in below us, which means there was nothing to catch me last night when I was doing acrobatics. My stomach curdles like cream mixed with orange juice, even though I try not to think about what could've happened. I made it, that's what counts.

Tam and Salyeh stand in front of me, watching one of the dock operators as she uses a crane to lift the gormling's tank out of the *Orion*'s cargo bay. The gormling itself seems pretty spooked—it's sloshing around the bottom of the tank in a panic, darting back and forth every time the tank sways, which just makes it swing more.

"Nadya, can you calm it down?" Sal shouts from the dock. "This would be over a lot quicker if it stayed still!"

I stuff my fears as deep as I can push them and reach for the gormling on the Panpathia. It's just a short distance on the web. I was okay last night. Surely nothing's going to come get me, right?

It's okay, I tell it. *If you stay still, everything will stop moving so much.*

The image of it in my mind glares at me. Its emotions run something along the lines of *I was born to swim. Imagine you were being thrown around in a tiny bubble of air two hundred feet under the ocean and think how calm you would be.*

It's got a point, but glaring at me seems to give it something better to do than stare at all the open space beneath its tank, and it calms down a little anyway. I hop off the Panpathia before anything notices me, and a few minutes later the crane operator swings the tank over the deck and sets it expertly on an enormous cart. I crutch over and press my hand against the glass. The gormling rubs its cheek against the other side, one last time.

I feel a little choked up. This fish and I've been through a lot together. I wish we could keep it, even though I know that tiny tank is a terrible home for it and we've got nowhere better to put it, plus we really need the money from delivering it to fix the *Orion* now that she's got a hole blown in her side.

"A remarkable specimen," says a friendly voice from the other side of the tank.

I look up to see who's speaking, and a short man with the fanciest clothes I've ever seen steps around the tank. He's got pale skin and wavy brown hair that cascades almost to the collar of a big silver cape on his shoulders. Beneath the cape he's wearing a white silk shirt and a purple vest. He smiles and reaches out to greet me with a hand gloved in silver-lined black velvet.

"Alan Salawag," he introduces himself as he shakes my hand. "Lord Secretary of Far Agondy." His voice reminds me of a piece of fleece that's been heated up in a steamer—fluffy and comforting. He's got piercing brown eyes, the kind that make the people who have them look smart, but when he smiles the sharpness goes away and they're as soft as his voice. He's also, I notice, got gills right where his neck meets his shoulders, so he's a skylung like me.

"Thank you for bringing this gormling to me," he says. "I've heard your voyage was enormously difficult."

Me, Sal, and Tam just look at him. We're not used to rubbing elbows with muckety-mucks. Eventually Salyeh coughs and says, "You're welcome."

Lord Salawag adjusts his cape. "You're the *Orion*'s skylung?" he asks me. "Awfully young to be doing the job on your own, aren't you?"

My gills burn. "Someone was teaching me, but we lost her to the pirates."

Lord Salawag winces. "Ah, I'm sorry. That's . . . awful, simply awful. It must have been terrible bringing the ship in by yourself. I'm impressed."

I shrug, but the burning in my gills stops. "I had help. We rescued a cloudling from the pirates."

Lord Salawag touches his chest in surprise. "Rescued . . . goodness, what a trip. Markus!" he calls, and a tall, burly guy even paler than Salawag, with tattoos up his arms and a beard that reaches the bottom of his neck, steps out from the secretary's crew and gives me a glare that could kill a rat. "Markus, give the ship's captain an extra ten percent and tell him it's to be shared out among his crew as a bonus. These kids have been through a lot." Salyeh makes a choking sound, and his eyes get big. Whatever Nic was getting paid, ten percent of it must be a lot.

The bearded guy makes a note on a clipboard he's carrying. As he writes, his collar slips, and I notice he's got gills too. Maybe Lord Salawag works with a bunch of skylungs or something.

"Thanks," I say, figuring if this guy's giving us enough money to make Salyeh choke, somebody should say it.

"I wish I could do more," Lord Salawag says, taking off his gloves and stuffing them into a pocket of his vest. "Your names?"

"Nadya," I say. "Nadya Skylung."

"Skylung," he says. "How interesting. Pleased to make your acquaintance. And the rest of you?"

Tam and Salyeh give their names, and I stand there trying to figure out what's interesting about my last name. "Tam, Salyeh," Lord Salawag says, "would you mind escorting Markus onto the ship to find Captain Vega and sort out payment? The others and I will wait here with Nadya."

Sal fidgets. Tam raises his eyebrows at me and opens his mouth, probably to suggest he or Sal stay too because we stick together around strangers, but I shake my head real slightly. I can take care of myself, and I want to keep my promise to the gormling about visiting. Buttering up Salawag a little ought to help me do that.

Tam frowns, but instead of whatever he was going to say, he just mutters, "Sure," and he and Salyeh lead Markus down the gangplank onto the ship.

Lord Salawag watches them go and sucks in a long, deep breath. "Ah, the cloudship *Orion*," he says wistfully. "I used to be a member of the crew, you know."

I blink up at him. I had no idea. Nic never mentioned it.

When he sees how confused I am, the wistfulness leaves his eyes, and he looks hurt and a little angry. "He never talks about me, does he?" he says. "Neither of them do, I bet." He sits on the edge of the cart with the gormling's tank on it, so we're eye to eye. "I was on the same crew Thom was, about fifteen years ago. I was the skylung in training, and he was the fireminder." He smiles. "We had some great times, chasing leviathans in the deep ocean, riding out the big storms in the fall, running the streets of Vash Abandi and T'an Gaban and all the other cities." The smile fades, and he looks at me seriously. "But when I was about your age, Nic got a whole lot stricter with us. He set all these new rules, told us what we could and couldn't do, started talking about discipline."

My mouth dries up. My heart flutters.

Salawag sighs. "I didn't like it, and I told him so. We argued a few times, and eventually he kicked me off the ship." He stands up, then gestures to the rest of his entourage. "Things worked out fine for me, obviously. I entered the civil service academy here in Far Agondy, and I was smart enough to make the most of my opportunities. But I still miss life on the open sea sometimes, and I wonder what it would've been like if Nic hadn't thrown me off the *Orion*." He looks up at the cloud balloon. "I miss the garden," he says softly. "I miss it a lot."

I can hardly breathe. Nic threw this guy off the ship just for arguing with him. What if he does the same to me?

"Tell me," Lord Salawag says, looking back down from the balloon. "How's he treating you these days?"

I cough. I don't know what to say.

Nic's booming footsteps on the gangplank interrupt us. "Alan!" he calls. "How nice of you to come yourself. I didn't expect it."

"Ah, Captain Vega," Lord Salawag says. He nods deferentially and shakes Nic's hand as he, Markus, Salyeh, and Tam come back from the *Orion*. "So good to see you well. When the ship was late, we feared disaster. Dockmaster Yamada told me about your troubles. That's why I came down to see you personally."

"You're too kind," Nic says gruffly, like he'd really rather Salawag hadn't come down at all. "As you can see, we've had quite a bit of damage. Yamada told you about the pirates?"

"Yes, of course. We'll have to speak to the Cloud Navy about making sure the shipping routes to the city are kept more secure. Trade, after all, is our lifeblood."

"Of course," Nic says. He's staring at me so hard I start to sweat. He must be guessing what Lord Salawag told me. Nic waves at the gormling. "He's unharmed. When can we expect our payment?"

Lord Salawag looks over the gormling again. "This afternoon," he says. "Markus will bring by the full amount, plus a little extra in consideration of your troubles. Will you be in?"

Nic clears his throat and rubs his collar with his thumb. "That's . . . very generous," he says grudgingly. "Thank you.

I'll be out most of the day, but he can give it to Thom or to Salyeh here if Thom's not aboard."

Lord Salawag smiles again and inclines his head ever so slightly toward Nic. "Wonderful. Please give my regards to Thom, and to Carla, James, and Brick, if you ever see them." I frown. I know Carla—she's the captain of the cloudship *Emerald Dream*—but I've never heard Nic or Thom talk about James and Brick.

Lord Salawag turns to the rest of us. "So nice to meet you all, truly. Good luck in your apprenticeships with Captain Vega here. Just make sure not to get on his bad side, eh?" He winks at Nic, but Nic doesn't seem to think it's funny. He takes a deep breath, like he's trying not to get angry.

I take a deep breath myself. My head's whirling from everything Salawag told me, and Markus is glaring at me like I'm a bit of mud about to throw itself at his beard, but this guy's gonna leave soon, and I have a promise to keep. "Can I come see the gormling?" I blurt. "Before we leave Far Agondy?"

Lord Salawag blinks, and then the smile's back on his face again, welcoming as a cup of tea after a cold day up checking plants on the catwalks. "Of course, Nadya. I very much want the gormling to be comfortable in his new environment, and a visit from you might help him adjust. Markus, put her name on the short-notice appointment list. Just come by anytime you're free, and Markus will fit you into my schedule wherever it's possible." He bows slightly, then walks off, his silver cape flapping behind him like the plumage of some kind of treasure bird.

Markus glares at me like my mud got all the way through his beard and went down his shirt onto his chest hair, but he scribbles a note on his clipboard before he stalks off behind Lord Salawag anyway. A couple dockhands head after them, pushing the squeaky cart with the gormling's tank on it.

The gormling looks back at me as it goes, and its emotions are so strong I can feel them without even trying. It's terrified, like we've all made some kind of horrible mistake.

I want to comfort it on the Panpathia, but I hesitate. It feels risky with all those shadow things skittering around. Still, as the dockhands round a corner and I lose sight of it, my heart twangs and I close my eyes and go searching for it in the nest of golden threads around me. I figure it'll be easy to find since it's so close by.

But it's not. Anything I might see is dwarfed by the sight of Far Agondy itself.

I've never been on the Panpathia in a place where there's so much life crammed together. Out on the ocean it's all dispersed, except in cloud gardens. Mostly I see lone little strands linking islands of light. Here in Far Agondy, the Panpathia's a golden web the size of ten mountains stacked together, reaching up into the sky and down into the earth. It looks like a shining version of a tent caterpillar nest—so thick you can barely see through it and made of millions of interlocking golden strands.

And, I realize as my stomach churns, there's something wrong with it. In one part there's a darkness, where the web looks white and brittle instead of gold and flexible. The skittering shadows are centered there, moving, whispering, peering out at the rest of the city, and at me.

I take a short, sharp breath and jump off the Panpathia, my heart pounding. I wish I could say something to somebody, but I'm not supposed to be on the Panpathia at all, and after Salawag's story, I'm sure not going to let Nic know I broke the rules again.

Instead I just gulp and try to listen as Nic gives out assignments for our next round of chores.

That afternoon, Nic calls me into his cabin. He's sitting at his big table under the iron chandelier, looking at the secret ledger Salyeh and I found after he was kidnapped, the one that says DIASPORA at the top of it. I know he's been trying to schedule a meeting but having trouble getting everyone together. He told me last month he was going to introduce me to the other people fighting the Malumbra, but I guess it'll have to wait.

The afternoon light pours in through the big windows at the back of his cabin and puts a little line of gold around his body. When I enter, he looks up, and his head blocks the light. He closes the ledger, takes his glasses off, and polishes them.

"Sit down, would you?" he asks, but I know it's more a

command than an invitation. I crutch to a chair opposite his and plop into it. "Tam and Salyeh tell me you spent some time alone with Lord Salawag this morning."

I nod, my mouth dry again. I don't blame them for blabbing. I'm actually kind of looking forward to talking to Nic.

"What did he tell you?"

I clear my throat. "He said he used to be on the crew of the *Orion*, back when Thom was. He said you kicked"—I choke—"kicked him off the ship."

Nic puts both hands on the table and closes his eyes for a second. Then he goes to the cabinet where he keeps a private stash of food and drink, fills a glass of water, and hands it to me. "That's one way of looking at it," he says. "And I'm not surprised he sees it that way."

I drink the water and my throat clears up enough that I could say something, but I don't know what to say. I don't know who to trust.

"Alan Salawag was an enormously talented skylung, Nadya, much like you," Nic says. "And he was overconfident and charismatic, much like you. The other kids on the crew followed his lead. He would have made an exceptional captain someday."

He sighs and looks down at his ledger, flicking some dust from its cover. "Except that he had a tendency to lead people into trouble. He made rash, foolish decisions in the pursuit of new experiences. He encouraged Thom to steal a watch in T'an Gaban and Carla to sneak into the lionwraith exhibit in the Deepwater Zoo with him. He nearly wrecked the *Orion* once when he persuaded James Daybreak, an older boy who was our starwinder, to thread a tiny gap between two rocky pinnacles outside the Free City of Myrrh. Initially I lectured him and assumed he would learn, but as he got older, he got more reckless instead of less." He looks me in the eye. "Eventually, I decided that his presence on the ship was damaging to the other kids, and I removed him from the crew."

My heart races. He must be telling me this for a reason. He's *warning* me. "You abandoned him?" I say.

Nic frowns. "No. I helped him get into the civil service academy here in Far Agondy. I paid his tuition for six years. I felt—*feel*—somewhat responsible for him. He seems to have mellowed with age. Certainly he's achieved an impressive position in the city."

"Who's Brick?" I ask.

Nic jumps, almost like I pricked him with a needle. He takes a deep breath, then leans against the table. "Brick—Brittany Brikowski is her full name—is a skylung like Alan. She was our engineer in training and Alan's best friend, back when they were crewmates."

I think about Pepper, and my guts shrivel again. "Why don't you ever talk about her? Did you kick her off the crew too?"

Nic twists his head to the side. He looks hurt, and I feel a little bad about running my mouth off. "Brick is a sad subject for all of us, Nadya," he says. He coughs, and his eyes get red and watery. "I did not remove her from the ship. We let her down." He pulls out the handkerchief he uses to clean his glasses and dabs at his eyes with it instead. "I don't want to talk about Brick today. But believe me that when we ask you to be careful, listen to our orders, and keep off the Panpathia, we have very good reason to do so."

CHAPTER 8

IN WHICH NADYA VISITS TAM'S OLD HOME, AND GETS MANY SURPRISES.

The next morning, I'm standing in a little waterboat with an engine that's way too big for it, trying to catch my breath as it crashes through the waves between the cloudship docks and the Far Agondy mainland. The city's skyscrapers loom in front of me like spikes of glass hair, all windows down the front with little bits of concrete sticking them together. The water smells like the bathroom when there's been a plumbing clog, but the sun is up and shining orange through a hazy layer of smoke. It's a beautiful day, all things considered.

Tam sits next to me, chewing on his thumbnail and staring at the city, the prosthetic leg he's making for me sitting in his lap. Thom's piloting the launch, which is what they call these waterboats. Aaron's standing in front, where the bow jumps up and down whenever we hit a wave, grinning ear to ear and trying to keep his balance. Pepper, Sal, and Nic are back on the ship, but Tian Li's here too, sitting across from

88

Tam staring at the skyscrapers and looking almost as lost in thought as he is.

I tug a little map Tam sketched for me last night out of my pocket and check our progress. The airship spires are out in the bay, south of Doubleflow Island at the heart of the city. We're headed to the west bank of the Doubleflow River, and there's a bunch of other neighborhoods on the east bank we're not visiting today.

Thom maneuvers us around a tugboat with some colorful shouting, and I think about what Nic said yesterday afternoon. I really, *really* want to know what happened to Brittany Brikowski, why Nic won't talk about it, and why it makes him think it's extra important for me to be careful, but I'm not sure when I'll get the chance to ask.

I sigh and slump down next to Tam. I'm a little peeved at him for not paying attention to Pepper and making the fight between us worse, but when I see the worry on his face, I let it go. He must be pretty preoccupied right now. Five years ago, he ran away from the workshop we're heading to after a machine he made hurt one of the kids there. He never even said goodbye, and now he's gotta go face Gossner—the woman who runs the workshop—plus the kid he hurt and a whole bunch of other kids besides.

Thom swings us around a garbage scow steaming off to dump a bunch of trash somewhere—probably the middle of the bay, if the smell is any guide—then between a couple fishing boats I hope are going way, way out into the ocean before they catch anything to sell to people. A few minutes later, he brings us into the part of the harbor for launches and other small boats. Tam and Tian Li leap off and tie the boat up, and I stare at my crutches and massage the Mighty Lady, fighting off a concert of stabbing pains in my missing toes and trying to feel hopeful about my prosthesis instead of sad about being on the boat when I'd rather be jumping around.

Once we're tied up, Tam helps me out, Tian Li gives Aaron a hand, and Thom pays the dock owner. Just as my foot hits the dock's slimy wooden planking and I start to worry about keeping steady on it, there's a loud whizzing overhead, like the wings of an enormous bumblebee heading straight for us. I duck, but Tam just cranes his head up. I follow his eyes and a second later a black blur screams over us on a line, catches another line, and slows to a stop on a platform at the end of the docks. The blur looks sort of like a big spider with its legs all bundled up, but as it unfolds I realize it's a person clipped to some kind of device on a steel cable. I straighten and look over my shoulder. The cable runs all the way out to the docking spire where the *Orion* is berthed.

"Whoa," I mutter.

"Those are the zip lines," Tam says. "They run all over the city. Fastest way to get around. Take an elevator up one of these skyscrapers, then a zip line across town wherever you need to go. Then do the same on the way back. It's genius. All us runners used to use them."

I look back up at the line, which bounces around above my head like a nervous flea. I've heard of the zip lines before, but I've never seen one used so close. "I guess," I say. Once, I

90

would've jumped on a line like that without thinking twice, but now I'm not so sure. "I think I'll stick with the ground."

"Me too," Thom says, coming over to join us. "You ready to go?" When we all nod, he sets off toward the end of the dock. "Good. We'll be taking streetcars and subways to get to Gossner's workshop." He raises his eyebrows at Tam. "*Not* the zip lines. I want to get everyone there in one piece."

Tam looks a little sheepish. He tries to impress Thom whenever he can. But the sheepishness fades pretty fast as we walk off the dock and Thom buys a roll of tickets for the streetcar lines. Soon Tam's back to looking preoccupied and worried, just like he was on the water.

Half the day later, we're standing on the thirty-third floor of a skyscraper, knocking on a big iron door. It was harder getting across the city than we expected. It's not made for people on crutches, and I kept getting bumped and almost losing my balance or having to hop my way down tiny aisles in the streetcars and subways. Plus there was a lot of construction and one of the main subway lines was closed. Thom got us lost trying to figure out a workaround.

But eventually we got here, to one of the biggest buildings in a part of the city Tam calls the Forge. Apparently most of these places are filled with factories, workshops, inventing guilds, and engineering schools. He says of the whole bunch, Gossner's is one of the two or three most important, and that she owns the whole skyscraper we're in. I'm still having trouble wrapping my head around that. This building's as tall as a mountain—how could one person own the whole thing?

On top of that, the hallway we're in is pretty strange. Usually every floor in a skyscraper has a bunch of apartments or offices in it. The hallways run in straight lines between the doors, and you have to figure out which one leads to the office you want. In the fanciest buildings, there's even a secretary outside the elevators, to tell you where to go.

But on this floor, there's just a little room with big windows looking out over the city and one door, with a sign next to it made of shining copper letters welded roughly to a stainless-steel plate.

GOSSNER

Tam gulps and rubs his hands on his overalls. He steps toward the door, then stops. He's breathing fast, and his hands shake a little.

"You want me to knock?" Thom asks gently.

Tam shakes his head. "No," he says. Quieter, almost under his breath, he adds, "It's gotta be me. It was my fault. I gotta deal with it."

He walks up to the door, which has a huge bronze ring that must weigh a ton in the center of it, and knocks three times. The sound echoes in the little foyer we're in, like the footsteps of a giant made of scrap metal.

A few seconds later, the door creaks open.

"Yes?" a boy asks. He only opens the door partway, so I can just see his face and the left half of his body. He's soft-spoken, a little shorter than Tam, probably a year or so younger than us. He moves confidently, thoughtfully, slowly, like he has all the time in the world to decide what to do about things. He's got a smooth, welcoming face and tan skin just a little lighter than Tam's. His hair's black, and his eyes are the deep brown of a rock outcropping with roots that stretch deeper than you can imagine.

Tam opens his mouth, but nothing comes out. He swallows, then tries again. "Hey, Rash," he says. His voice shakes like a shivering cloud frog. "I'm, ah, looking for Gossner."

The boy raises an eyebrow. "Do I know—" He startles, and then his eyes widen and his jaw drops as far as Tam's did. "Tam. Tam Ban. Holy third axle of Goshend's skytrain. We thought you were dead!"

Tam coughs and scratches the back of his neck. "No," he says meekly. "Not dead. I just left. How . . . um . . . how've you been?"

"Good," Rash says. "Come in, come in!" He opens the door all the way, and I see the other half of his body. He's missing his right arm partway above the elbow, and I realize why Tam was so nervous. This must be the kid who got hurt by his machine. "Hey, Alé!" he shouts. "You'll never believe who's back! Somebody go get the Goss!"

Tam glances at me, takes a deep breath, and walks through the door. The rest of us follow into a room that looks like a mixture between a squirrel nest and a playground. There's metal everywhere—the beams of the skyscraper are exposed, enormous steel columns like the ribs of a leviathan jutting

93

from floor to ceiling every twenty feet or so in a grid. The ceiling itself is four stories high and vaulted, so we're in a massive, cavernous space. Instead of floors like most places would have, there's iron catwalks and platforms with little holes drilled in them, so you can see all the way up. Zip lines and staircases and lifts and swings run between them haphazardly, and it looks like the kids who work here sleep anywhere they want—there's sleeping bags and little tables and hammocks and dressers and mirrors spread out all over the place, with no plan whatsoever. The far wall is all windows, facing east toward Doubleflow Island, where the biggest skyscrapers of all tower over this one.

"Sorry," Rash says, bustling back to us. He sucks his teeth and grins. "I forgot to get your names. It's just so exciting to have Tam back. The Goss is gonna flip when she sees him. She was so sad when he disappeared. Who are the rest of you?"

"Thom Abernathy," Thom says, reaching out to shake his hand. "First mate of the cloudship *Orion*." He introduces me and Tian Li, then Aaron, "our general hand." Aaron, who's been staring openmouthed at all the kids running around this ironwork wonderland, puffs his chest out like a bird who's found a fat, juicy worm. He must be proud he got included in the list of crewmates.

"Nice to meet you," Rash says. He nods at Tian Li, who smiles back. "Navigator, huh? I'd love to pick your brain about a few things. I love maps." He turns to me. "And a *skylung*." He grins. "Wait till I show you what we've got on the third floor!"

Tian Li shrugs nonchalantly. She's looked a little uncomfortable ever since we got to Gossner's skyscraper. Rash's excitement must be catching, though, because after a second she smiles a little and says, "Yeah, sure."

I look up toward the third floor, but all I can see there are the catwalks and platforms, except in one corner, where there's a whole room of iron sealed off from the rest of the workshop. I'm about to ask Rash what it is when all the motion around us stops. The workshop goes silent, and a woman's booming voice calls out, "Tam Ban, you rascal! I can't *believe* you left without saying goodbye! Where in the world have you been?"

I follow the voice, and at its source I see a woman with a smile like a copper pipe, big and bold and bright. She's a little taller than Tam and rounder than Nic, and she's got light brown skin and big brown eyes and long black hair pouring off her head. Her boots clank like they've got steel toes, her overalls and the welding apron over them are covered in grease marks and oil stains, and if the way she tosses her gloves down and scoops up Tam and squeezes him is any sign, her heart's every bit as big as her skyscraper.

"It's good to see you," she says, and she ruffles his hair and puts him down again.

"Tam has been with us, Machinist Gossner," Thom says smoothly, "working as our mechanic and a general hand on the cloudship *Orion*. He told us," he continues, clearing his throat and raising an eyebrow at Tam, "that he was an

95

orphan and had no place to stay, but that he was good with machines."

Tam looks down. "Sorry, Goss," he whispers. "I just . . . I couldn't . . ."

She claps him on the shoulder and pulls his chin up so he looks her in the eye. "You're a free child, Tam Ban," she says seriously. "I said that when you joined us here, and it's never changed. You work for board, you work for training, you work for a bit of wages, and you don't owe me a thing but your respect and courtesy." She flicks him in the forehead. "*Which*, I might add, was seriously lacking in your departure. I expect you'll make it up to us by joining us for dinner tonight, whatever your current living arrangements are." She glances up at Thom, as if asking whether that's okay. He nods.

"Yes, Goss," Tam says, still looking down. "I will."

"*And*," she goes on, "you'll stop moping and start catching up with the kids here who remember you. You've seen a lot, I imagine."

Tam looks up. The whole workshop's staring at him. He stammers, "I . . . but . . ." He looks at Rash, and at the place his arm used to be. "How . . ."

Gossner's eyes glint, and she spins and pushes Tam toward Rash, who catches him one-handed. "You can start," she says mischievously, "by talking with Rashid, who's always wanted to show you what he did with the machine you left behind."

Tian Li and Aaron and I end up with Tam and Rash, while Thom and Gossner talk about some business of Thom's that has to do with the World Beyond, where the fire spirits he and Pepper summon come from. Rash races up one of the staircases from the landing where Gossner met us, taking the steps two at a time, grinning wildly. "Wait till you see what I did with the cleaning machine, Tam. I mean, it's a monster now—it can do practically a whole floor by itself!"

Tam stops climbing for a second, then runs after Rash. "You mean you didn't destroy it?"

Aaron, who's hanging back with me while Rash and Tam and Tian Li take off on their two good legs apiece, whispers, "What machine, Nadya?"

I watch the others and feel a little sad, a little left behind. "Tam used to live here," I explain. I clue Aaron in about Rash losing his arm and Tam running away.

"Hang on," Rash says as they get to a landing. He and Tam are warming up to each other as they start talking machines. "Let's wait for the others."

Tian Li, who's looking at the workshop thoughtfully, raises an eyebrow as I get to the platform. "So Gossner owns this whole place?"

Rash nods. "Yep! Designed it herself, when she was younger."

"Where'd she get the money?" Tian Li asks.

I frown. Tian Li has a thing about money. Where she comes from, some people have a lot of it and some people have none at all. She told me once she wants to go back and change that, like it's her personal life quest or something.

"Um . . . ," Rash says, scratching his chin. "I dunno, actually.

99

I mean, she makes a lot selling her inventions and doing custom jobs for people and stuff, plus hiring us out as runners and fixers, but I never really thought about how much it must've cost to build this place. Maybe she got a loan or something?"

He shrugs and leads us upward again, like where Gossner got her money's no business of his. "Sorry about all the steps, Nadya. There are swings and lifts for people with leg problems or who don't like the stairs, but the swings in this part of the shop are being reconfigured, so you'll have to crutch it for another few platforms. We change the layout all the time. The Goss says it's good for us to think creatively in three dimensions. We'll get the swings set back up before dinner tonight."

"No problem," I say, even though my arms are sore already and my hands are cramping. I stare around at all the machines, the catwalks, the little nooks where kids sleep, and feel a little sad. Pep would've loved it here. "So you guys can do whatever you want?"

Rash nods. "Just about. The Goss tells us to stop doing something or break it down or put it back the way it was every once in a while, but most of the time she just checks to make sure it's safe, then laughs and tells us to carry on."

"And she pays you?" Tian Li asks.

"Yep," Rash says. "Pretty much the best gig you can get as a kid in this town, short of being born with a silver spoon in your mouth. We all feel pretty lucky. Me, I might never have figured out I could do all this if the Goss hadn't showed me. We're not all geniuses, but you can't help but learn here." He gets to a small platform and stops by a sleeping nook. "Okay," he says, "just a sec. I need to grab my arm for this."

He reaches into his blankets and pulls out a prosthetic arm attached to a chest harness. It's made of black iron and looks—honest to Goshend—like an anatomical drawing of the inside of a biological arm. It's got a whole bunch of little rods and screws and springs and gears that rotate and compress and stretch out. He shrugs into the harness and takes a minute adjusting the arm. It looks like it has to line up just right. "I've figured out how to get a lot of functionality out of this over the years," he says. "Watch." He twitches a muscle in his shoulder, and the fingers in the arm close. He twitches another, and they open. Other twitches can make the wrist rotate right to left, or left to right, or the elbow move up and down.

"I'm pretty lucky," he says, looking at me more seriously. "Most people who lose a limb don't have the Goss to help them build prostheses, or a workshop full of smart kids to lend them ideas and extra hands." For the first time, he looks at my leg, and I realize he's the only person I've seen so far in Far Agondy who didn't treat it like the most important thing they saw about me. "You're lucky too, now that you're here. Bet Tam's building you a leg, and you came to get help with it, right?"

I nod, a bit flummoxed. How's this kid *know* so much?

He grins. "She'll get it sorted for you. I've seen her build legs for money, and she always does a great job. Bet she'll do one extra special, since you're a friend of Tam's."

Tam looks down again when he says that. He's getting embarrassed so easily today. It must really be hitting him hard to be back here.

"So is this where you sleep, then?" Tian Li asks. She nods at the pile of blankets, the floppy mattress, the tower of books and newspapers, and the pile of gears and rods and half-built gadgets that seems to be the sum of Rash's worldly possessions.

"Yep." Rash spins to face her. "We kinda sort ourselves into families, since there are so many of us. I sleep up here with Alé. We're best friends. We have a lot in common." He flexes the arm one more time, then seems satisfied. "Right," he says. "On to the machine!"

Rash shows us a lot more than just the one machine. First he takes us to the expanded version of the cleaner Tam built, while Tam stares at it and breathes hard and looks like he's trying not to cry. The thing has a driver's seat now, a steering wheel, and a whole row of brushes and mop heads and dials and gauges. After that Rash brings us to a reclining bicycle he's working on, with a big basket in the back to help kids haul inventions or repair jobs around the city for Gossner. Then we're off to the kitchen, where a crew of eight—including his friend Alé—is prepping dinner for what looks like forty people. Finally, he takes us all the way up to the roof.

We head through a locked door out onto a rooftop terrace as wide as the *Orion*'s deck six times over. The wind's pretty fierce, and it takes me by surprise and almost blows me down the stairs, but Rash catches me and holds me up with a smile until I get my balance back. He's surprisingly strong for a kid his size, but so are Tam and Pepper. It probably comes from working with machines all the time or something.

The view from the roof is mind-blowing. We can see the whole city, and since the sun's setting, it looks like the bay is on fire. The electric lights around and inside the buildings turn on like enormous lightning bugs sparking up. The sky-scrapers glimmer like fire-kissed stalks of corn covered with morning dew, and the docking spires out in the bay loom like the spines of an enormous leviathan, winking at us with their red and green navigation lights. Launches and boats cross back and forth in the harbor, and cloudships are still coming in and leaving, even this late in the day.

"Wow," I say as the sun slips below the horizon and leaves the buildings in twilit shadows. The view sorta reminds me of the night sky, and I almost mention it to Tian Li. She's looking at the places between the skyscrapers, though, where the buildings are dark and low and smoky, lit only by the reddish glow of the fire spirit under the city. I figure she's got other things on her mind.

Rash, however, is beaming. "Isn't it great?" he says. "But it's only half of what I brought you guys up here to see." He walks toward a big tarp with a bunch of lumps underneath it, then whips the tarp off dramatically. Underneath are six machines that look like giant wings with harnesses. I squint, not sure what they're for.

"You're building gliders?" Tam says. He runs his hands over one. "Do they work?"

"Sure do," Rash says. "Watch this." He picks one up one-handed and throws it across his shoulders, buckling it as he goes. "You just have to be careful about knowing what the wind does between the towers, or you can get into trouble pretty fast. I'd offer to take you guys out, but the Goss put the kibosh on that after one of Alé's friends from across town nearly got turned into a pancake against a building. So I'll just have to show you instead."

He turns to Tian Li. "Hey, double-check my straps, would you? Just make sure there's no buckle showing."

Tian Li looks over the handful of buckles keeping the harness secured to Rash's chest. "Looks good to me," she says.

"Thanks," Rash says, and then, with a glance at Tam, he runs toward the edge of the balcony.

I've gotta admit, my heart jumps into my throat when he leaps off the building and swan-dives into the air. But the wings on the harness extend and fill with air, and he only falls about six feet before they catch him and he's flying, gliding in a smooth circle out toward the building across the street. It looks like a blast, and I find myself bouncing up and down, wishing I could join him.

"He's losing altitude," Tam notes with a frown.

He's right. Rash drifts toward the street every time he circles. He seems to notice, and he banks suddenly and changes direction, shooting up the street toward an intersection. When he gets over it, he tips his wings again, and smooth as a hawk, he catches some kind of updraft that carries him skyward in slow, lazy circles. He stays in it till he's maybe thirty feet above us, then wheels gracefully around and starts gliding our way. As he closes in on the terrace, he drops his legs down from the little strap they've been resting in and tilts the harness up. The wings flare and set him gently on his feet, right in front of us.

"Whoa," Tian Li says.

Even Tam's smiling. "That's incredible!" he adds, running over to Rash, who's sweating a bit but grinning ear to ear. "What's the glide ratio? I mean, it looks like you could keep going for a pretty long way, and then when you hit those thermals . . . How'd you get the trusses in the wings to bear the strain? How'd you figure out the steering?"

Rash laughs and unbuckles the harness. He starts to reply, but he gets cut off by a loud throat-clearing from the stairs back to the workshop.

"A-hem!" Gossner says. She's standing on the stairs, arm resting across one knee, shaking her head. "If you're done showing off, Rashid, everybody else has been waiting for dinner for about ten minutes."

Dinner's great. I mean really great. There's a huge buffet line with about eight different dishes. Tam does me a favor and fills my plate, since it's hard to crutch around and get food at the same time. I take big spoonfuls of this green vegetable-and-cheese glop that Rash suggests, a couple sausages, and green salad to start, and then we go back for baked macaroni and cheese, some sliced ham, and a fruit salad of strawberries, pineapple, mango, blueberries, and melon. I end up sitting with Aaron and Tam on one side of me and Alé and Tian Li on my other. Rash sits next to Tam.

Tam eats quietly. Some of the other kids ask him questions, and he tries to put on a brave face, but I can tell he's still not totally comfortable being back here. Must be weird. This used to be his home, his family. Then he ran away, and now we're his new family and the two are meeting and he's sorta caught in the middle.

Thom sits up at the head of the table, having a pretty deep discussion with Gossner. Maybe it has to do with the history Thom was asking about earlier. Looks like they've got a lot in common, even though I bet Gossner's got fifteen years on Thom.

Kids are just starting to line up for dessert when Aaron speaks for the first time since we sat down. "Do you know anyth-th-thing about kidnappings, Rash?" he asks quietly.

Rash, who just got up to head for the dessert line, stops and sucks his teeth. He sits back down and sets his plate on the table. "How'd you hear about that?"

Aaron stares at him blankly. "It h-h-happened to me. Nadya saw it h-happen to my sister too."

Rash blinks. All of a sudden the noise and life and smells and great food seem duller, and my fears crawl out of my stomach and wrap their tentacles around my heart like an angry octopus. "We found Aaron in chains on a pirate ship," I explain. "And on the Panpathia I saw a girl in Far Agondy getting grabbed by a shadowy man. We think she was his sister."

Rash leans back in his chair and taps his fingers on the table. "There've been kidnappings," he says. "The runners all say to be real careful and go in twos and threes over by Bleak Forest and the Silver Stream. I don't get out much though. Alé, what do you hear about it?"

Alé has been friendly as a summer breeze all through dinner, blinking behind thick eyebrows, explaining things to me, and asking about the *Orion* and what we see in the other cities. She's got skin almost as pale as mine and long, crow-black hair that she likes to tuck behind her ears.

"Bad things," she says. "A new gang lord came to town a while back, carved out a territory in Bleak Forest, then expanded into the Silver Stream. The police have been having a nightmare even containing him, let alone getting order back into those parts of the city, and the other gangs have fled. The kidnappings started soon after he had his territory secured. They happen all over the city, always kids, always skylungs or cloudlings." She looks at me, evaluating, calculating. "You should be careful, Nadya. Don't go out alone, don't go out at night, and never go into Bleak Forest or the Silver Stream."

I swallow. "Where're those places?"

"On the other side of the Doubleflow," Rash says, "within sight of city hall. It's been a real embarrassment to the Lord Mayor that she can't keep order in her own backyard. Apparently she's furious about it." He eyes the line behind us, then gets up. "I'm grabbing some cake. You want anything?"

"Sure," Alé says, "get us each whatever you're having," and he takes off. Tian Li follows a second later so he'll have an extra set of hands, and Tam and Alé and Aaron and me just sit.

Alé observes me, spinning her fork around. "You look like you're thinking." She's a little older than me, and it shows sometimes. She hasn't taken her eyes off me since we started talking about the kidnappings. "What about?"

I cough, trying to decide whether I can trust her. But I figure I don't really have a choice. My options for getting out and about are pretty limited right now, and this might be my only chance to ask some questions. "The kidnappings. We've gotta do something." I nod at Aaron. "His whole village is gone. He's a cloudling, from Cloudlington."

Alé stops twirling her fork, then whistles. "Wow. I'm sorry."

He shrugs. "Th-th-that's okay. But can you h-h-h—" He stops and frowns. "Can you give us some advice or someth-thing?"

Alé nods. "We can, but . . ." She looks up and down the table at all the other kids. Everyone seems absorbed in their own conversations, but there are a few who might be listening to us. She leans in closer. "Ask if you can spend the night. The Goss will need time to help you with your prosthesis anyway, and she'll be fresher for the work tomorrow morning. Plus it's dangerous on the streets after dark. We can talk more privately once everyone's asleep."

I'm all set to agree, until I remember Tam and how uncomfortable he's been. I look over at him, and he stares at his plate. But then he nods, and I figure we've got a plan.

It's surprisingly easy to persuade Thom to let us spend the night. He and Gossner are still talking when Tam and I go up to their table to ask, and he says it's okay with him if it's okay with her, and she says we'll work on my leg tomorrow morning after breakfast, and that's all the discussion there is.

I get back to the table feeling excitement and dread swirling in my gut, like there's cake and spinach mixing around in there—which, come to think of it, there is.

Rash grins when we tell him how it went. "Killer!" he says. "You guys can bunk with us. There's plenty of room and we've got some spare blankets and cots." Kids are starting to put away their dishes, and he gets up to join them. "I've got clean-up duty tonight though. Alé, can you get them settled?"

"I want to help," Tam says suddenly. He gets up. "If you guys don't mind, I mean."

"Me too," Tian Li says. She starts gathering plates and forks and glasses around Tam.

"Great!" Rash says. He claps Tam and Tian Li on the shoulders. "Come on, dish buddies! Let's get scrubbing."

The two of them take off for the kitchen, leaving me, Alé, and Aaron at the table. Alé gets up and brushes her hands off on her overalls, then tosses a dark-green corduroy jacket with tons of pockets sewed onto it over her shoulders. "Well?" she asks. "You ready?"

I scratch my head, looking around at all the kids cleaning up. It's amazing how smoothly this place operates. Everybody gets along so well too. I miss Pep more than ever. She'd be right at home running around with Tam and Rash, asking questions about glide ratios and steam pressure. But instead I'm here, and she's on the *Orion*, because she took the heat for all of us.

Then Alé starts off toward the sleeping platform, and soon I've got other things on my mind again.

It's exciting bunking down with Rash and Alé. Alé scrounges up a couple extra mattresses from neighboring platforms, then spreads out blankets. "We use these in winter," she says. "But this time of year we only need about one blanket each."

Their platform's pretty small, so all the mattresses get jammed together. We're basically all going to sleep in a big pile. The platform's got railings everywhere except where the two catwalks enter and exit it, so I'm not too worried about falling. Alé catches me looking and smiles. "Rash and I will sleep on the edges," she says. "Just in case. We're used to it up here."

I nod, and then I settle down toward the middle. It feels *great* to get off my crutches and rest. Even though they got the swings set up by dinner, I've crutched farther today than ever before. My armpit's rubbed raw, my hands have blisters, and my forearms and shoulders are killing me. My missing leg aches, and my other leg feels exhausted.

Alé sits next to me with a tired *whuff* while Aaron peers through the railings at the kids getting ready for bed above and below us. "Long day, huh?" she says. She pulls off her boots, and when she takes the left one off, her leg just pops straight out, no foot attached.

I can't help it. I stare, even though I hate it when people do that to me.

Alé starts giggling. "I knew it! I knew it!" She rolls onto her side, then sits up. "I knew you didn't know!" She grins. "Rash and I had a bet going, and now he's got to make my bed for a week."

I nod, still not sure what to say. I've got so many questions, but I dunno how I'd feel if some kid I just met started asking me about my leg, even if she was missing part of hers too.

"Want to see the prosthesis I made with the Goss?" Alé asks. I nod and she hands me her boot, which has a zipper down the front, and unzips it. "It's all one piece to make it easier to get on and off, but it unzips so I can work on the mechanism. Sorry about the smell."

"What smell?" I mumble. It mostly smells like gear oil and leather, with just a little bit of funk. "My shoe stinks a whole lot worse after a day like today."

She laughs again and pulls her legs up underneath her. "I lost my foot to a car," she says. "It came screaming around a corner as I was stepping off the curb"—she slaps one hand into the other—"and *bang*, that was it. I was already working for the Goss as a runner, so she paid for my doctors and helped me figure out how to build my own prosthesis. She's a genius." She grins. "She'll do a great job with yours, I'm sure."

I nod, looking at the mechanism inside Alé's boot. It's a

long piece of metal bent at an angle about the same as if you were walking and put your weight on the ball of your foot. It probably works like a spring, and it's got another bit of metal beneath it that looks like a heel. On top of it there's a complicated mess of springs, and then a cup and sleeve.

"Yours will probably be a lot like that," Alé says, pointing. "Just with a rod where your shin would be and a cylinder to fit your residual limb and knee." She rolls across the sea of mattresses and rummages in her clothes until she finds something. "Here," she says, "it's clean," and she tosses me a sock. It's made of some kind of rubbery material. It stretches and shifts, but it's super tacky, like it wouldn't slip at all against metal or plastic. "This is the key to the whole thing, the biggest part I bet Tam's prosthesis is missing. The Goss didn't get the chemistry right till about six months ago, and it makes a huge difference in how well her stuff works."

"Thanks," I say, and I return the sock. I look down at the Mighty Lady and flex her back and forth. She barks like she's been jabbed with a needle, and that little bit of pain pokes a hole in a dam inside me, and suddenly there's tears in my eyes. I've told myself over and over that I'll walk again, run again. But I don't think I've really believed it until now. Alé's prosthesis is so good, and she's so good at using it. Maybe I'll be like that too someday.

I glance up and she's watching me, looking sympathetic. "I lost my leg to pirates," I say quietly. It's the first time I've told anyone. "They kidnapped Thom and Captain Nic, plus our tutor, Mrs. Trachia. Tam and me snuck onto the pirates' ship to rescue them, but we found Aaron there too, and we got caught after I broke him free. The pirates shot at us and hit my leg, and it got infected. Nic had to amputate it."

I take a long, deep breath after I finish, staring at the Lady. I can still remember what it was like to have my leg. It wasn't that long ago. But I'm starting to get used to being like this, and if I'm totally honest with myself, sometimes I realize how big a change that is and it scares me.

Alé stares at me, wide-eyed. "Goshend's eyeballs," she says. "That's awful. But you *saved* that kid? From pirates? You're a hero."

I shake my head. Nic thinks I'm so reckless I might be a danger to the crew. Pepper thinks I'm a terrible best friend. I might've saved Aaron, but I haven't done anything to save his sister.

So, no, I wouldn't say I'm a hero at all.

Our conversation turns to other things—I ask about the food, the city, and how Alé found Gossner, and she tells me they grow some themselves and get a big delivery every day, the city's the best place in the world, and she was five years old when her parents died in a warehouse fire by the harbor, and Gossner knew them and took her in. I ask who does the laundry for all these kids and where the bathrooms are, and Alé smiles and says the bank of washing machines is the size of a bus, then points out a little room with plumbing pipes coming out of it a couple catwalks over and says there's a few bathrooms on every level.

Eventually Rash, Tam, and Tian Li show up. Rash and Tam laugh like old friends, and even Tian Li's in a better mood. She and Alé stay up talking about the city for a while before we turn in for the night, and I borrow some paper and a pencil and write a note to Pep. Rash says Gossner has little flying messenger machines I can use to send it out, and I'd like to get it to her tonight if I can.

Hey, Pep,

Wish you were here. Gossner's tower is pretty cool. There's a lot of machines and stuff, and the kids are all into gears and steam like you. I miss you. Tam's doing okay, I think. He and this kid Rash we're with get along really well. I met a girl named Alé I think you'd like too. After Nic stops being such a jerk, we should come back and all hang out or something.

I sigh. So much for the easy part.

I'm still trying to figure out why you're mad at me. I want to be a better friend, I just don't know how. I don't know if I can help it if people don't listen to you around me, but I guess I can try. Maybe they'll listen.

My stomach crunches up. I don't feel like this note is going very well. But if I don't finish it now, I'll just get stuck trying to get the words perfect, so I finish it as quick as I can. Better to say something than nothing, right?

Anyway, I hope Nic isn't being too hard on you, and you're having a good time with Sal. It was really awesome when you saved us all from getting in trouble. I think you're a great friend.

Rock on,
Nadya

I fold the note up and hand it to Rash, who attaches it to a little iron bird with a clockwork heart. He winds it, then flicks a few levers and drops it off the edge of the platform. My heart jumps, but a second later its wings start to flutter, and it sails out an open vent at the top of the workshop.

I thank Rash, then lie down and stare at the ceiling, thinking about Pep, Nic, and kidnappings. Rash and Alé don't want to tell us what they know until everyone's asleep, and I figure with how busy my brain is right now, I'll just stay up until they're ready.

But the sound of a few dozen other kids dropping off one by one, breathing soft and slow or snoring, is pretty hard to resist, and eventually I fall asleep anyway.

I dream about Aaron's sister calling for help, and my gills burn. *I'm trying!* I call out to her. *I'm trying, but it's hard!*

The shadowy man holding her turns toward me, and I try to run, but I fall down and have to scramble away on my hands and knees. He grabs me, and I hitch in my breath to scream—

"Hey," Tam whispers urgently. "Hey, Nadya, wake up!"

I take deep breaths and open my eyes. I'm facedown, tangled in a pile of blankets. My head's about three feet from a gap in the railing at the edge of the platform. Rash, who was supposed to be guarding it, must've rolled away in his sleep. Tam's got me by the arm, and my foot's against his chest, so I think maybe I've been kicking him.

"You awake yet?" he grunts.

"Yeah," I whisper back. "Sorry." I move my foot, and he lets go of my arm and rubs his chest.

"Geez, you kick like a backfiring dump truck," he says.

My gills burn, but I decide to take that as a compliment. "Thanks," I say. Next to me, Rash lets out a loud snore. "Think we should wake the sleeping engine boiler over there?"

Tam grins. "Probably. I'll get the others." He turns to crawl over to Tian Li, Aaron, and Alé, but I realize this might be the last chance we get to talk alone for a while, and I grab his ankle before he goes.

"Hey," I say, "are you okay? Being here, and all?"

His grin fades, and his eyes dim. The soft orange light of the boilers down below hits his face like sunset on a cliff. "I think," he says. He runs a hand through his hair. "I mean, most of the time I am. Rash doesn't blame me at all, says if he'd listened to my rules in the first place he never would've lost his arm. Goss doesn't either, although she seems a little mad I left without saying anything. And the other kids don't look at me like I'm a monster anymore. They want to ask me all kinds of questions about the Cloud Sea and cloudships and pirates and the world outside Far Agondy." He shrugs.

"So if I let myself, I can feel like everything's okay. But every time I do that I feel guilty, like I shouldn't be getting off so easy. So I dunno. I'm okay. But I'm not great." He glances up. "Thanks for asking, Nadya."

"No problem, Tam," I say. "We gotta stick together, y'know?"

"Yeah," he says. He smiles. "Yeah, I do."

It takes a few minutes for everybody to wake up. Alé gets her prosthesis on, and I find my crutches. Soon we're all standing by the stairway leading up from their platform.

"Okay," Rash whispers. "We're headed to the third level. We've got a spot there where we can talk without anybody hearing us." He looks at me apologetically. "We won't be able to use the swings, because they're so loud. Think you can crutch it?"

I nod. I'm still sore, but I'm not gonna let that stop me. "Of course," I say. "Let's go."

Alé grins. "Follow me," she whispers, and she leads the way out.

She takes us on a long, winding path that keeps us from running through other people's sleeping nooks. "It's great sleeping wherever we want," she whispers as we stop for breath on a platform full of buckets of rusty bolts and scrap metal, "but it makes sneaking around at night pretty hard."

When we get up past the second level, Rash pulls me aside and points out our destination. It's the room I saw before, a big black rectangle probably a hundred feet long and thirty feet wide, suspended from the roof in one corner of the building. Only one catwalk leads up to it. There's no lights shining there and the boilers are far below, so I can't see any details.

"What is it?" I ask.

"A surprise." He gives me a big, goofy wink. "Remember that thing I wanted to show you? That's where we're headed."

I stare at it as we work our way up, trying to figure out what it is. Some kind of room, obviously. But what could be in there? A swimming pool? It's definitely big enough. But why would they put a swimming pool up by the ceiling?

I still don't have it figured out by the time we get there.

The entrance is kinda spooky. We're up by the windows, so there's a great view of Far Agondy's electric night, all those skyscrapers with their dandelion brightness, but it's still pretty dark up here. The room we're entering is made of cast iron, welded together so tightly I can't even see the seams. It must weigh a bazillion pounds—there's support rods attached to it every six feet or so in a grid. I'm amazed the roof can take all that weight, but I guess they must build things pretty strong around here.

The door's design is really familiar. It's got a big wheel in the middle that looks like it has to be unlocked and cranked open and shut. Just in front of it there's a shelf with a bunch of masks.

"Here, put one of these on," Alé says. She starts handing them out.

I stare, blinking. The masks are made of black rubber, with little glass eyepieces so you can look out. They cover

118

your mouth, and attached to the mouthpieces are black hoses about a foot long, with canisters at the end. Rash and Alé show Tian Li and Tam how to get theirs on.

I stand patiently and wait my turn, but when Tam and Tian Li are done, Rash just grins. "You and Aaron won't need them," he says. I recognize the design of that door, and my stomach twists up in a knot. This can't be what I think it is. It *can't*.

"Come on," Alé says. We bundle into a waiting room just like the one on the *Orion*, and Rash cranks the outside door shut. Alé pushes a big green button. The air hisses and whooshes as it's sucked out, and then there's a chime and the inner door unlocks. My gills open up, and we step into something that's definitely, one hundred percent, undeniably a cloud garden.

CHAPTER 9

IN WHICH NADYA WRESTLES WITH HER FEARS, AND LEARNS ABOUT A MAN NAMED SILVERMASK.

I can't believe my eyes. The cloud garden up here in the roof of Gossner's workshop looks as bright and green as any I've seen on a cloudship. The trees stretch to the ceiling. Birds in dozens of colors flit between them, chittering and chirping happily. A lizard skitters up an iron support beam next to me and sticks its tongue out to taste my cheek, then runs away. There are two sun-in-a-jars, one at each end of the garden, and food crops take up about a third of the space. I see tomatoes and corn and beans and lettuce and spinach and carrots and more. I scoop up some soil and run it through my fingers. It feels moist and heavy, perfect for growing.

A cloud garden, in a skyscraper. There are six kids in here, and four of them shouldn't be able to breathe the air.

"Goshend's tangled beard," Tian Li says beside me. Her voice sounds all muffled through the mask. "Is this what the *Orion*'s garden is like?"

I nod, swallowing. My mouth feels a little dry. I've told Pep a hundred times how much I wish I could share the garden with her. So why don't I like seeing other people here? "Pretty much," I say. "Except this one's bigger. And greener." Maybe that's it. I've been so worried about whether I'm doing a good job with our cloud garden and whether I could ever be as good as Mrs. T, and this garden's like a big neon sign saying, NOPE, YOU'RE A FAILURE. "Who takes care of this?"

"Rash and me, mostly," Alé says. The mask covers her mouth, but I can tell she's grinning, proud as a cloud bird with a nest of new chicks. "The Goss comes up sometimes too, and there's a few other kids who help out with the food."

"Isn't it great?" Rash asks. He claps me on the back. "This is one of our biggest successes. Nobody's ever had a cloud garden without a skylung or a cloudling to run it before!"

I feel a little woozy. "Yeah," I say. "Great." There's a soft-looking patch of grass a few feet away. "Mind if I sit down?" I crutch over and do it without them answering, trying to work some spit back into my mouth. No skylung. No cloudling. Nobody to talk to the plants and animals. And they're *still* doing a better job than me.

"These masks are incredible," Tam says behind me. "How do they work? Do you think I could have one? Or make one? I mean, then Nadya and Aaron wouldn't be stuck doing all the garden work in our balloon. This is amazing!"

I touch my gills. "It isn't *amazing*, Tam!" I snap. "It's just a stupid box!" I lurch up and crutch into a stand of trees. I feel like crying, and I don't want to do it in front of anybody else, plus I don't want to insult Rash and Alé any more than I just did. But I'm so mad and confused I think if I'm around anybody else right now I'll just keep snapping and snarling.

I squeeze past the trees into a stand of bushes with bright, speckled flowers shaped like pitchers, brushing tears out of my eyes. I've spent my whole life trying to learn how to run a cloud garden. I had Mrs. T to teach me. I thought I was getting really good at it. She *said* I was getting really good at it. But now she's gone and my garden's not as good as this one.

I can't do anything right. I can't take care of a cloud garden, I can't keep my best friend from being mad at me, and Nic's worried I'm gonna be a danger to the other kids on the crew. My whole life I've told myself I could do anything, but maybe I've always been wrong.

Dumb and lucky, Tam called me once when he was really mad at me, and even though he apologized, it still stings sometimes. Maybe I was never really any good at taking care of the *Orion*'s cloud garden, and it was always just Mrs. T.

I throw my crutches at a tree and immediately regret it. The plants here didn't do anything wrong. They just grew, like they're supposed to. I reach for it over the Panpathia. *Sorry,* I whisper. *I'm just mad about a bunch of stuff. It's not your fault. Are you okay?*

The tree stays completely still. In our garden, the plants don't talk, but they do things like sigh or rustle their leaves or straighten up or slump. I frown. Something's wrong here. I look around at the other plants and animals on the Panpathia.

They're all bright and golden, just like they should be, with little gold strands linking them.

A lizard crawls up by my toes, and I try to find its mind. *Hello?* I ask. *How are you?*

The lizard tilts its head and blinks at me, then scuttles off. The plants behind me shiver, but it's just from the air circulating. *Hello?* I ask again, louder. *Is anybody there?*

Hello . . . , a voice whispers back at last. It sounds like a saw being dragged over a bed of nails, and it feels like a worm wriggling into my ear and biting.

I shake my head, trying to get rid of the feeling. *Hi,* I respond. *Do you live here? What are you? Where are you?* If whatever that voice belongs to lives in this garden, then maybe Rash and Alé aren't the great caretakers I thought they were. That voice doesn't sound like it belongs to something healthy.

Just a friend, the voice whispers, but I don't believe it. This thing doesn't have friends, whatever it is. Just victims. I take deep breaths and look around at the trees, the lizards, the birds, trying to figure out what and where this thing is.

Something dark and shadowy skitters, far off on the Panpathia, and suddenly I remember where I am: in the middle of Far Agondy, not in the *Orion*'s cloud balloon. It's not safe here. There are nasty things all over the web in this place.

The voice chuckles, and even though I know I should leave the Panpathia, I can't stop listening. It's like when a mouse stares into the eyes of a snake. Sometimes you just freeze.

You're close, the voice says. *I can feel it. One of the skyscrapers just down the way. And so strong. You remind me of . . . It couldn't be. But you are. You ARE!* The voice works itself up higher, shouting like a hurricane wind. *You're the one who escaped! The one it wants!* It laughs, a whirlwind banging a hundred garbage cans together. *Oh, how marvelous. Stay put, will you? Just stick right where you are, and I'll have someone there to get you very soon.* Whatever's behind the voice smiles, and it sounds like a drawer full of knives being opened. *And then we'll sit down, you and I, and have a long chat about what happened on the cloudship* Remora.

Something grabs hold of my mind and pulls it on the Panpathia. I fly through Rash and Alé's garden and out over the city, sliding along slick golden strands. A face looms out of the darkness. It's a silver mask, two big eyes carved wide-open, staring, and a snarling mouth with jagged, sharpened teeth.

Hello, the voice says. *So nice to make your acquaintance . . .*

I finally get my mind in gear and jump off the Panpathia. Goshend be good, there's nothing keeping me there like there was on the *Orion* last month.

"Tam," I squeak. I open my eyes and I'm still surrounded by the eerie brightness of Rash and Alé's strange, silent cloud garden. "Tian Li, Aaron, Alé, Rash . . ." I can't find my voice. The lizard I saw before skitters toward me, and I flinch away and crawl back. Everything in this garden feels wrong, and if I stay put another second, that voice will send something to get me. I have to go. I have to go now.

I nab my crutches, wobble to my feet, and head for the door as fast as I can.

124

"Nadya!" somebody calls, but I don't care. "Nadya, what're you doing?"

I crutch to the door and lean on the wheel, but I can't get enough weight on it to make it turn with just one foot to brace me. I suck air in and out of my gills faster than I need to. The world spins. My face tingles. I can't get out. I'm stuck here. Something's coming for me, and I can't get out!

"Come *on*!" I scream. I jump and use my whole body to get the wheel to turn, and finally it loosens. I fall down, but I pull myself right back up again and start to tug the door open.

Tam reaches over my shoulder and pushes it shut. "Nadya, what's going on?"

I turn to face him and he looks like a monster, the kind of thing that silver-masked creature would send after me. "Let me *go*!" I shout, and I push him away. "Just let me go!"

Tam backs off, hands up. "It's the mask, isn't it?" he asks. He pulls it up so it's not covering his face anymore. He stands there, holding his breath, and looks at me, eyes clear and brown and deep. My chest heaves. My head spins.

But he looks like Tam again, and I start to calm down. I nod and close my eyes. "You can put it back on," I say. "I'm just not gonna look, okay?"

I hear Tam fiddling with the mask, and then he takes a few long, deep breaths. "Okay," he says. "What happened?"

I keep my eyes shut, but I reach out for him. I need a hug, and I'm glad he's there to give one to me. I tell him everything that happened, and he hugs me until I'm done explaining. Then he says Rash and Alé were talking about the kidnappings before and he thinks they might have an idea what's going on.

I let go of him and wipe the tears from my eyes. I can still hear that masked man's voice in my head, nails and saws and wriggling shadowy things. I shudder.

"You okay, Nadya?" Tam asks.

I take a deep breath and nod, and then we head off to find the others.

I still don't like looking at the masks. I've calmed down, and I sit next to Tam, but mostly I try to focus on Aaron because he looks the way I expect him to. Everybody's sitting in a circle under one of the sun-in-a-jars, where Rash and Alé have some chairs and benches set up.

"I'm sorry," I say to them. "I'm really sorry I called this place a stupid box." I take a deep breath of warm, moist, plant-scented air, then let it out shakily. "This garden *is* amazing. It's just . . . what's the thing you've spent the most time working on, your whole life?"

Rash scratches his face. "My inventions, I guess," he says.

Alé nods. "Me too."

"Well, imagine if we invited you over to the *Orion*, and we were showing you around and all having a great time, and then I took you into a room and there were all your inventions, except I'd done them better, and everybody got all excited and I started telling them how easy it was to invent stuff like this if you just read this one book I had about inventing."

Rash grunts. Alé leans back and looks up at the ceiling. "That'd feel pretty bad," she says after a second.

I pick at some dirt on my pant legs. My hands feel cold. "The thing I've worked on the most in *my* whole life is learning how to take care of a cloud garden. I thought I was good at it. But when I saw how good you guys were, I got scared that maybe I wasn't, and then I got mad and took it out on you, and I shouldn't have done that and I'm sorry."

Alé shrugs. "No big deal," Rash says. "You should hear some of the names Alé calls my inventions." She socks him in the ribs.

I take a long, deep breath. There's more I gotta say. "Okay," I start. "So, I tried to talk to the plants and animals in here, but they couldn't talk back—"

"We know," Alé interrupts. "We had another skylung over once and he said the same thing. We think it's because they don't have anybody around to talk to. We want to get sky-lungs to come in every once in a while and see if they pick it up."

That explains that, at least. "And then I heard this voice," I continue. "This really awful voice, and it said it was looking for me and it knew who I was and what happened with the pirates last month. When I saw the thing it belonged to, it had this big, nasty silver mask on. Does that make any sense to you?"

"Silvermask," Rash breathes. Alé whistles.

"Yeah, a silver mask," I say. "What's it mean?"

"Sorry," Rash says. "That's the name of the gang lord we were talking about earlier. The new one behind the kidnappings. They say he's a skylung, and that's how he finds his victims." He puts his head in his hands. "We shoulda told you. Oh, man, we shoulda just told you. I'm sorry, Nadya."

The walls of the garden close in, looming over me like the fingers of an enormous, evil hand. "Could he get me here?" I bite my lip to keep it from quivering. If he says yes, I think I'll probably lose it.

"No," Alé says quickly. "Not here. It's too far out of his territory, and the Goss has the place locked up. He'd need an army to break in, and he doesn't have one yet." She stands up and starts pacing, like she's thinking real hard. "I bet he knows that. I bet he said all that stuff to spook you into running so you'd end up on the streets alone where he could get you." She tugs at the cuffs of her jacket. "We need to protect you. Rash? Can we?"

Rash nods and slaps his thigh. "Abso-freakin'-lutely. I'll get word out to the other Dawnrunners first thing tomorrow."

"The what?" Tam asks.

"That's what we brought you up here to talk about," Alé says. "Rash and me put together a group of kids to fight back against Silvermask. We call ourselves the Dawnrunners, but we have to be real careful not to let the Goss know about it or she might stop us. We're mostly kids who run messages and deliver things and do odd jobs around the city."

Rash, who's sitting underneath a big palm tree, cuts in smoothly. "When the kidnappings started, we needed a way to fight back. The other kids in the network tell us where the abductions are, and we arrange protection for any sky-lung or cloudling who has to head into dangerous territory. Sometimes we get help from adults or the police, but usually it's just a gang of five or six kids. Silvermask's thugs never work in groups of more than two. We don't know why, but we figure maybe it's because otherwise they'd be too easy to spot. They kinda . . ."

He trails off, like he's not sure how to describe it, and Alé picks up. "They *feel* wrong, when they get close to you. They act like they don't have minds of their own, do stuff like walk into garbage cans and knock them over. And they get really spooked by fire. Some of us think they're like puppets, that Silvermask controls them over the Panpathia somehow."

"That's not how the Panpathia works," I say, but then I re-member the Malumbra making me walk around in my cloud garden when it got its shadow in my mind last month, and I'm not so sure anymore. "Er, maybe. Aaron, does that make sense to you?"

Aaron's sitting sort of curled up, with his knees tucked against his chest. He's focused very hard on the plants behind Alé. "Yes," he says at last. "It sounds like the people who came to town and took everybody."

My stomach sours, and we all sit beneath the silent palms, thinking. "So Silvermask would have Aaron's sister, then?" I ask eventually.

Alé tugs her cuffs again. "Best chance, anyway. We don't think Silvermask takes the kidnapped kids out of the city.

We're not sure what happens to them." She stops pacing and looks at me, and I flinch. That mask. I really don't like it. "But how'd he know who you are? How'd he know what happened with you and the pirates?"

"The ones who escaped the *Orion*!" Tian Li says. She slaps her hands together and curses colorfully. "He must've helped them, or they must've gone to him or something."

"But how'd *they* know?" Tam asks.

I grimace. "We weren't exactly quiet around them." I could kick myself for it now. We could've been a lot more careful. "They probably pieced together the story from listening to us." I remember seeing them sleeping sometimes, and I'd just crutch right past, blabbering on about whatever to whoever. Maybe they weren't really sleeping after all. Maybe they had a plan, and this was it.

"So does Nadya just stay here, then?" Tam asks.

"No!" Rash, Alé, and I all say at once. Tam flinches.

"We can't risk keeping her here. Silvermask knows where she is, and he'll start messing with us. He might kidnap other kids, even," Alé explains. "We can't protect everyone all the time, and we can't tell the Goss or your officers what we know because then the Goss would bust us for starting the Dawn-runners."

Tam's face twists, but he doesn't disagree. He just stares at the ground.

I swallow and look around. The garden doesn't seem quite so spooky anymore, but I still don't like it. "Besides," I say, "I don't wanna stay here if he knows where I am. The *Orion's* home. If I have to hide anywhere, I want to be there."

Everybody goes quiet for a few seconds. "How do we get her outta here, then?" Tian Li asks.

Alé plops onto the grass, leans back, and yawns. "We wait till morning, after Tam and the Goss get her prosthesis figured out. Silvermask'll be watching the building, so we'll use a decoy through the front and get you out another way."

"Like what?" I ask.

She sits up. I can hear the smile in her voice. "Oh," she says, "I've got something in mind."

CHAPTER 10

The next morning, I'm standing on top of Gossner's building on the other side of the roof from where Rash's gliders are, feeling a hot breeze gust up from the street and nervously watching a zip line bounce over my head.

"Don't worry," Alé says, laughing. "I do this all the time. We'll be totally fine."

I gulp, looking at her hair blowing around like the branches of an angry willow and her jacket buttoned up tight with all the pockets zipped shut, and nod. She's checking a thin metal box that sits on a steel cable. Inside the box are three grooved wheels, with the cable running along the grooves. The whole thing comes apart in two pieces to snap on or off the cable. A short piece of super-tough woven material called webbing runs from the box to a metal clip, and that attaches to a safety belt that goes around your waist and legs, just like the ones we use on the *Orion*.

Alé clips the webbing to her belt, then opens the roller and snaps it onto the cable. She gives it a test pull back and forth, and it moves smoothly.

It looks sturdy enough, but catapulting through the air thirty stories above the street still makes me nervous. "Tam used to do this?" I ask.

"Yep!" Alé says. "Loved it too."

I haven't seen Tam since we spent a couple hours after breakfast working with Gossner. She took a whole bunch of measurements of my leg, some for the sleeve and some for the cylinder. Then she spent a long time going over the mechanics of the prosthesis so we'll understand how it'll work once she's done modifying it. Not all of it made sense to me, but I figure I'll sort it out once the leg's ready. Gossner said it might take a while to make the sleeve and do all the refinements, but she promised to have it before we leave port. Looking at Alé walking around, I can't wait.

"Okay," Alé says after checking all the buckles on her safety belt. "That does me. Let's get yours rigged up."

I crutch over to her. There's another zip-line roller on the ground next to her, and she shows me how to get it on the line, then tugs the webbing through a buckle until it's the right length to clip to my safety belt. The leg loops on the belt ride around my hips, between my thighs and my torso. My crutches I'll hold against my chest.

Alé checks a few things and tests out the roller, then grins at me. "All set," she says. "You ready to fly?"

I nod, and somewhere under the horde of butterflies in

my stomach, I'm a little excited. I've seen people zipping all over town on these things, but I've never gotten to try one. And they do look like fun, even though it means screaming around at a million miles an hour three hundred feet above the ground.

"You'll do great." She checks her watch and leans over the edge of the building, peering down. "They should be leaving any minute now."

The plan to distract the Shadowmen, which is what Rash and Alé call Silvermask's gang, is complicated. Early this morning, Rash took off in one of his gliders to talk to the Dawnrunners, and they found a girl who looks a lot like me. She and Rash are going to leave the building before Thom and the gang, acting like they're in a big, scared rush. They'll race into the street and grab a motorcab, which will take them a few blocks away, where they'll rendezvous with six other Dawnrunners dressed like me. Then they'll all split off in different directions and make their way to safe houses the Dawnrunners have set up across the city.

My stomach flips and flops. That's a lot of kids I don't even know taking a huge risk for me. But when I mentioned it to Rash, he shrugged. "They're excited to try this," he said. "A lot of these kids have lost friends and family to Silvermask. They want to stick it in his eye however they can."

I'm still not totally comfortable with it, but here we are, getting ready to go. We told Thom that I really, really wanted a chance to try the zip lines out with Alé, and I made all kinds of promises about not getting into trouble or going off on my own, and said I'd get back to the *Orion* before they would. When he still wouldn't give in, I flashed some pretty good moon eyes and pouted and told him I understood but I just felt so cooped up and Mrs. T always said I should see the world. Eventually he caved.

It occurs to me that's exactly the kind of thing that got Alan Salawag kicked off the *Orion*, and I have second thoughts. Maybe we shouldn't be doing this. Maybe I should go back down and tell Thom the truth. We can trust him to keep Rash and Alé's secret, can't we?

"There they go," Alé says.

Rash and a girl with blond hair run out the front of the building into a black motorcab waiting on the corner. The cab takes off quickly, and sure as spit someone near the door steps into the street and points at it, and then a couple other cars pull out of an alley and follow as it races away.

My neck gets goose bumps. "It's real," I say. "They're after me." It's too late now to change the plan. Rash and the Dawnrunners are already putting themselves in danger. I can't chicken out.

"Come on," Alé says. "We gotta get out of here before they realize what's up." She steps onto the roof's stone railing. "You got your tailhook ready?"

I look behind me, where there's a hook on a short rope hanging from the back loop of my safety belt. Its job is to catch a wire as we get close to our landing zone. There's another wire that catches the roller, but this way, in case it snaps, there's still something to slow me down. "Yep."

"Great," Alé says. "I'll go first. It's real easy. See the signal light?"

There's a light at the landing this zip line runs to. If it's green, the wires are set to catch you and you're good to slide. If it's red, you can't go or else you'll end up slamming into a crash pad at the landing. Alé says that's a real nasty way to stop, that at least one kid gets a serious injury from it every year and adults, who are heavier, have died.

I swallow and nod.

"Great," Alé says. "Then all you gotta do is hold the webbing to stay upright and remember not to scream. Just let gravity do the rest. Like so!" Alé sticks out her tongue, grabs her webbing with one hand, and holds up two fingers on her other hand like they're wolf ears. Then she leans backward until she falls off the building. My heart tries to jump out of my throat and grab her, but the roller and the webbing and the cable catch her and sling her forward, and soon she's sailing over the street, through an alley that leads to another skyscraper eight blocks away. Before I know it, she's halfway there.

"Okay," I tell myself. "Okay, Nadya, you can do this."

I crutch over to the railing, sit on it, and stand up, holding my crutches like they're a life preserver and grabbing the webbing so hard it makes my fingers hurt. "Okay," I say again. I can't see Alé anymore, but the light's red, so she must've hit the wires and arrived. A few seconds later, the light turns green. "Just jump."

My leg doesn't seem to be listening. "Just jump," I repeat. I look down. It's a long, long way to the street.

I shut my eyes, take a deep breath, and jump.

My stomach leaps like I left it on the building, and I shriek before I remember that Alé told me not to scream. It feels like I drop a hundred feet before the cable catches me, but it's probably only ten or twelve, and then I'm whizzing forward faster and faster, the wind ripping at my hair and tugging my breath away. I spin around so my shoulder's in front and I can breathe a little easier, and I open my eyes.

I'm flying.

I mean, I've been in a lot of flying machines by now, but this is the closest I've ever been to *really* flying, like Rash in his glider. There's nothing between me and the ground but air and my tailhook dangling behind me. I'm moving as fast as a striking hawk, passing over oilcars and horse cars and steam cars and streetcars and people and shops and food carts and all the packed-in life of Far Agondy. I feel like shouting, but I settle for laughing instead. What a rush!

The cable levels out, and I just barely see the wires for the roller and tailhook before they snag and slow me down. My safety belt tugs on me, but the system must be designed pretty well, because it doesn't squeeze too hard. The building rushes toward me slower and slower, and then the wire lets go and I roll gently through a window on the twenty-second

137

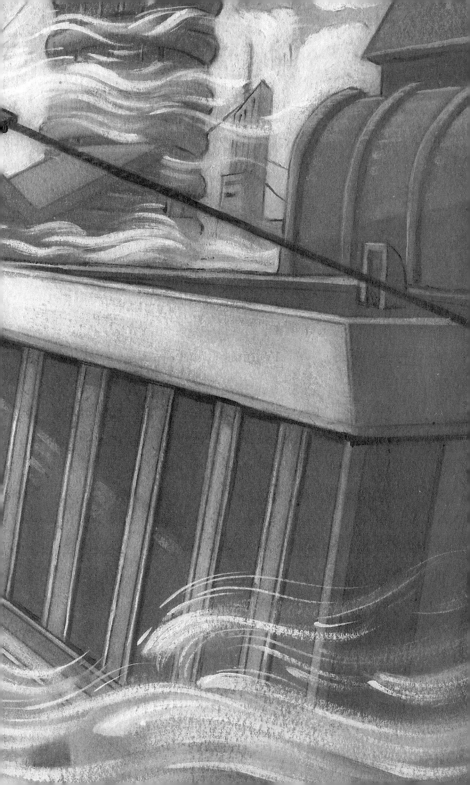

floor and bump against a big, thick pad the size and shape of a feather mattress.

Alé's standing below it on another pad, already off the wire, her roller clipped to her belt. "Well?" she asks. "How was it?"

I'm still breathing hard, but I grin. "It was *great!*" I shout. "You really get to do this every day?"

"Sure do," she says, laughing. "Best part of my job, by a hundred miles."

There's an iron platform just the right height for me to stand on next to Alé, close enough to the zip line you can reach it with your foot if you stretch, but far enough that you won't crash into it by accident. Alé grabs my ankle and guides me toward it.

And then things start to happen very fast.

Somebody grabs me. I'm not sure where he comes from, but all of a sudden there's a man in a long black overcoat with a shadowy face wrestling with Alé over my leg, and I'm spinning toward the other side of the crash pad where he's standing. His eyes are dark as wet plum pits, like the leviathan's I saw in the ocean, and I shriek and swing a crutch at him. It smacks him in the jaw, but he just grunts and keeps pulling. Alé loses her grip on my leg, and the guy yanks me toward him. He unsnaps my roller and yanks it off the cable, dropping me onto the crash pad with a thump.

The guy's still got my leg, and he pulls me toward him, so I let go of one crutch and hold the other in both hands, slamming it on his fingers, screaming, hoping somebody's around on this landing to hear me.

The man lets go after I hit his hand for the third time and reaches into his pocket. He pulls out a long knife, and I freeze. I feel like I'm back on the *Remora* staring into the barrel of a gun, except this time I've got nothing to fight with and nowhere to go.

"Crawl back, Nadya!" Alé shouts. "Crawl back!" She jumps onto the pad in front of me, pulls something out of her coat, and gives it a savage flick with her wrist. A long, thin rod slides out of a rubber-coated handle in her hand, and she swishes it toward the shadowy guy's wrist. It lands with a heavy *thwack*, and he drops the knife.

"Get to the next zip line!" Alé points over her shoulder, where another line leaves through an open window about ten feet away. "Hurry! There might be another one coming!" She keeps swishing that rod of hers, and the shadowy guy stumbles back a few steps. She gets him in the leg, then the face, then the leg twice more in the same spot. His knee gives out, and he falls down and lies there staring at her, like he's not sure what's happening.

The crutch I dropped is next to the guy Alé's fighting, so I leave it behind, snap my roller together, and slide off the crash pad, hopping and stumbling on one crutch toward the next zip line as fast as I can. When I get there, I fiddle with the cable, trying to remember how Alé attached the roller. At first I can't get it to click back together, but eventually I realize

I've got it backward. There are now two guys coming toward Alé, and she's swinging that rod like it's a sword to keep them back, but they're starting to surround her and it won't be long before they have her.

"Just go!" Alé shouts. "*Go!* I'll follow, I promise! But I need you out of the way!"

I just barely remember to check for a green light before I jump off the platform and let the zip line carry me off. I spin back to see what Alé's doing, but I'm moving so fast I can't see her at all, so I turn to see what's ahead of me instead. I really hope there aren't any shadowy guys in this building, because I don't think I could hold them off with my crutch the same way Alé uses that rod.

A few seconds later, I hit the wires and slow down, and this time when I bump into the crash pad I hit the catch on my roller right away, flop down, and roll off the pad. I end up on my back, looking at the all-clear light.

It's still red.

"Shoot," I mutter. "Shoot, shoot, shoot!" I scoot off the platform and stand, then search for the mechanism that resets the wire. I don't even know what it looks like. There's a couple chairs, a table with some switches by it, a message board . . .

And there, a winch over by the base of the platform, attached to the safety wires. I crutch over to it, but with how fast those guys were closing in, I think I'm probably going to be too late. I'm trying not to hyperventilate and think about Alé getting kidnapped and me getting lost in the knife-forest maze of Far Agondy's skyscrapers when I hear someone screaming at the top of their lungs, coming down the zip line toward me.

"No way," I whisper, and then Alé comes flying down the cable, not even using a roller, just holding on for dear life to a metal chain she must've been keeping in one of those pockets of hers. She zooms in feetfirst, lets go of the chain, and thumps into the crash pad hard enough that it shakes the platform.

Immediately, she falls back onto the pad. She tries to get up, but her leg buckles. *"Mmgh,"* she mutters. "Goshend's stinkin' fish breath, that hurt. Nadya, close the shutters. See the winch by the window?"

I follow her eyes and spot another, bigger winch next to a track that looks like it closes two huge shutters over the window we came in through.

"We close them when big storms come in. Do it now. Just turn it to the left."

I crutch over and lean on the winch. It's heavy, but it's oiled well, and after a bit of grunting and struggling to get the right leverage, I get it turning. Two enormous iron storm shutters slide along the track and thud together with a thunderous *boom*.

"Okay," Alé says from the platform, sitting up and wincing. "That oughta buy us a little time." I crutch her way, and she smiles at me weakly. "Think I busted my ankle. The real one. I can't believe none of us realized they'd be watching the zip lines. Sorry they almost got you."

I spend a few seconds staring at the big doors I just closed, breathing hard, letting the fear-octopus crawl back into my stomach as I tell myself that nobody could possibly get through all that metal. Then what Alé said sinks in, and I turn back to her. "'Sorry'? You were amazing! You saved my life! How'd you learn to fight like that?"

Alé shrugs. "Just practice with the Dawnrunners, I guess." She flops onto her back, staring up at the ceiling. "It's not much fun in real life though."

We sit quietly for a few seconds. It wasn't fun for me either.

Just as my leg tires out and I'm looking for a place to sit down, Alé grunts and rolls onto her side. "We'd better keep moving," she says. "Any chance we could share that crutch?"

CHAPTER 11

IN WHICH NADYA RETURNS TO THE *ORION*, AND MEETS A SKYLUNG NAMED RAJ.

The rest of our journey to the *Orion* isn't pretty. Alé's ankle swells up like a puffer fish. She can't walk on it, so I go first, then slide my remaining crutch across the floor so she can use it, and we rinse and repeat. By the time we get to the docking spire and I can borrow a cart to wheel us home on, using my crutch like a paddle to push it, it's early afternoon. I've totally blown my promise to Thom, and sure enough, Nic is standing on the deck as Alé and I approach, crossing his arms over his chest and glaring.

For a second I'm sure he's about to tell me not to bother coming back to the ship, but he must still be his old self somewhere inside, because when he sees that we're in trouble he thumps up the gangplank to us. "Here," he says. He offers his arm to Alé as we get off the cart. "What happened?"

Alé and I talked it over on the way here and figured we

didn't need to lie. We just won't tell the whole truth. "My name's Aléjandra Figueroa," Alé says. "I'm one of Machinist Gossner's runners." It's amazing how different she sounds when she's talking to an adult. Like she's grown up three years. Nic nods. "I said I'd show Nadya the zip lines this morning," Alé continues, "but we got ambushed by kidnappers from one of the gangs in the city. We got away, but I hurt my ankle." She lifts it up for Nic to see.

Nic glances at me worriedly and rubs his forehead. "We'll treat you on board," he says, "and we'll send word to Machinist Gossner to have someone come get you. I'm glad you're both okay." He turns toward the ship, Alé leaning on him and limping because we have to leave the cart on the dock. I think maybe I'm going to get away without a scolding at all until he looks over his shoulder at me. "This is why I don't want you out on your own, Nadya, breaking and bending rules." He sighs. "I won't question Mr. Abernathy's decision this morning, but I know you well enough to guess you played on his sympathy." His eyes narrow. "So, let me be plain: If I suspect again that you're taking advantage of Mr. Abernathy's grief over losing Mrs. Trachia, or his feeling of responsibility for you now that she's gone, I will take drastic measures. This is your last chance. Am I understood?"

I swallow and look down, gripping my crutch as hard as I can, my gills burning. "Yes, sir," I whisper.

"Good," he says. He stops partway down the gangplank, like maybe he's going to say something more, maybe apologize, maybe just tell me again that he's glad I'm okay. But then a spasm of fear crosses his face, and he continues on in silence.

I spend the rest of the afternoon up in the cloud balloon with Aaron. Nobody has time to head ashore for more crutches, so I crutch-hop from plant to plant, making sure everybody's got enough water and checking on the soil. The plants are still struggling, and I look through Mrs. T's notes for an hour or two trying to figure out why until I finally get it. I've been so worried about doing a good job that I'm *over*fertilizing the plants. That's why their lower leaves are turning yellow and some of the roots are getting black. Luckily, if I let off the fertilizer for a while the garden should right itself.

I lean back and breathe a sigh of relief. That's one problem solved, even if the rest are stacking up faster than I can count. Everybody on the ship's wound tight as a watch spring, about ready to pop. Tam and Pep looked sick to their stomachs when I told them what happened. Sal tapped his hands on his legs nervously, and Tian Li seemed about ready to rip something in two from frustration. Thom took it especially hard. He put on his first-mate face, but I'm learning to see through it, and I could tell he blamed himself for letting me go, even though I tricked him into it.

I keep thinking about Alan Salawag as I work, wondering if I'm really like him, wondering whether Nic's going to throw me off the ship, and worse—whether he'd be right to.

Aaron's up here with me, but we don't talk much. He seems kind of distracted too, and I don't want to bug him by asking what's wrong. I bet he just needs time to work through it.

Sure enough, partway through the afternoon, I hear his footsteps behind me.

"Nadya," he says, "you don't h-h-h—" He swallows. "You don't need to try to rescue my sister anymore. It's okay."

He's standing in the shade of an enormous palm tree, its fronds hanging around his head. His fists are balled up. "It's too dangerous. I don't want anybody else to get h-h-hurt." His voice quiets down to a cloud-feather whisper, and he starts to cry. "I just wanted h-h-her back."

His tears hit me like a flash flood. I'm bruised and hurting after my run-in with the Shadowmen, but it's just on the outside. Alé's ankle will heal. So will my pride, and probably even my relationships with Nic and Thom. But Aaron's sister is gone unless we find her.

"Shh," I say, and I crutch over and wrap my arm around his shoulder. "I'm not giving up." As I say it, I realize it's true. I can't give up. What am I gonna do, just run away? Never come back to Far Agondy? Spend the whole rest of my life looking over my shoulder for Silvermask, wondering whether his gang has its tentacles in the other cities too? Wondering whether more pirates are going to come after me?

"But Captain Vega . . ."

I push back from Aaron and put on *my* first-mate face, which I've still got even though I'm not gonna be first mate anytime soon. "Captain Vega doesn't know everything. And he can't be everywhere all the time. We're gonna crack this, Aaron. We're gonna beat Silvermask, take down his gang, and get your sister back, okay?"

Aaron nods and wipes his nose. He smiles up at me, snot puffing in and out of his nostrils. "Thank you, Nadya," he says. "You really are a hero. Just like Alé says."

I let go of him, lean on my crutch, and chew a piece of my hair that's dangled down by my mouth. I don't *feel* like a hero. I still *feel* like I can't get anything right and I'm in way over my head. I want to curl up under my blankets and wait for somebody else to fix things. I miss the days when I thought I could do anything.

But I guess those days are over, and if I've got to be something other than Nadya Skylung, Invincible Queen of the Air, I guess I'll take Nadya Skylung, Hero to Small Children with Missing Sisters.

I'm just starting to think about how I can follow through on my promise to Aaron when Tam's voice breaks the quiet from the speaking tube in the wall. "Nadya!" he shouts. He always talks into that thing way louder than he needs to. Maybe *I'll* borrow one of Rash and Alé's masks sometime so he can come in here and understand that he doesn't need to shout.

I cross over to the tube. "Yeah?"

"Captain Vega wants you and Aaron down on deck. There's a visitor here for you."

I glance at Aaron and take a deep breath. The fear-octopus crawls out of my stomach and waves its tentacles menacingly. I'm feeling pretty mistrustful of strangers right now. But you can't spend your whole life being afraid, right? And all in all, meeting a stranger on the deck of the *Orion* with Nic and Tam right there is a pretty small risk.

I have plenty of time to look at the visitor as Tam lowers me to the deck. He's a tall man, built like an ironmonger, all huge arms and legs and a barrel chest. He has wavy black hair that reaches about to the back of his neck, light-brown skin, and a small, well-trimmed beard that clings tightly to his chin. He wears green trousers and a dark-red long-sleeved shirt with buttons up the front, work boots, and a belt with a big golden buckle. He chats amiably with Nic as I come down, laughing and smiling and gesturing to a sack near his feet. Nic's more serious, but his movements are pretty relaxed. He must know this guy well.

"Nadya," Nic says as I'm unbuckling from the swing, "this is Captain Raj Varma, of the cloudship *Golden Dawn*. He's just back from reporting Mrs. Trachia missing to the Cloud Navy. He's a close friend of hers."

Raj bows his head. "It's a pleasure, Nadya. Zelda spoke of you often."

My heart races. One of the last things Mrs. T said to me, as I was getting ready to leave her with the pirates on the *Remora*, was *"Find Raj. He'll teach you."*

"Nice to meet you too," I say. I can see his gills, now that I'm closer. They move when he does, and every once in a while there's a flash of pink visible when they open as he turns his neck. "Are they going to track her down?"

Raj tugs a few hairs in his beard. "I don't know. They'll pass the information on to their captains, but the Cloud Sea is a big place. Honestly, I think Zelda's most likely to rescue herself." He smiles broadly. "Now, Captain Vega tells me Zelda wanted me to teach you more about using the Panpathia. Are you ready to learn?"

I want to keep pressing him about Mrs. T, but I also really want to know more about the Panpathia. My thirst for knowledge wins, and I nod.

"Excellent!" He claps. "I think I can show you a few things, but I'd prefer not to do it on deck. Is there a good place for a lesson?"

"You can use the galley," Nic suggests. "It should be another few hours until dinner. Will that be long enough?" The sun's starting to slide toward the horizon, but I guess maybe Nic's thinking we'll have a late dinner tonight.

Raj laughs and shrugs. "Who knows? It could be twenty minutes, or it could be two hundred." He points with his chin over my shoulder, where Tam and Aaron have reached the deck. "A lot depends on you and your young friend there, if he's willing to come. I hear *he* may have a few things to teach *me*."

A few minutes later, we're sitting around the table in the galley. The windows face the docking spire rather than the sea, but they still let in enough red-gold light from the afternoon sun to see pretty well. Raj settles down at the head of the table, leaving Aaron and me to sit on either side of him.

"Well," he says. "I hear you had a rather exciting morning."

I nod, my gills flapping a bit. "Yeah. Kidnappers. Know anything about them?"

"Nothing more than what's in the newspapers, which isn't much," Raj says. "We've only been in port a few days." He leans back and drums his fingers on the table. "You're quite direct, for someone your age," he says. "Don't lose it. It'll do you good."

He cracks his knuckles and looks over at Aaron. "Now," he says, "in a moment, I'll answer any questions you have for me. But first, a toast." He pulls three glass bottles out of his sack, each with a metal cap and a fizzy brown liquid inside. "Medzin's Cola," he says, smiling, and he pops the caps off the bottles with his thumbs, one by one. "One for each of us. Have you had it before?"

I shake my head and sniff the mouth of the bottle he hands me. It smells sweet and tart, like a mixture of root beer and lime syrup. Aaron does the same.

He chuckles. "You're in for a treat, then. I won't spoil it. But before you drink . . ." He holds up his bottle. The sunlight shines through the liquid and makes it glow, and the laughter leaves Raj's eyes. "To Zelda Trachia, a fine human being, a fine skylung, much loved and much missed. May Goshend's hand shield her, Goshend's breath sail her, and Goshend's anger never find her."

I raise my bottle and tap it against his. "To Mrs. T," I echo, choked up, thinking of her climbing through the broken window on the *Remora* so she could stay there in my place. "A true hero."

Aaron lifts his bottle and adds it to the toast, but he doesn't say anything. He just watches us, like he's not sure what to do. Raj tips his bottle back, and I do the same.

It's like drinking the sunset. The cola starts off fizzy and sweet and kind of sticky, like any other cola, but it changes as it moves over my tongue and down my throat, golden sweet and thick and soothing like honey and then fruity and thin like strawberry juice and then sharp and clean like a dissolving peppermint. "Whoa," I say, thumping the bottle down. "What *is* this stuff?"

Raj takes another sip. "Liquid gold, I find. There's a lot of money to be made buying it wholesale here from Medzin and selling it across the Cloud Sea. But we're here to talk about the Panpathia, and the Malumbra, and how to fight the one on the other." He raises an eyebrow. "I assume you have a few questions?"

Do I ever. I barely know where to start. "Thom told me the Malumbra's like a leviathan that lives between the worlds and eats minds. But where did it come from?"

"Who can say? Where did the worlds come from? Where do our minds come from?" Raj shrugs. "There are some mysteries no one has solved."

I frown. That's not much of an answer. "Well, do you know how it controls people, then?"

He drums his fingers on the table again and nods. "A little. It reaches into our world from the space between and touches minds. If you're on the Panpathia and it contacts you, it has direct access, so it can cloud your mind very quickly. But it can also possess people—even ones who can't use the Panpathia—by touching them physically with one of its skylung or cloudling drones."

"What's a drone?" I ask, sipping cola and feeling it explode on my tongue.

"That's what we call people whose minds are taken," Raj explains. "The Malumbra controls them directly, in contrast with its servants, who work for it of their own free will. It's the drones you can spot by the darkness in their eyes."

"Servants?" I sputter, spitting cola across the table. "There are people who work for it on purpose?"

Raj's nostrils flare. "Yes," he says angrily. "There are. And I hope you never meet one."

My stomach flips, and I look at Aaron. "We saw a man last month with darkness in one eye, the captain of the pirates we fought."

"Captain Vega told me," he says, frowning. "My best guess is that he was under partial control. I've never heard of that before, though. The Malumbra must be changing its tactics, and that worries me."

Anything to do with the Malumbra worries me. I get caught up thinking about the time it touched my mind, until Aaron says, "Wh-wh-what h-h-h-happens to someone if it clouds their mind?"

Raj grimaces. "We don't know. It takes a long time for the Malumbra to assume full control, and it seems the process is reversible in its initial stages. But for people who have been possessed for years, or decades?" He shakes his head. "It may consume them entirely. We'd have to return to the Roof of the World to find out, and no one has been able to do that safely."

Aaron looks at the floor. His chin quivers. I put my hand on his shoulder.

"What about just a month or two?" I ask. "We think his sister was kidnapped by the Malumbra's drones."

Raj's shoulders slump and his voice softens. "Ah, I didn't know. I'm sorry."

Aaron keeps his eyes locked on the floor. "Th-that's all right. But do you think sh-sh-she's still okay?"

"I hope so," Raj says. His eyes drift toward the window, like he's thinking about someone off the ship.

We all stay quiet for a little while, and then Raj clears his throat. "If that's all of your questions for now," he says, "I have one for you, Aaron. Captain Vega told me you burned the Malumbra's shadow out of Nadya. Can you tell me how?"

Aaron answers quietly. "It's a lot of imagining," he says. "My mom said it draws on your h-h-heart, how you see yourself inside." He fiddles with the cap from his cola. "Wh-when you see the sh-shadow, you start by clearing your mind, like it's a big empty f-floor and you're sweeping the fears off it." He looks up. "Does th-that make sense?"

I stare at him. That sounds hard. Whenever I think about the Malumbra, my mind has more fears running around it than an ant colony has ants.

"I think so," Raj says gently. "Please, continue."

Aaron stops fiddling with the cap. "After that comes th-the really h-hard part. You have to see yourself as something big

155

and strong and bright. I see myself as a lion, with th-th-three heads and six legs and paws full of claws." He blushes a little and looks up at me, and I do my best not to smile. "Th-then you wrap yourself in th-the Panpathia's light and you *be* the animal. 'Light always wants to burn sh-shadow,' th-that's what my mom said. And a big, strong animal will always ch-chase away a threat. So you ch-chase and fight and burn."

Raj nods. "Hmm. And what happens if you don't win?"

"You *h-have* to win," Aaron says. "If you don't, you're the wrong animal. That's the wh-whole point."

Raj leans back, eyebrows furrowing.

But I think I get it. "It's like if you were trying to figure out how to be a bird without knowing what a bird was, right?" I say. "And you only knew that birds could fly. If you imagined yourself as something that couldn't fly, then you'd know you weren't a bird and you had to keep trying."

Aaron smiles. "Exactly!" he says.

I get a sinking feeling in my stomach. The fear-octopus pokes its head out and hisses at me. If clearing my mind of fears sounds hard, *this* sounds impossible. I can barely imagine myself as somebody worthy of staying on the *Orion* right now. How in the world am I going to imagine myself as something that can beat the Malumbra?

We sit quietly while the cola fizzes. Raj strokes his beard.

"Hmm," he says at last. "Hmm, hmm, hmm." He stands up and paces. "This will take some doing, I think. Thank you, Aaron, for sharing. If it's all right with you, I'd like to pass the knowledge on to a few other skylungs."

"You're welcome," Aaron says. He licks his lips, then looks up. "Raj," he asks, "h-h-have you ever met a servant of the Malumbra?"

Raj's face tightens and his nostrils flare again. "Yes," he says shortly. "Though there aren't many." The sinking sun makes deep, sharp shadows on his face and neck. "It promises them things they want, and they justify horrible acts to get them." He takes a deep breath and reaches for his cola again. "But for now, let us turn our minds to brighter things, and I'll see if I can teach you some useful tricks."

Raj shows us how to find someone by holding their image in our mind, then feeling along the Panpathia for a vibration that reminds us of their footsteps. It's pretty tricky, especially here where the web's so dangerous and we can't spend much time on it, but after we play a few rounds of hide-and-seek around the ship, I get the hang of it. It's not as exciting as burning shadows and fighting back against the Malumbra, but I have to admit it would've come in handy on the *Remora*. If Mrs. T had taught me this, maybe I would've found everyone more quickly.

After our lesson, Raj debarks, promising to come back and teach us something else. He tells us we're doing a great job, and that we can get in touch with him anytime we have more questions.

"I've got another question now," I say as he's about to head up our gangplank and back to his ship, which is moored at a different spire. "Do you know anything about my parents?"

There's been so much going on in Far Agondy that I haven't thought much about them. Nic told me last month that he thought their cloudship crashed outside the city of Vash Abandi and that it was carrying something special. Maybe Raj will know something too.

Raj pauses, looks at his hand on the ropes along the gangplank's edge, and sighs. "Not much," he says. "Just rumors, a few names. Your parents' ship was called the *Brightening*, and it left the Roof of the World from Arnvang, the city that surrounded the Tree of Whispers." My heart thumps. The Tree of Whispers is the heart of the Panpathia. Nic told me all the strands on the web lead back to it.

"Your parents were first-rate cloud gardeners. They specialized in crossbreeding plants and creating new strains that produced wondrous things. The first fire-opal plant, for instance, came out of their lab."

My imagination takes off like a robin that's spotted a worm. The things Raj is telling me mix with the few memories I have of my parents. I can picture them dashing around the world, collecting plants and breeding them, or working hard at chemistry benches in a dazzling city, the huge boughs of the Tree of Whispers over their heads. "Do you know their names?" I ask.

Raj shakes his head. "People called them the Plant Doctors, and that was the only name attached to the rumor I heard: the Plant Doctors escaped from Arnvang on the Day of Shadows, carrying something that could heal the Tree of

Whispers. Captain Vega and Mrs. Trachia spent years trying to track them down. They found the wreckage of the *Brightening*, and you, but no more."

"The Day of Shadows?" I ask. I've never heard that name.

Raj shudders, and he looks at the horizon, where the sun's just dropped below the sea. "That's what we call the day the Malumbra took over. It was full of chaos and terror. Friends turned on friends, and family turned on family. There was fire and panic and death and flight." His eyes look like gravestones, scoured by wind and hard years. "For those of us who survived, it was the worst day of our lives."

I think of my doorknob, with its picture of a tree crawling up the front of it. I think of my mother, pulling it off a big silver safe and telling me to hold on to it, saying she'll be right back. I wasn't born yet when the Malumbra took over the Roof of the World, but I know when the worst day of my life was.

Raj puts a hand on my shoulder. "I'm sorry, Nadya," he says softly. "I wish I knew more about your family. I lost my parents, my sister, most of my aunts and uncles and cousins and friends." He kneels and takes my hands, rubs my knuckles gently. "But let me tell you of the other things I've seen in the last twenty years. We are coming back, like a plant that's been trodden on reaching for the sun again. There are skylungs in every city around the Cloud Sea, and in some beyond. We talk. We make things. We trade. The fall of the Roof of the World was a terrible thing, but it was not the end of our story." He lets go of my hands and stands, tall and proud as an ironwood tree. "It was only a dark moment, partway through. We are writing the next chapter ourselves, day by day, and we will make it whatever we wish."

He bows his head to me, and to Aaron. And then he walks into the deepening dusk, his eyes twinkling like stars, and leaves me thinking sad thoughts about home.

A storm blows in soon after Raj leaves. It starts off soft, just rain and a bit of wind, but by the time dinner's cleaned up it's raging hard enough to shake the docking spire. There's lightning and thunder everywhere. With the weather this bad, there's no way Gossner's going to make it out to bring Alé home, so we get ready for her to stay overnight. Nic and Thom suggest she stay in Mrs. T's old room, but when I offer to let her share my cabin instead they leave the decision to her, and she takes me up on it.

She seems excited about staying over. Tam helps us battle through the wind and the rain to my cabin, then says good-night. We're both pretty wet, despite the rain slickers we have on, but Alé still grins like she's on the biggest adventure of her life. I turn up my oil lamp, show her where to hang her slicker, and grab a couple towels from my dresser for us to dry off with.

161

"Thanks," Alé says. The floor shimmies underneath her, and she nearly loses her balance. "Think I'm gonna sit down." She slumps into my desk chair and takes one of Nic's empanadas, wrapped in a napkin, out of her pocket. "Mmm," she says as she wolfs it down. "Man, this is good. Like the ones my dad used to make. Does the floor move around this much all the time?"

I finish with my towel and drape it over the footboard of my bed. "Just during storms, and even then it's not usually this bad. We try to run around dangerous weather, and even if we get caught in it at sea, there's room for the *Orion* to move with the wind. We only get shaking like this when we're tied up in port and a storm hits, or if we have really bad luck in the open."

Alé nods, wrestling with her boot, then plonking herself on the floor so she can pull on it harder. She wiggles her hurt ankle a little. "Ow. Goshend's eyeballs, that hurts. Captain Vega thinks it's just sprained, but it might take weeks to heal." She slides onto her back and puts her foot up against the wall. "He wants me to keep it elevated. Says it'll help."

I only half pay attention, reaching under my bed for some extra blankets for her. She keeps talking.

"So you guys really see the whole world, huh? What's it *like*, having that kind of freedom?"

I snort, tugging out two heavy blankets I reserve for winter and storm nights and nabbing a spare pillow from my bed. "What freedom?" I grumble. "We just go where Nic tells us to."

Alé reaches over to the coat hooks and fishes around in one of her pockets, then pulls out a rubber ball and starts bouncing it off the wall. "I picked up on that," she says. "He seems kinda strict."

I roll my eyes. "'Kinda' doesn't even start to cover it. Lately he—"

There's a *rumble* and a *thump* from the deck below us, and I stop talking.

Alé spins away from the wall and sits up straight. "What was that?"

I put my finger to my lips and keep listening. It's probably just thunder or the ship straining against its mooring lines. But the deck below's where the hole in the hull is, and it sounded like maybe something came aboard. I strain my ears, trying to pick up anything below us, but there's so much noise from the storm I can't hear much else.

Then there's another *thump*, softer, and creaking timbers. Alé reaches for her boot and starts putting it back on.

"I dunno," I say. My heart pounds. "Maybe somebody's sneaking aboard." But who?

The fear-octopus pounces. "The Shadowmen," Alé and I say at the same time.

I can't believe we didn't think of it before. Silvermask knew who I was. He knew what happened on the *Remora*. He must've gotten the name of the *Orion* too, and if he had that, it can't have been that hard to figure out where she was berthed.

I vault off my bed and grab my crutch. Nobody's on watch because of the storm, so if I don't raise the alarm, no one will.

"Stay here," I tell Alé. "Lock the door, and scream bloody murder if anybody tries to get in."

"Wait a sec!" Alé says. "You can't just *leave* me here!"

"We've only got one crutch," I say, "and I know the ship better than you do."

Alé curses, then reaches into her coat pocket. "Then you'd better take this." She tosses me the collapsible rod she used to fight off the Shadowmen in the skyscraper. "I made it myself. There's a button on the side. Just hold it and flick it out, and then hit them as hard as you can wherever you think it'll hurt the most. The side of the leg just above the knee's pretty good. So are the ears and the face."

I find the button and try it out, then tuck it into one of my pockets. "Thanks."

Alé nods. "Go get 'em," she says, and as I'm heading out the door, she slides under my bed to hide.

Then I'm out on the deck, and the storm's screaming, and I have to fight to stay upright. The wind races over Nic's cabin and splashes rain into my eyes. The cloud balloon shifts, and water cascades onto the hood of my slicker and nearly takes me down. This storm's as bad as I've ever seen in port. The deck groans and shifts, and I'm really wobbly on one crutch. My balance hasn't been right ever since I lost my leg.

I do a lot of slipping and sliding, and halfway across I fall, bashing my chin and biting my tongue. I end up scooting across the rest of the deck, but eventually I get to Nic's cabin. I knock twice, then twist the knob and barge in.

Nic's sitting at his table, head in his hands, staring at

nothing. He jumps when the door opens. "Nadya," he says with an exasperated frown, "what have I told you about entering without permission?"

"Sorry, Nic—Captain . . . *urrgh!* Look, I think those kidnappers are back, on the ship, looking for me!"

"What?" Nic says. He stands up and reaches for his coat on the wall. "What do you mean?"

"This guy Silvermask. He's kidnapping skylungs and cloudlings, and I think he wants me specifically."

Nic walks over with a confused look on his face. "You? Why . . . ?" He shakes his head. "Never mind that for now. Who do you think is on the ship, and where, and why?"

I take a deep breath and try to calm down. "I heard some thumps below me, and then boards squeaking, like someone was sneaking around down there."

A look of instant relief breaks over Nic's face. "Ah. It's probably just the storm, Nadya. Tam was frightened about the hole in the hull a few days ago and thought there were intruders too, and that's where Pepper was when she was out of bed. I can understand why you're worried after today. But it's probably nothing. I'll just go check it out and make sure."

I shake my head. "You don't understand, Nic. Silvermask is *after* me. He saw me on the Panpathia and he told me he was coming for me and the whole reason I went on the zip lines today was to avoid him in the first place! They're *here*, I know it! This is serious!"

Nic looks at me hard, like there's books writing and unwriting themselves in his mind as he tries to figure out how far to trust me. My gills burn. I wish I hadn't lied to him. I wish I hadn't snuck around. I wish I hadn't ever pushed the line or broken rules or talked back to him, because I need him to trust me right now, and I don't know what I'll do if he doesn't.

Finally, he nods. "Okay," he says. "We'll get Thom and check the ship. And later you can explain what's going on, and give me the whole truth this time."

I bounce on my toes, still worried. "Fine, but hurry! Alé's alone in my cabin. What if they go there first?"

Nic starts for the door, pauses, then pulls a walking stick with a heavy brass knob at the top from behind his cabinets. I've only ever seen him use it in port, but after watching Alé with her little rod, it occurs to me it's not just for walking around—you could give someone a pretty good thump with that if you had to. "Then we'll go to your cabin first," Nic says. He opens the door.

Alé screams.

The door to my cabin is open across the deck, and Nic takes off toward it like a cannonball. There are two shadowy shapes inside, and I can see Alé kicking at them beneath my bed.

"Get Thom!" Nic shouts. "And have the others raise the alarm with the dockmaster!"

I watch Nic go for a split second, torn. I want to help. Alé gave me her rod, so she's got nothing to protect herself with, and those goons must think she's me or they wouldn't be bothering with her at all. But it would take me ages to get across the deck again. Nic's her best shot right now, and I'm

166

the only one who knows what's going on and can bring help.

So I turn and crutch down the stairs to the mid-deck as fast as I can, screaming at the top of my lungs. "Thom! Tam! Sal! Tian Li! Pep! Everybody, get *up*! There's goons on the ship! Get up, get up, get *up*!"

By the time I hit the landing on the deck, Sal and Tam are already there. "What's happening?" Tam asks. "What's going on?"

"Those guys who tried to kidnap me are back," I say breathlessly. "They've got Alé, and Nic's fighting them in my cabin. Somebody's gotta go help and somebody else needs to raise the alarm!"

"I'll get the dockmaster," Sal says, and he takes off up the stairs. I wonder why he's not going to help Nic until I remember his vow to Goshend never to harm another human being again. I grind my teeth. Sure would be handy if he could bend his vow right now, but he's a faster runner than Tam anyway, and I guess bringing help is pretty important too.

"Okay," Tam says. He takes a deep breath, like he's psyching himself up. He didn't like tangling with the pirates last month at all. "Okay, here I go."

Just as he's starting, Thom bursts out of his cabin carrying a walking stick like Nic's. "Move!" he barks, and we jump out of the way as he thunders by. I hear him sprinting across the deck above our heads a second later. Alé's not screaming anymore, but I can hear Nic and Thom shouting and lots of big, heavy footsteps.

"Coming through!" Tian Li shouts a second later, and she flies up the stairs in Thom's wake. Pepper's right on her heels, carrying the cargo net from her ceiling that usually has her stuffed animals in it.

That leaves Tam and me. "Okay," Tam says again, breathing hard. "Are you gonna be all right alone, Nadya?"

I nod. "I'll stick with Aaron in Sal's room. We'll be fine. Just go help them!"

Tam swallows, and then he takes off up the stairs too.

My heart's still thumping. I wish I could go up there with him, but everybody would have to protect me once the goons figured out who I am. So instead I crutch over to Sal's room, clenching my fists in frustration, and head inside.

Aaron's sitting up on his cot, staring at the door. "Is th-there a fight, Nadya?" he asks.

"Yeah," I say, my arms shaking. "It's those goons from before." I lock the door behind me and crutch over to him. "They came back. But everybody's taking care of it." I sit on the cot next to him, and then there's more thumping above me and Pepper shouts in pain. I wince and try not to cry. *Please be okay,* I think. *Please, please, everybody be okay.* A siren starts up from the dockmaster's office down below, and I figure the dock's security guards should be here any minute. Everybody just has to hold out a little longer, and maybe the Shadowmen will get spooked and leave.

"Hear that?" I say, wiping the tears away. "It's gonna be fine. That's the security coming. Everything's—"

The hallway creaks, and I shut my mouth and freeze. *Oh no, oh no, oh no,* I think. *Don't hear, don't hear, don't hear.*

Somebody tries the doorknob. My heart jumps into my throat, and Aaron shrinks up against me. "If they get in," I whisper, "I'll try to distract them. You run, okay?"

Aaron nods. Whoever's out there shakes the doorknob more forcefully. I take Alé's rod out of my pocket and extend it, then hop up on my foot.

There's a few seconds of silence, except for the shouting and thumping above us. I hear the voices from our side more than I hear the voices from theirs now, and everybody sounds calmer. I think we're probably winning.

The door crashes open. A big, booted foot plunges down in a sea of splinters that used to be the wood around the lock. It's attached to a large man with a long black coat. There's another man behind him in the hallway. They look at me and Aaron for a second, then inch forward. Their eyes are dark as midnight.

One of them speaks with Silvermask's nails-on-a-saw voice. *"Found you,"* he says, and he chuckles. It sounds like a bucketful of bolts rattling around in an engine. *"Oh, you led me on quite a chase, but here you are, both of you together. Remarkable. We'll just take a little trip, shall we?"*

I stand my ground and wait for them to get close enough to hit with Alé's rod. The bigger guy steps forward, and I thwack him in the leg just like she did, but he doesn't seem to feel it. When I swing the rod again, at his face, he catches it and yanks it out of my hand. *"That won't work again. These men are more tightly under my control. They won't be confused or distracted by little stings."*

Aaron jumps up next to me, but I hold him back. "The window," I whisper to him, nodding toward Salyeh's porthole on my right. "Try for the window."

And then, against every instinct in my body, I pick up my crutch and jump straight toward the two guys in the door, swinging it like a club.

Silvermask stops taunting me. His goons step aside and let the momentum of my swing spin me around. I almost fall, but I catch myself on the wall and try again. This time the big guy ducks under my crutch, puts his shoulder against my hip, and lifts me up in one smooth motion.

Aaron's to the window, and he's got it open. I scream and bite and claw, but I can't do much from this position except pull this goon's hair and yank on his ears and try to kick him in the gut or the crotch, and he just stands and takes it. The other goon walks calmly past us and plucks Aaron up beneath the armpits, then slings him over his shoulder too.

There's no more talking. The goons hustle out Sal's door toward the hole in the front of the *Orion*. I'm still hollering and shouting and kicking and biting, and Aaron's doing the same, but it doesn't seem to matter. The goons get onto the ropes between the *Orion* and the docking spire. I can see how they got in now: There's a rope ladder dangling through the spire down to the water, where they have a launch tied up, bobbing wildly on the crashing waves. Nobody thinking for themselves would chance the bay on a night like this, but these guys aren't thinking for themselves. Silvermask is controlling them, just like Rash and Alé thought.

The goons inch carefully along the ropes. I buck and twist, trying to get free, but this guy's got too strong a grip on me. I'm pointed back toward the *Orion*, and I can see the fight on the deck now in the orange light from her lamps and the white of the floodlights. The security guards are arriving, and it looks like the other Shadowmen are giving up. They're starting to jump onto the ropes and head toward the launch.

We're almost to their ladder. They're gonna take me to Silvermask, and then I dunno what's going to happen. I lose my breath for a second. I feel tiny and meek, like a mouse.

No, I tell myself, realizing I've got one last chance. *You can't be like a mouse.*

If Silvermask is controlling these guys over the Panpathia, he must be using the Malumbra's shadow to do it. And maybe if I can burn the shadow out of them, I'll be able to get free.

I close my eyes and step onto the Panpathia. Sure enough, the strands coming off the guy carrying me feel dark and cold, like a blizzard tainted with an oil slick.

Okay, Nadya, I tell myself. *Big and powerful.* But my mind freezes. The fear-octopus shoots out and wraps itself around my brain. All I can think of is that leviathan I saw last week and how it lost to the shadow. There's nothing big and powerful enough to beat the Malumbra. Nothing in the world.

I feel light and heat on the Panpathia in front of me. Aaron must've had the same idea I had. Dimly, I'm aware of the guy carrying me stumbling and slowing down. I catch a glimpse of Aaron as a lion, slashing through shadows, his claws trailing fire and light.

But behind him there's something else.

A silver mask appears, and the body of a man flows out of the shadows behind it. Silvermask walks toward us gleefully, tugging on the poisoned purple strands of the Panpathia that lead to his goons like a puppeteer. He wears a black suit, and a black cape flaps from his shoulders. The clothes are so dark they look like little gashes of nothing in the fabric of the world.

Hah, Silvermask breathes. *So this is how it was done.*

Aaron roars and charges at him, but Silvermask doesn't seem worried.

Impressive, for a child, Silvermask says. *Still, there's so much you don't know.*

Silvermask reaches behind himself and pulls on his too-black cape. As he tugs, it stretches around him until he's cocooned in an egg of darkness. The egg grows and grows. It's the size of a room, then a house, then bigger. Eight enormous legs erupt from it. Its body squeezes into an hourglass shape, and eight eyes bubble up on the front. By the time Silvermask is done growing, he's a spider the size of the world's biggest cloudships. I could drop into its eyes and be lost forever, falling and falling in the dark . . .

My heart seizes. I've seen this spider before, when I was looking for Mrs. T on the Panpathia last month. It was just over the horizon, hunting kids like me.

Aaron's lion skids to a stop. He can't possibly win. Silvermask is too big. Quick as the lightning around us, Silvermask lunges toward him.

Run, Nadya! Aaron shouts. As Silvermask pounces on him, Aaron swipes at the strand of the Panpathia leading to the man carrying me. Sunset light bursts along it until it hits us like dawn on the end of a sledgehammer. The goon carrying me curses. His arms go limp, and I leave the Panpathia because I have to focus on what to do with my body. We're still at the very edge of the *Orion's* slip, on the ropes in front of the ladder down to the launch. The safety net's below me. I push as hard as I can at the man's head and roll off his shoulders. I fall about twelve terrifying feet before the net's cold, wet, scratchy rope catches me, and then I tumble down it until I'm resting at its bottom, twenty feet below the *Orion's* keel.

I jump back on the Panpathia.

Aaron! I shout. I try to follow the strands to him, but they're all jumbled. *Aaron!* Maybe I can figure out something that will beat that spider. I have to try.

But all I can find are the cloud gardens of the ships around me. In the distance, the tortured web of Far Agondy's Panpathia hangs like an enormous, twisted chrysalis of brightness and shadow, fire and cold. There's no other skylungs. No cloudlings.

The spider and the lion are gone.

CHAPTER 13

IN WHICH NADYA FESSES UP TO NIC, AND A NEW PLAN IS MADE.

It takes them half the night to find me. Nobody thinks to check the net under the ship, so I spend hours down there, getting wetter and colder, occasionally trying to crawl up the net and failing because the slope is too steep and the rope is too slippery. The whole time I know Aaron's getting farther and farther away, and I lie there, feeling like dirt, until the storm quiets down enough that someone might be able to hear me and I start yelling.

Thom comes down to get me. Apparently Nic's making a report to the dockmaster at the base of the spire and talking to the Far Agondy police. Tam and Tian Li lower Thom on a harness, and he runs down the rope to me so fast he almost falls.

"Nadya," he breathes when he gets to me. "Goshend be good. Are you all right?"

I nod, but I hold my stomach and feel like crying and

throwing up anyway. "They got Aaron. I couldn't stop them. I'm sorry. I'm sorry!"

Thom scoops me up and hugs me. "That's not your fault, Nadya," he says. "And you're all right. That's so much better than we thought things were ten minutes ago."

I blubber and cry a little more, and then Thom says, "Your face is like ice. Let's get you inside and warm, okay?"

A few minutes later they've hoisted me up to the *Orion* and plunked me on a stool in the kitchen next to the oven, which Thom called a fire spirit into to help me warm up faster. I have a blanket around me and a cup of hot tea, but I'm still shivering, and I feel like I've been run over by one of the big steamrollers they use to flatten the streets in this stupid, overgrown, evil city.

Everybody's gathered around watching except for Sal, who ran to tell Nic that they found me. Pepper's got her arm in a sling.

"I tried to get one of those guys with my net," she explains when she sees me looking. "But he jerked it away so hard that it pulled my shoulder out of the socket." She closes her eyes, and her lip quivers. "Nic says it'll be fine though."

I swallow. "I'm sorry," I say.

There's a chorus of "Don't apologize" and "We're glad you're safe" and "It's okay, Nadya," but Pepper doesn't join it. She just looks away. I feel like she punched me in the nose, but I don't blame her.

"You don't understand," I say to everyone else. "I didn't tell Nic and Thom that Silvermask was after me. This is my fault."

Thom, who's standing near the edge of the kitchen behind everybody, rubs his temples. "You didn't tell us what, Nadya?" He looks pretty haggard. He's been up all night, and I don't know how hard it was for him fighting those goons but it must've been rough.

"Silvermask," I say. "This gang lord Alé and Rash told us about. He's after me because of what happened on the *Remora*. I think he must've been the boss of the pirates, or maybe the one buying kids from them. It was his guys who tried to kidnap me this morning, and his guys who attacked us tonight."

Thom takes a deep breath. "That's . . ." He grunts, then rubs his eyes. "You, me, and Nic will talk about it later," he finishes. He shakes his arms out, then heads toward the stove, where I smell coffee brewing. "For now," he says as he goes, "I'm just glad you're safe."

Later comes in about two hours, when Nic gets back from talking to the police. He looks even worse than Thom—wet and bedraggled and exhausted, completely at the end of his rope. But he trundles me into his cabin anyway. I'm glad to see that there's dockyard guards all around the ship when Thom brings me up on deck, but there aren't any policemen, and that worries me.

"First things first," Nic says as we sit at his table, "I'm glad you're okay. The police are looking for Aaron, but the detective I spoke with said there've been a lot of these kidnappings, and they're having a hard time finding the kids. They've already put as many people on the case as they can."

My stomach shrivels. "That's not enough! They got Aaron! It was my fault!"

Nic sighs. "To them, Aaron's no more important than any of the other kids who were kidnapped. And I can't change that, even though I'd like to."

I shrink back in my chair. The old Nic wouldn't have given up like this. He'd have found a way.

"So," he continues, "what haven't you told us? Start at the beginning."

I take a deep breath. I see the bags under Nic's eyes, and how shaggy his eyebrows have gotten. His shirt's not tucked in and his bed's not made and papers are scattered over his table. Behind him, Thom sways like he can barely stand, his eyes bloodshot, stubble on his face. They're under so much stress. I don't want to make it worse by lying to them.

So I tell them everything. I talk about how I've been using the Panpathia and it's cold and dead here. I tell them about Aaron's sister and how I promised to rescue her, whether Nic wanted to let me or not. I fess up about Gossner's workshop and Silvermask, and after swearing them to secrecy, I tell them about the Dawnrunners and how they helped me escape. Then I tell them how hard it's been to have them come down on me and the rest of the crew, to threaten us with being thrown off the ship.

Through the whole thing, they don't interrupt me once. Nic doesn't scold me. Thom doesn't sigh or put his head in his hands or clear his throat or anything. It's like old times again.

"Thank you," Nic says when I've finished, and he stands up

and faces the windows at the aft of his cabin. The storm has passed, and the city lights are twinkling brightly.

"I'm sorry you've been dealing with all that alone, Nadya," Nic says. "And I'm sorry for my part in it." He reaches for his glasses, finds his pocket empty, and settles for smoothing his shirt. "This is a difficult time for me and Thom. I have always had . . ." He clears his throat. "A tendency toward too much discipline, I suppose. It comes from my upbringing, which I won't go into now. Zelda and Thom balanced it. For the record, Thom disagrees with what I've been doing lately, but without Zelda here to add her thoughts, well . . ." He finds his glasses on the table and tucks them away. "I've been over-ruling his objections, which I should know better than to do. I owe him an apology as well."

Thom snorts. "You can deliver it along with a big old bonus next week," he says, but he winks at me as he does it, and even Nic smiles a little.

"I'm old, Nadya," Nic continues. He closes his eyes, and his face looks pale and stretched. "Too old to be fighting the Malumbra. I should long ago have retired to someplace warm and safe, where my biggest worries are boredom and the weather." He lowers himself into his chair gingerly. His forearm, I notice, has the beginnings of an enormous bruise on it. "But the fight isn't over, and that means my part in it isn't either."

He folds his hands in front of him, and I finally see the old Nic in his eyes—warm, kind, and thoughtful, plus smart and strict and disciplined. "Now," he says, "I have realized—late,

178

as usual—that this has become your fight too. It's you the Malumbra wants, through this Silvermask who must be its agent. It's you who'll be fighting long after I'm gone. So tell me, what would you like to do?"

The first thing I do is get everybody else in on the action. We move from Nic's cabin back down to the galley, where there's room for all of us to sit. I ask Nic to catch everybody up and make his apologies while I brew tea in the kitchen. Pepper cries when Nic tells her he's sorry for being so hard on her, and Tam cries too when he tells Nic how he lied to him to create a diversion for me when he was doing bed checks.

By the time I finish the tea and Tian Li brings it in for me, the crying and apologizing are done. Thom nods at me approvingly, like he's saying, *I don't know how you did it, but I'm glad he's back.* I smile and shrug, because I don't know how I did it either, but I'm really, really glad Nic's back to normal too.

Alé's still with us, sitting with her leg propped up between Sal and Pepper, which is good because she knows the city better than anybody else here, and she knows the Dawn-runners, who I'm hoping will help us get through this. I've got the beginnings of a plan, but I don't know how to fill in the gaps.

"Okay," I say when the tea's all passed around. "So Aaron's missing. That's mission number one, the biggest thing we've gotta take care of." The fear-octopus floats around in my chest as I think about that, but the busier I am—the more I'm *doing* things about what scares me rather than just *thinking* about them—the less I feel it, so I figure I'll just keep doing as much as I can. Tian Li and Salyeh nod. Tam frowns. Pepper sips her tea and stares out the window. "To get Aaron back," I say, "we've gotta figure out where Silvermask is taking the kids. Then we've gotta get in there and rescue him, and hopefully everybody else too."

Alé blows the steam off her tea and looks up. "That's what the Dawnrunners have been trying to do for months." She tugs at her cuffs. "But all we've got is a neighborhood where we think he might be, based on where the kidnappings are happening."

"Well, let's start with that," Tam says. "Where is it?" Nic rummages in a cabinet and pulls out a map of Far Agondy to lay down in front of Alé.

She points to an area of the city called Bleak Forest. "Here," she says. "Bleak Forest used to be a big-money part of town, back when Far Agondy was a timber port. But around the time the silver mines opened upriver, the forests dried out and the timber barons lost their shirts. So it's mostly old, dilapidated mansions that nobody lives in anymore. Most of the kidnappings are clustered in and around Bleak Forest, and the farther away from it you get, the fewer of them there are. So we figure Silvermask must be set up in one of these old mansions, but we don't know which, and we can't get in there to see for ourselves because the Shadowmen control the whole territory."

I nod, craning my head to look at the map. Bleak Forest is a big blob the shape of a peanut, just east of the Doubleflow

River. "Nic, do you think if we can find the right place, the police will help?"

Nic frowns. He's put on his glasses to look at the map, and he peers through them owlishly. "I'm not sure. The detective I spoke to seemed . . . demoralized. I think they've more or less given up on solving the kidnappings for now. If the kids fell into their laps, I'm sure they'd do something about it, but I'm not sure they'd risk a confrontation with a dangerous gang without clear evidence."

"Are there skylungs on the force?" Salyeh asks.

Nic puts his glasses back in his pocket. "I suppose there probably are, at least a few in a city this big. Why?"

Sal leans forward on his elbows and raises his eyebrows. "Well, could Nadya find Aaron on the Panpathia, then show the police skylungs the way?"

I shiver, thinking about that giant spider and how it got Aaron, even though he was so good at chasing shadows off the Panpathia. "I could try, but it's dangerous. Silvermask can do things on the Panpathia I don't understand—control people, take them over."

"That's the Malumbra working through him," Nic cuts in. "And I'd rather not put Nadya up against the Malumbra, Salyeh. It took down skylungs much more experienced than her at the Roof of the World." He sighs. "It was a good idea, though."

I tap my fingers on the table, looking at the map. "Well, is there another way we can track them to their base?"

Pepper straightens in her chair, looks at me, then looks back down. She chews her lip nervously.

"Pep?" I ask. "Have an idea?"

She opens her mouth, closes it again. "I thought . . . it's dumb. Never mind."

"Come on, Pep," Tian Li says. She nudges her with an elbow.

"Well," Pepper says, and she looks up at me and there's so much confusion and fear and hurt in her eyes that I remember all of a sudden that she's still mad at me and I don't know why. "We know they're looking for Nadya, right? So what if we use her as bait, and we track one of them down, and we catch him and get him to show us where his hideout is, or we chase him off and follow him home?"

Everybody's silent. My stomach churns. For just a second as Pep looks away, I wonder whether she only came up with this plan because it might not work and I wouldn't be around anymore. But she seems so torn up about it I bet that's not it. She can't be *that* mad at me.

I don't like the plan. Nic and Thom are very clear that they don't like it either. Everybody else agrees.

But we talk for hours and don't come up with any better ideas, so eventually that's what we decide to do.

CHAPTER 14

IN WHICH NADYA TALKS WITH PEPPER, AND TRIES OUT SEVERAL INVENTIONS.

After we all get some sleep, I find Pepper. She's alone in her room with the door open, throwing clothes into a bag. We figure we might need to hole up for a few days at Gossner's if things go badly, so everybody's getting ready.

"Hey," I say. "How're you doing?"

Pepper grunts. "I'm okay. I've been talking with Thom about how to fight the Shadowmen with fire spirits. He says he thinks it can be done, but I need to learn to make my contracts with the spirits more specific first."

I imagine Pepper calling up an army of fire spirits the next time we tangle with the Shadowmen. It's a warm thought. "That's great. How's your arm?" It's not in a sling anymore, but she's still babying it as she sorts her clothes.

Pep rotates it and grimaces. "It hurts, but not as much as it did before. It's not as bad as Nic thought."

"That's good," I say. "Can I sit?"

Pep waves at her chair, frowning at a blue shirt and some orange socks. "Sure."

She seems distracted, but I'm not sure when we'll get a chance to talk again, so I just dive right in. "Did you get my note?"

The shirt and the socks fly into the bag, and then Pep rolls onto her bed and stares at the ceiling. "Yep."

I frown. I sorta figured she'd be doing a little more than grunting one word at a time. "And?"

She rubs her knuckles into her eye sockets. "And I'm glad you're trying to figure it out, but you still don't *get* it." She rolls over to one side. "The suggestion I made today? It's the first time anybody's listened to any of my ideas in months."

I flap my mouth open, but Pep glares at me. "Just *lis-ten*, Nadya. Stop talking so much." I shut my mouth, but that stings. I don't talk that much, do I?

"And it's a terrible idea," Pep continues, "and it probably won't work, and then nobody will trust me for months again. Everybody thinks I'm just your sidekick. I'm the fun one. I'm the easygoing one. Nobody takes me seriously."

My stomach squirms. "That's not—" I start, but Pep glares at me again and I remember I'm supposed to be listening.

She pivots around and dangles her feet over the floor. "And you're always the first to say how bad my ideas are. I say something, and you're like, 'No, Pep, blah-blah.' Or 'That's not it, blah-blah-blah.' And everybody takes your lead. Even

Aaron pays more attention to the others than to me." She kicks up off her bed, grabs her bag, and walks past me toward the hallway. "So if you want to know what's wrong, that's it. And since you're so great, why don't you see if you can fix it?"

Pep's words sit in my gut like hunks of coal all morning, burning and crackling. She's got a point, but she's also being *mean* in a way she never has before. I'm all worried about whether I talk too much, and whether I don't take her seriously enough.

I'm so preoccupied I almost bump straight into Sal and Tian Li on my way to the cloud balloon. The two of them are sitting on one of the capstans out on deck, watching the cloudship traffic around the docking spire. They look kind of serious, and I figure I won't bother them, but I still overhear what they're talking about as I go by.

"Then Gossner told me what she *does* with all that money. Helps orphans, sponsors schools and hospitals, that kind of thing. It's like she's trying to make up for everything that's wrong in the city all by herself."

Salyeh frowns. "Isn't that a good thing?"

"It's *okay*," Tian Li says. "But it's not *working*. The city's still so messed up. So maybe trying to change things all on my own in T'an Gaban wouldn't work either." She scuffs her feet on the deck. "I want to get out and see more of Far Agondy, even the bad parts, figure out what's wrong and what isn't."

Salyeh nods. "Well, maybe if we . . ."

But by then I'm working my way up the ladder and out of earshot, and even though my ears burn and I want to hear the rest, they're my friends, and I figure I'll respect their privacy.

We pick up new crutches for Ally and me—it's a huge relief to be on two again—and head back to Gossner's to hash out the rest of the plan, bold as brass under the late-morning sun, all of us together, Nic and Thom swinging their walking sticks just in case. We don't spot any Shadowmen, but we're sure they're watching. Alé and Rash grudgingly let Gossner in on the Dawnrunners, and she rolls her eyes at them and asks just how dense they think she is. After a quick, awkward conversation, they make up and we get planning.

Gossner's got an even better setup for making plans than we do on the *Orion*. Her table's about twenty feet long and ten feet wide, made of huge wooden boards set up on enormous iron legs and all sanded and lacquered and nicked and old as you can imagine. It sits beneath a three-story window that looks out toward the skyscrapers on Doubleflow Island. Behind them, on the other side of the river, Bleak Forest sprawls in smoky shadows.

"They'll know you're here," Gossner says, leaning back in a big wooden chair on wheels that can swivel and rock. "They've been watching the place ever since you left."

"We know," I say. "We figured coming back here was a good way to get their attention."

Gossner picks up a pencil, then starts rolling it around between her knuckles absentmindedly. "So there's a whole bunch of them out there, probably getting ready to storm the place. How do you want to do this?"

I start sweating, thinking about what's coming, and glance at Alé. She lays out the plan. "We want to modify Rash's bicycle so Nadya can use it with just her hands, since her hurt leg's still healing. They won't expect her to be that mobile, so they'll have to scramble to get after her. We've mapped out a route for her that leads to a police station, where we think the Shadowmen won't follow. They're always careful about getting caught." Alé pulls out Nic's map, which we brought from the *Orion*, and traces my route. It runs along a couple major streets, then through some alleys, and it zigs and zags a lot. The Shadowmen will have oilcars, but I'll be more agile on my bike. That should let me keep them confused and lose them in the alleys.

Gossner looks over the route, then shakes her head. "Your map's old," she says. "This street's not there anymore, there's a building here, and the road's all torn up here." She grabs a red pencil from the table and starts making changes to my route. "This should work though. How are you going to catch one of these guys?"

Thom answers smoothly. "We're going to have ambushes set up along the way. Three teams, each of which will have a chance to nab one of Nadya's pursuers and get away with him. We're getting some help from Captain Varma and his crew, and we're hoping these Dawnrunners will be in on it as well."

Gossner frowns. "These guys are dangerous. No offense,

but I'm not sure you and your kids will be able to handle them."

Nic, who's seated across from Gossner, leans forward. "Our crew has tangled with these men and others like them and come out on top." He taps his walking stick on the floor for emphasis. "Don't underestimate them."

Gossner blinks under her big eyebrows like she's calculating something, then shrugs. "Well, suit yourselves. It's a decent plan. But Goshend help you if it doesn't work." She looks out at the workshop. "And don't think you're using any of my kids. They live here, and if they get on the wrong side of these Shadowmen, they may never walk the streets safely again."

Alé starts to protest, but Gossner levels a glare at her that could melt a glacier, and she closes her mouth. "That goes for you two too. You're free to do what you want, but you're not free to recruit anybody for this scheme within these walls, got it?"

Alé huffs, crosses her arms, and looks away, but after a second she nods.

"Rashid?" Gossner asks.

Rash looks like he wants to argue too, but he says, "Fine."

"Good, then," Gossner says. "That's settled. You're welcome to use the workshop to get that bicycle modified. In the meantime, Nadya, your leg's ready for its first fitting." She smiles. "Would you like to come try it on?"

While Rash, Alé, and the others head off to work on Rash's bicycle, I crutch over with Tam and Gossner to her personal section of the workshop. "That was fast," I say breathlessly. "I thought it was gonna take like a month!"

Gossner shrugs. "I work faster than most, and I couldn't sleep last night, with the storm and Alé missing. So I stayed up to work on it and keep from worrying." She glances at Tam, as if to suggest how hard it must've been on her when *he* disappeared, and he hunches his shoulders like he's trying to disappear inside his overalls.

"So, like, it's ready for me to use?" I ask.

"Probably not. But it's ready for you to try on. Then I'll make some final adjustments." We get to a set of big iron doors in a metal cage the size of the *Orion*'s cargo bay. It's an interesting setup—Gossner can see out to check what's going on elsewhere in the workshop, and the kids can see in to check whether she's there and what she's doing, but nobody can bother her or mess with her stuff. She unlocks the door with a combination of numbers and a key, then swings it open.

On top of a metal workbench toward the back of the space, surrounded by drill presses and stamping machines and augers and lathes and scrap metal and a forge and empty metal vats with a million rainbow stains on them, is the leg Tam built for me. Next to it there's a footlong sleeve made of that rubbery stuff Alé showed me two days ago.

The leg's a little different now. Some of the black iron pieces Tam banged together on the *Orion* have been replaced by shining steel ones that look like Gossner made them here with her way-more-advanced tools. The cylinder is smaller.

The mechanisms in the foot and ankle have been simplified, so it's really just a few sets of springs and a couple levers, like the ones in Alé's foot.

"Tam has great ideas," Gossner explains as we walk over to it, "but he has a tendency to overcomplicate his designs." She smirks at him. "What did I always tell you?"

Tam sighs. "'Simple works. Simple is easy to make. Simple doesn't break. It's not done till you can't make it simpler.'"

Gossner laughs and pats him on the back. "Exactly. So I simplified the leg a little bit to make it more reliable. Still, yours was amazing for a first go."

Tam brightens. "Really?" he asks, and then he gets up close to the leg. "I thought so too, but I get what you did here. I was using a lot of extra pieces."

Gossner turns to me, still smiling. "So, are you ready to try it on?"

"Sure," I say. "I'd love to."

"Hop on up, then!" Gossner pats the workbench next to the leg, and I set my crutches against the bench and jump up, then turn around so my injured leg hangs down.

"Great," Gossner says. "We'll start with the sleeve." She hands it to me. "Just to get used to the feeling. See how it's different on the inside and outside?"

I nod. On the inside, it's tacky and sort of sticky, like it'll keep a good grip on my skin. On the outside, it's covered in smooth felt.

I hand it back to her, and she starts to put it on me. "The easiest thing to do," she says, "is to start with it inside out and then roll it up your leg." She demonstrates, putting the sleeve against the Lady and then rolling it upward. It gets about halfway up my thigh before it stops, and she grabs a pen from the workbench and makes a couple marks on it. "I always fab them too big," she explains, "and cut them down afterward for a better fit." She finishes making marks and steps back to look at me. "There. How's it feel?"

I lift my leg up and down, rotate it, flex and extend my knee. It's like wearing a thick sock that fits really well. "Pretty good," I say.

"Too warm?" Gossner asks. "Too tight? Too loose?"

I shake my head. "No, I think it's about right."

Gossner grins. "Great."

Tam beams. He looks excited, like the promise he made me on the *Orion* last month—that he'd make sure losing my leg never kept me from doing the things I love—is about to come true. I don't think we're quite there yet, but I'm glad he's happy. Without his help, and without him coming to Gossner's to face his past, I'd never have made it this far.

"Let's try the prosthesis next," Gossner says. She fits it against my leg, moving slowly and carefully, not pushing too hard. "How's that feel?"

"A little sore," I admit. The Lady's still kinda swollen, and when the top of the cylinder presses against my knee, it smarts.

Gossner makes a note on a piece of scratch paper. "I'll enlarge the cylinder a little, then. Your leg will change size sometimes, depending on how long you've been standing, how hot the day is, and other factors I don't fully understand yet. The best way I've found to deal with it is to make the cylinder a little too big, then have you fill the gap by putting on extra socks as necessary." She finishes scribbling and looks back at me. "Is it so tight that I shouldn't continue?"

I shake my head. "No way. I want to see how this thing works."

Gossner laughs and presses a button on the cylinder. "See this?" she asks, and I nod. "This opens a one-way valve that lets air out. Now, as you put your leg into the cylinder, I want you to listen."

I nod and press my leg into the cylinder so that it moves up over my residual limb—it feels more natural to think of it that way here, with Gossner being all technical about things—toward my knee. There's a little hiss, like air leaking out of a balloon, and then a big, wet farting sound. Even though my stomach's fluttering, I laugh a little. So does Tam.

"Great. That's far enough," Gossner says with a smile. She scribbles down a few more notes. "That sound was air escaping from the cylinder as your leg pushed into it. Now I just let the valve close"—she lets go of the button—"and we should be in business. How's the leg feel?"

I practice lifting and lowering it. It's weird to feel weight below my knee again instead of just an occasional twinge of pain or pressure from my missing foot. But it's also exciting. I *remember* this. It's only been a month since I had my leg, and I was already starting to forget what it was like. But this is pretty close, except it's a little heavier and it's not nearly as flexible. "Great," I whisper. "It feels great."

Gossner claps and smiles. "Wonderful! Now, I want to demonstrate the purpose of that little valve, if it's okay with you." I nod, and she holds the foot of the prosthesis. "Try to pull your leg out of it."

I do, gently at first, expecting it to come off pretty easily. It doesn't budge.

"Try as hard as you can, Nadya," Gossner says.

I reach down and press on the top of the cylinder, trying to pry it off my leg. It won't go. Every time I think it starts to move, I feel suction on my residual limb and it keeps the leg attached.

Tam looks almost giddy. "It's a vacuum!" he says. "Gossner, that's genius!"

"I know," she says lightly. She lets go of the leg. "Because your leg forced all that air out of the valve, there's less air in the bottom of the cylinder. When you try to remove your leg, something has to fill that space. Since there's no air around to flow back in, the cylinder pulls itself back onto your leg again. Now, press the button and try taking it off."

I reach down and press the button, and the prosthesis comes off as easy as anything. Air hisses back into the cylinder through the valve as I pull it out. "Wicked," I say, breathing quick and brushing hair out of my eyes. "Can I try walking on it?"

"That was going to be my next suggestion," Gossner says. We put the leg back on, and she helps me stand. "Okay," she says. "Now put your weight on it, gently. Go as slow as you want. We'll start with standing before we walk."

I lower the prosthesis and put weight on it. It pinches a little, and I wince.

"Still too tight?" Gossner asks.

I nod, and she asks me where and makes a few more notes. "Okay," she says. "Now just practice balancing. Tam, would you hold her hands so I can look at her from a distance?"

Tam nods and takes her place in front of me. His fingertips feel warm and a little sweaty. He looks me in the eyes and grins, and I can't help grinning back. We're *doing* it.

"Looks good from here," Gossner says across the workshop. "How's it feel?"

I try shifting my weight a little bit and nearly fall, but Tam catches me. "Whoa," I say. Before I put weight on the leg, it really did feel a lot like my old, biological one. But this isn't the same at all. "It's, ah, different. I can't really feel it the same way."

Gossner nods. "That's normal. Try just rocking back and forth, heel to toe."

I do. That feels much more natural. It's not quite like having my old foot back, but it's sort of like being on stilts.

"Good," Gossner says, "very good!" She walks over and stands alongside me. "Tam, stand on her other side, please, and offer your arm like this." She holds out her arm so I can lean on it if I need to. Tam mimics her. "Now," Gossner says, "are you ready for your first step?"

I nod, my heart pounding. "Let's do it."

"Good. Take it slow. Just try walking normally. Put your weight on your heel and let it roll toward your toe."

I take a deep breath, balancing on Tam's and Gossner's arms, and swing the leg. It's awkward. My hip strains to move all that weight. I guess it's not used to it anymore. But the exercises and stretches Nic has me doing must be working pretty well, because I *can* do it. The leg swings. When I move my weight onto the prosthesis, the heel lands first and rocks me forward onto the toes, like it's getting me ready to take another step. I wobble a little, but Tam and Gossner catch me. I can imagine walking in this thing. I can imagine climbing in it. It'll take a while to master, but I think it's going to work, I really do.

"Great," Gossner says, "you're doing great. Let's keep going for a while, and then we can go see how the others are coming along with that bike."

We only get a few dozen steps in before my leg tires out and the Mighty Lady swells up, and Gossner tells me it's time to get out of the prosthesis. She and Tam help me take it off, and she suggests I do some of Nic's stretches before I go. I do, and Tam watches, grinning the whole time. I grin back. I can't help it.

Gossner points us toward Alé, Rash, and the others, who are in a room similar to this one half a floor up and about a hundred yards away. "You go ahead," she says. "I have some ideas I want to jot down. Most people I work with just need these legs for walking and standing. But you I think could use something special."

She waves us off and closes the door of her workshop behind us.

"Wow," I say as I head over. Tam walks next to me, hands in his pockets, looking thoughtful. "That was great. Thanks, Tam."

He shrugs. "Ah, Gossner did most of the work."

"Yeah, but you brought me to Gossner, and you're gonna be with me to help with this thing once we leave."

Tam shrugs again, but a smile sneaks over his face like a nervous kitten. I look up ahead, and Pep's underneath the bicycle, covered in grease and gesturing with a wrench while she works.

"Hey," I say, slowing down, "do you think I put Pep's ideas down sometimes?"

He scratches his head. "Um," he mumbles. "Well, sometimes, yeah."

I feel like he just whipped my leg out from under me.

"Not a lot," he hurries to say. "Just . . . you could follow her lead every once in a while, y'know? Like, sometimes you insist on your way, but hers is just as good. Maybe pick your battles, I guess is what I'm saying."

I let out a big, lip-flapping sigh. Trust Tam to be totally honest, even when I wish he wouldn't be. "Thanks," I say, looking up at Pep again. She and Alé are laughing. I bet Alé listens to her ideas better than me. "I'll try."

CHAPTER 15

IN WHICH A PLAN GOES VERY WRONG.

Late that afternoon, I'm wheeling Rash's now-hand-cranked recumbent bicycle out of the ground floor of Gossner's building, my heart fluttering, my hands sweating, and my tuna sandwich and spinach salad on the verge of climbing up and breaking for daylight.

What's a hand-cranked recumbent bicycle? I'm glad you asked, because I had no idea until Rash showed it to me.

Recumbent is a fancy word that means "lying down," which is how you position yourself when you use the bike. Most bikes have the seat up high and the pedals down low. This bike's the opposite. The seat's down between the wheels, and the pedals are up high where the handlebars would be, so I can use my hands to move them and steer at the same time. There's two wheels behind me and one in front, which makes the whole rig a lot more stable. Once you get it going, it can really fly. It's got a bunch of gears, and when we tested it and I hit the high ones, I was going so fast I could barely stop myself with the hand brake before I hit the end of the little track Gossner has along one side of her workshop.

I think it'll work to outrun the Shadowmen. I know they won't be able to keep up on foot, and it's a lot more maneuverable than a car. I just hope they don't have any gadgets we haven't thought of yet, and I'm still terrified of something going wrong. I really, really don't want to end up kidnapped by Silvermask. I don't know what he's got in mind for me, but I'm pretty sure it involves giving me to the Malumbra.

"All good so far?" Tian Li asks. She's the only one coming out with me for the first part of the run, where we expect to pick up the Shadowmen. Everybody else is plotting an ambush with a team of Dawnrunners somewhere along the route, except Rash. He's back up in the tower with Gossner and Raj, to help me if things get sticky.

You there, Raj? I ask tentatively over the Panpathia. It's risky keeping contact with him like this, given that Silvermask is out there on the web somewhere and probably looking for me, but we all agreed it was better than being totally on my own.

Absolutely, Nadya, Raj says. *I'll be right here if you need anything.*

I let out a deep breath and watch the street. I'm getting a few funny looks from pedestrians on the sidewalks, and occasionally a car buzzes by me a little close for comfort, but mostly it's just a sea of strange faces passing without looking twice. I guess in a city this big, people must see kids on un-usual inventions all the time.

"There they are," Tian Li says, pointing across the road to a little vendor stand selling newspapers and candy, where two shadowy-looking goons have stepped off the sidewalk and are moving our direction.

"Just the two?" I ask.

"That's all I see," she says. The goons start to cross the street toward us. "You ready?"

I swallow. "Guess I have to be, huh?"

Tian Li puts her hands on the back of my bike, then leans down and smiles. "You'll do great, Nadya. You got this. Now go!" When the guys get halfway into the street, she plants her feet and gives the bike a big shove, and I shoot forward, past their grasping arms and out into traffic. I nearly turn the bike over because I have to swerve around an open manhole cover, and steering while pedaling in the real world is a lot harder than I expected it to be.

Once I'm clear of that, I look back. The two goons are chasing me all right, just like we planned, and as I look at the rest of the street, I see more of them. Another pair is working their way up the sidewalk to my right, moving pretty fast. I shift up a gear and really start cranking on the pedals. My first turn's coming up. I'm supposed to go left into an alley just before a big intersection where the street I'm on meets a thoroughfare that leads downtown.

As I approach the turn, I hear squealing tires and jerk the

bike to my right. A car swerves into the spot I was in just a second ago, and I catch a glimpse of a shadowy goon driving it. I hit the brakes to drop behind him and shoot left again, all the way across four lanes of traffic, dodging a vegetable truck and a street mime as I zoom into the alley we picked out.

Okay, I say to Raj over the Panpathia. *I'm on my way, and they're following me.*

Good, he says. *We can still see you from the roof. You're doing great. The car's circling around to try to cut off the other end of the alley, but you'll get there first. Just go straight and maintain your speed.*

I nod, starting to breathe hard. My arms are buzzing. They're the biggest risk of this whole scheme—they aren't used to this kind of work, and my shoulder's barely healed. If they wear out, I'm stuck up a cloud balloon without an engine.

I shoot out of the alley into an open street just ahead of the car with the goons in it, which is screaming around the corner. I shift again a couple of times. Now that I'm heading straight, I can work up some real good momentum as long as nothing gets in my way, and for now, it's all clear. I keep racing down alleys and zipping across thoroughfares, Raj feeding me directions as I go.

Excellent, Nadya, he says as I navigate a roundabout and turn onto a narrow cobblestone street that jars my teeth. *The first ambush is coming . . . shoot. Hold on.* I clench my jaw to try to keep my teeth from clacking. The first ambush was supposed to happen in an alley on the next block.

There's more construction here than we were expecting. The road's blocked off, and there's a fissure down to the cavern where the fire spirit under the city lives. It looks like the street collapsed and they're repairing it.

My heart clenches as I judder around on the cobblestones. *Y-y-you m-mean I-I'm h-heading straight t-toward a CLIFF?*

Yes, he says. *But Rashid's spotted a bridge across it. It's narrow, probably meant for construction workers on foot, but you can make it.*

I frown. I can see the end of the street now. There's a huge chasm where the road should be, and the bridge he's talking about is only two or three feet wide, made of rickety planks. It's got handrails, but they won't stop this bike if I make a wrong move. *Is th-th-there a-another w-way?*

One moment, Raj says. I'm about to stop pedaling and let the bike coast when a car roars behind me. I look over my shoulder and recognize it as one belonging to the Shadowmen.

The fear-octopus jumps out and wraps around my face. *Th-they're r-right on my t-t-tail!* I call out. *Raj!*

There's no other way, he says. *We can see more of them on the right and left of you. You have to cross the bridge.*

The bike slaloms on the cobblestones. It's really hard to control. I can barely keep that little bridge in the center of my vision, let alone try to line myself up.

You can do this, Nadya, Raj reassures me. *Just stay centered and believe in yourself.*

The car engine roars. The bike fights me. I get closer and closer to the chasm, zooming downhill. My arms feel like lumps of iron from struggling to keep the bike straight. Just as I think I'm lined up, I hit a cobble that bumps the bike to the right. For a second, I'm flying straight toward a three-hundred-foot drop into a cauldron of fire and smoke.

The fear-octopus takes control. I can't do this. There's no way.

I grab the hand brake as I hit the bottom of the cobblestone street, sending the bike into a screeching turn to the right. I feel the whiff of a hand just missing my head as the car behind me slams to a halt before it goes over the cliff.

I didn't make it! I shout to Raj. *Tell me where to go next!*

I pedal up toward full speed again, but there's another car in front of me, parked sideways blocking the street. Two goons spill out of it carrying a huge burlap sack. The car behind me starts up again, and my only choice is to duck into an alley too narrow for them to follow and head back uphill.

Raj curses. *Where are you?* he says. *Are you okay? We can't see you.*

There's no engines behind me, but this alley's long, and going uphill is killing my arms. The bike's slowing down a lot. *I'm in an alley,* I wheeze. *They'll be after me again soon!*

Another alley opens up to my left and I take it. Maybe if I go far enough I can find a place where there's no chasm and get back to the ambush teams.

We still can't see you, Raj says. *Can you head back toward the collapsed street?*

I'll try, I say. The alley spills into a wider street, and I turn downhill. I'm just getting moving again when a Shadowman dashes off the sidewalk and tries to catch me with his jacket like it's a net. It hits me in the face, but the bike hits *him* right in the stomach and I'm moving so fast it knocks him down. Unfortunately, it also knocks the bike up and shoves it to the side. For a second I'm balanced precariously on two wheels with the jacket wrapped around my face. I careen across the street and down an alley before the bike finally flips and I tumble onto the pavement.

I jump right up, worried I might be in the middle of a busy street.

But there's no traffic. No horns, no squealing tires, no swerving. No voices yelling, no policemen blowing whistles. Just silence that feels very, very wrong.

I'm in a big loading area behind a bunch of buildings. Shadows cover everything. I can't even see the sun, the walls above me rise so high. It smells like garbage and oil, and the hair rises on the back of my neck.

The other side of the loading area is full of Shadowmen. There must be at least two dozen, milling around by two cars and two motorcycles, maybe thirty yards away.

Like they were waiting for me.

"Oh no," I whisper. "Oh no, oh no."

I scramble on hands and knees back to my bike, which is still on its side. Footsteps thump toward me. Engines crank. But still there's no yelling, no shouting, no voices saying, "There she is!" or "Get her!" or "Great job, Frank!"

There's just a cold, dark feeling on the back of my neck and then Silvermask in my ear. *Hello. I'm so glad you came out to play.*

His iron-screech voice just about takes my leg out from under me, but I don't have time to be afraid, or to think about how all those guys I ran into must've been put there to make me run into this ambush. I plant my shoulder against the bike and push, and it flips upright again. I jump into the seat on top of the Shadowman's jacket, then get turned around and head down the alley.

Engines thunder behind me like storm surge breaking on tall cliffs. The motorcycles enter the alleyway, followed by the two cars.

Raj! I shout over the Panpathia. *Raj, I need help!*

The response sounds like he's a hundred miles away. . . . *arely hear . . . omething block . . . e . . .*

What a friend you have there, Silvermask says. *Almost strong enough to get a message to you straight through me.* He laughs. *What a joy. I think I'll track him down and see how he does when I'm a little closer.*

I can almost see him now, a giant spider perched on the Panpathia between me and Gossner's tower. He must be interfering somehow so Raj and I can't talk to each other. Which means I really am all alone, with Shadowmen chasing me in a part of the city I don't know at all, and no idea where my friends are to help me.

It's okay, it's okay, it's okay, I tell myself. *I just have to stay one step ahead of them.*

I get to the end of the alley, and the guy I knocked down earlier lunges at me. I swerve around him and take a hard right, heading downhill again and praying there's no chasm when I get there. The turn slows me down, and I have to crank extra hard to get up to speed. The motorcycles roar out of the alley behind me, but they're going so fast they have to stop to make the turn, which buys me a little more space. I can't see the cars, but I bet they'll catch up fast now that we're in the open again.

Raj! I try again. *Raj, can you hear me?*

. . . es. Keep talk . . . ending Ra . . . at do you see?

I try to look around, but there's a lot to concentrate on. *I'm heading downhill on a little street surrounded by big brick buildings. There's an intersection ahead. No chasm. It's got a statue in the middle of it. Where should I go?*

There's no response. I head straight toward the statue. The engine sounds draw awfully close. The motorcycles are almost on me, and the cars are closing in too. My shoulder feels like it's about to fall apart, and my arms are exhausted, but I keep pushing and pushing, because if I slow down even a little I'm pretty sure that'll be the end of Nadya Skylung.

I shoot into the intersection, and Raj's voice comes clear again. *Turn right, Nadya! Turn right at the statue! Can you hear me? Turn right!*

I'm almost past the statue, but I grab the brake to make the turn and just barely keep the bike upright. The tires screech like angry owls and I arc across the intersection, dodging a truck and two bright yellow cars on the way.

Okay, I say, panting, feeling tingles down my spine at how close I came to the wheels of that truck. *What next?*

Go straight ahead. The road will dead-end at a set of stairs down to a promenade by the Doubleflow River. Take them, then turn right again and stay parallel to the water. Get in with the pedestrians and make the cars follow you. Ra . . .

Raj's voice goes dead.

Raj? Raj! I shout. My arms are so tired they feel like fraying pieces of rope. I'm slowing down. I can't help it. I see the end of the street and the staircase ahead, with the river just beyond it. I hit the curb as fast as I can to jump it, even though it makes me bite my tongue, and start rattling down the stairs. At its bottom there's a wide, paved promenade about twenty feet above the surging brown waters of the Doubleflow. I turn right and ride parallel to it like Raj said, weaving around pedestrians and street performers. The cars rattle and bang down the stairs behind me, honking their horns. People nearby start yelling.

Raj, where are you? I call. *Raj, help!* My arms are getting worse. I can't keep this up.

Uh-oh, Silvermask says softly. *Got your friend. And soon you too. Won't be long now.* I can feel him trundling over the Panpathia toward me, so big he shakes the web and makes the whole city tremble.

Raj! I shout again. *RAJ!*

And then I have to let go of the Panpathia because Silvermask has almost gotten to me. I'm all alone, listening to the Shadowmen's cars race up behind me and trying to come up with a new plan. I don't see how to get away. I start sobbing. I can't catch my breath.

"Nadya!" somebody shouts.

I must be hearing things. I look up, blinking tears away and trying to find the voice in the crowd. There's a *swish* above my head.

"Nadya, I'm here!"

It sounds like the voice is behind me now, and above, but it's hard to tell. I glance over my shoulder and see a car coming up fast with a Shadowman hanging out of the door, reaching toward me.

"Nadya, hands up, legs clear!"

I don't understand. I can't put my arms up. I have to keep pedaling. And what does "legs clear" mean? I want to ask, but I'm breathing so hard I can't get the words out.

"Hands *up*! Legs *clear*! Trust me! *Now*, Nadya, *now*!"

I shut my eyes and stick my hands up. I take my leg and residual limb off their footrests and try to make sure they're clear of anything. I feel like I'm giving up, and I'm sure the Shadowmen are going to get me.

But it's not the Shadowmen who nab me.

There's an enormous *whoosh*, and Rash grabs my wrists and hoists me out of my bicycle.

"Oof!" he grunts, and I have the sensation of my stomach falling away and my body rising. The jacket on my seat wraps around my ankle, and I dangle out of reach over the Shadowmen as they grab the bicycle and haul it into the back of their car, then race off down the riverwalk. I blink a few times, my body swirling with strange sensations and my mind full of so many emotions it goes blank. Eventually I figure out that

Rash is in a glider, there are big wings above me to either side, and I've been rescued.

Rash grunts again and head-butts some kind of switch. The glider changes direction and sails over the river. The wind ripples past us, cool and refreshing. "Can you grab the harness?" he asks. My arms are shaking, but I get my fingers around the leather straps, and he lets go of me with his flesh-and-blood hand—his prosthetic one stays locked in place—and winds a strap around my torso and underneath my armpits. It's not much to trust my life to, but it might hold me for a second if I lose my grip. "Okay," he says. "Now we go home."

He hits that switch again, and the glider banks right and sails over a garbage scow on the river. We gain altitude, riding sickly sweet, stinking hot air off the piles of trash. I glimpse the Shadowmen standing outside their cars on the riverwalk, staring at us, and I shiver and shake and cling to Rash's harness for all I'm worth, trying not to think about how close that was, wondering whether Silvermask really got to Raj.

Rash doesn't say another word. He just grunts every once in a while. He's breathing hard. It must be a lot of work to control the glider with two people in it. He gets up as high as he can and glides over to another thermal and then another, rising and rising, and when we're up high enough, he wheels around and takes us back toward the glimmering glass dagger of Gossner's tower, while the sun starts to set and turn the whole city and its hundred thousand windows gold.

CHAPTER 16

IN WHICH CONSEQUENCES ARE HEAVY.

As Rash lands at Gossner's tower, a crowd gathers to meet us. Alé's there, and a bunch of Gossner's kids, plus Tam. I dunno where the adults and the rest of the crew are, but I'm most worried about Raj.

Got him, Silvermask said, and I really hope he was lying.

Rash flares the glider and comes down softly. I slip out of the line he tied around me while the other kids run up to give him a hand. Tam and Alé catch me.

"Where's Raj?" I ask breathlessly. "Is he okay?"

Tam purses his lips. "What? He's fine. He just looks tired, maybe a little gray."

My guts tumble like the pieces of paper that blow around in alleys here. Nic told me last month that people touched by the Malumbra at the Roof of the World got sick and then better, and then they started acting like something was controlling them, just like the Shadowmen. "I've got to get to him," I say. "Where is he?"

Alé sighs. "He's on the second floor at the big table, having some tea."

"Thanks," I say. "Can you—"

But Alé's way ahead of me. She hands me her crutches and sits on a bench that runs along the railing. "Somebody will bring me another pair. Just go." She tugs on her cuffs. "I hope everything's all right."

I could kiss her, and Rash for that matter, since he saved my life, but I've got to get to Raj. He was only on the Panpathia at all because of me, and if anything happened to him it's my fault.

Tam comes with me as I crutch toward the nearest swing. "What happened?" he asks. "My team got the signal to come back to base, but when we got here the place was total chaos, Rash was gone, and everybody said you were in trouble."

"I chickened out," I say, struggling over to the swing. "And then they almost got me." Alé's crutches are too big for me because she's taller, and they're really uncomfortable. "Can you get me down?"

Tam helps me into the seat of the swing, hands me the crutches, then starts the crank that lowers it. We keep talking as I drop away. "What do you mean you chickened out?" he asks.

I feel like dirt. I could've made it onto that bridge. Raj was sure of it. But I lost my nerve. "The route ran over a big

211

chasm. Raj found me a bridge over it, but I was too scared to take it. Then I got chased. Raj was giving me directions on the Panpathia, and . . ." I swallow. It's hard to say out loud. "I think Silvermask got him."

The swing reaches the second floor, and I grab the crutches and start moving. Tam runs down the stairs and catches up. "What? How?"

"On the Panpathia," I say. We're coming up on the room where the windows are now, and not knowing is killing me. Raj sits calmly at the end of the table, his hand rising and falling mechanically as he sips his tea, facing the window and staring at the sunset on the glass face of the building across the street.

When we get to the table, I slow down. I don't want to startle Raj. He looks like he's thinking hard. I open my mouth, then close it, looking for the right words.

"Hello, Nadya," he says. "Hello, Tam." He takes a deep breath, then lets it out. "I'm glad you're okay."

"Thanks," I mumble. "Raj. I'm sorry. Are you . . . are you all right?"

Raj lifts the cup again. His hand shakes. Slowly, he lowers it. "No," he says. "I don't think I am."

My heart turns into lead and falls through my feet, past the floor, and all the way to the bottom of Gossner's tower.

"You were touched by the Malumbra once, weren't you?" Raj asks.

Shaking, I nod. I slide into the chair next to him, and Tam

follows my lead. My arms feel limp, like cables someone just took all the tension out of. "Yeah," I say. "When I was looking for Mrs. T's mind on the *Remora*, before we boarded it."

He sips his tea, sets it back down. "What did it feel like?"

I swallow. "Like fingers of ice, creeping over my head from the back of my skull. And then my body started doing things on its own."

Raj shudders, and his shoulders slump. "I was afraid of that." He stares sadly into his tea.

"What happened?" I ask.

"I could feel him coming toward me, but I needed to keep giving you directions, so I stayed on the web until I could see him, and then I stayed longer. When he reached me, I tried to transform myself and fight, but . . ." He waves limply at the window. "It didn't work. I couldn't envision myself as anything strong enough to beat him. Have you seen him, on the Panpathia?"

I nod, trembling. That spider. Huge fangs. Giant eyes. Legs as big as the steel columns holding up Gossner's tower.

Raj takes another sip of tea. "Then you know how terrible he is. How could any of us face a monster that size? If he's just one of the Malumbra's servants, no wonder the Roof of the World fell." He puts his face in his hands. "What will I tell Dhruv?"

I don't know who Dhruv is. His husband? His business partner? His brother? His son? I've put him in so much danger, without even thinking about his life and the people who rely on him. He has a whole crew. What'll happen to the *Golden Dawn* now? What will happen to *him*? "I'm sorry, Raj," I blubber. "I should've listened, I . . ."

He waves my apology away. "Thank you, Nadya, but you're a child, and I am not. I will take responsibility for my own foolishness. We should never have put you in such danger. Our first duty is to live, and live richly, not to save the world."

Those words hurt, worse than I think he imagines. He means them to make me feel better, but all they do is make me feel tiny and afraid and even more like I messed up. "Maybe I can help," I say numbly. "Aaron burned the shadow out of me. Maybe he could burn it out of you too."

Raj shakes his head. "Thank you, but Aaron isn't here. And I've no idea how we'll ever find him."

I can't stand this. Raj's hand shakes again, and he puts it in his lap.

"Nadya, I think we should go," Tam whispers.

I keep staring at Raj, thinking about what he said.

"Nadya," Tam whispers again, and he tugs on my sleeve.

I let him lead me away. "We can't let it end like this," I say.

He looks at me sadly. "What else can we do, Nadya? This was the best plan we had."

"I don't know. But we have to do *something*. We can't just let him turn into a Shadowman or whatever's about to happen! He *helped* me!"

Tam takes a deep breath, and after a second, he nods. "Okay," he says, "but what do we do?"

I'm just starting to turn my mind to that problem when

Pepper runs toward us from the staircase. "Hey," she says, panting. When she sees Tam and me, she looks like she's just been punched in the gut, but she presses on anyway, pushing a big wave of hair out of her face. "Have you guys seen Tian Li and Salyeh? Everybody else is back, but nobody knows where they are."

It's pandemonium again for a few hours. The sun goes down, and Salyeh and Tian Li still aren't back. Rash gets in his glider and takes word out to the Dawnrunners. Nic and Thom contact the police and give descriptions and their last known whereabouts. Salyeh apparently never showed up to his ambush crew. I was the last person to see Tian Li.

"Do you think they were kidnapped?" I ask Nic as we pore over a map, marking all the places we've searched for them. Outside, darkness is falling over the city like a blanket of pitch-black silk, and the electric lights are winking on.

Nic frowns over my shoulder toward Gossner's private workshop, where Raj is secluded. Raj said he didn't want to be around anyone else so he couldn't pass the shadow to them. "I don't know," Nic says softly. "I hope not."

I put my head in my hands. This is a nightmare. Raj is sick with the Malumbra's shadow, Tian Li and Salyeh are missing, and we're no closer to finding Aaron and rescuing everybody than we were this morning. Our whole plan was a complete disaster, and then when it went wrong, I screwed up and made things even worse.

I'm staring at the floor, flexing my residual limb and feeling for the first time in a while like maybe I deserve the aches and pains in my missing foot, when shouting starts up downstairs.

Everybody around the table—Nic, Thom, Gossner, me, Pep, Tam, Rash, and Alé—jumps up. Fast as an otter darting after a fish, Gossner scoots to the edge of the platform, where she can see the door.

"They're back," she says breathlessly. "It's them."

I feel like I might just fall into pieces, so I flop back into my chair and tilt my head toward the ceiling. I'm not much for praying, but I don't mind thanking Goshend, or his daughter, or whoever else might be responsible, for this one.

A few minutes later they're walking up to us, beaming. Tian Li's flushed and practically bouncing, and Salyeh's got a grin a mile wide on his face.

"We did it," Tian Li says. "We know where their base is."

My heart vaults into my throat.

"What?" Tam sputters, slapping a hand to his head. "Ha—how?"

Salyeh takes a deep, satisfied breath. "It was Tian Li's plan. I ditched my ambush team, since I swore never to hurt anybody, and met up with her a few blocks away from Gossner's tower. We looked at a map this afternoon and figured out there's really just one bridge between the area where we set the ambushes and Bleak Forest, so we thought we'd be able to tail the Shadowmen from there if they gave up or something went wrong."

Tian Li walks triumphantly up to the map Nic and I were working on. "And that's just what happened. A little after the ambushes were supposed to take place, we saw a whole convoy of Shadowmen headed across the bridge like their tails were on fire. We heard sirens from the riverwalk, so we figured something had gone wrong and followed the cars." She plunks her finger down on an intersection. "This is where they went. Arachnya House. Corner of Fifty-Second Avenue and Timberline Street."

Nic takes his glasses out of his pocket and puts them on. He looks at the intersection, then peers at Salyeh and Tian Li, shaking his head. "You two shouldn't have put yourselves in danger like that." Thom, behind him, nods vigorously, and Tian Li's grin fades.

"But we did it," she protests. "We—"

"I know." Nic takes her hand and squeezes it. "And given everything else that happened today, I am so very glad you did." He pulls her into a hug, then does the same with Salyeh. "But I want both of you to promise, next time you think of an improvement to our plans, that you will *tell* us, rather than just going off on your own."

Salyeh, looking a little sheepish, nods. Tian Li just laughs. "Fair," she says. Then, after a second, she frowns. "What do you mean, 'everything else that happened today'?"

"I screwed up," I say. I put my head in my hands again. "And now Raj is sick and we have to get Aaron back soon or he might not ever get better."

Tian Li's eyebrows huddle. "How . . . ?"

Nic clears his throat. "We'll fill you in later." He looks down at me and sighs. "For now, I think we're all long overdue for some food. Machinist Gossner, would you mind if we troubled you a little longer?"

Gossner smiles. "I'd love to host you."

Dinner ought to be delicious. I worked my tail off today, and I haven't eaten anything since lunch. But I can barely bring myself to touch the food. I eat mechanically, putting down half a sausage and a bit of salad with some kind of sesame oil dressing on it, then a couple pieces of fruit. Tam watches me the whole time with a big frown. He tries to talk to me, but I don't even remember the conversation by the time dinner's over. All I can think about is Raj getting sicker and sicker alone in Gossner's private workshop, and how in the world we're going to get Aaron back and save him.

As we're getting our beds ready—the whole *Orion* crew is sleeping down by the workshop boilers, where enormous columns of flame get piped up from the fire spirit under the city to create steam—Tian Li finally corners me and asks what's wrong.

"I told you," I say miserably. "Raj is sick. And I don't know how to fix it."

She squints at me. "But we know where Silvermask is now. All we have to do is get the police to go after him. That's where Nic and Thom are right now. It's practically over!"

I shake my head. "I don't think the police will do it."

Everybody goes quiet. The crew, plus Alé and Rash who're down here chatting with us, all turn to face me. But I've been running this over in my head all night, and I'm pretty sure I

218

know what's gonna happen. "Look," I say, "we think Silver-mask was in charge of the pirates, right?" Everybody nods. "And the pirates had an agent in the Far Agondy customs inspectors. Why would they stop there? If they could get somebody in the customs office, why not the police? I bet that's why none of these crimes have been solved and the police seem demoralized. Somebody, high up, must be stopping them from doing their jobs."

Alé shuffles her feet. "We've thought the same thing before," she says quietly. Then she looks up. "But maybe we're wrong. Maybe if the evidence is good enough—"

The doors to Gossner's workshop open, and we crane our heads toward the receiving area. It's Thom and Nic. And they don't look happy.

"It's just like I thought," I mutter after Thom and Nic explain what happened. They went to the police station, and the detective assigned to our case referred them to his captain, who dragged her feet through the whole thing. First they had to wait an hour, then they had to sign a bunch of paperwork. Then the captain said she'd need more evidence, because she'd have to get a warrant from a judge who'd want something more solid than the word of two kids. Then she spent twenty minutes scolding Thom and Nic for doing anything on their own, and especially for involving kids in a case about kidnappings. She said if it was up to her she'd have them both locked up for child endangerment, and that if she got word that any of us kids were doing anything like this ever again, she'd see to it we never got to come back to Far Agondy.

Nic looks pretty shaken. Thom paces by the boilers like a

scorpion somebody poked with a stick. Gossner's down with us, watching the flames and drinking a glass of something golden, thinking. Everybody else just seems kind of shocked, flopped on chairs or the old couches down here. They were so sure that the police would help us. *I* think most of the police probably would if they could, but their hands are tied, and we need to find a way to untie them.

I've been thinking about it too, and I might just have a way.

"I can talk to Alan Salawag," I say. Everybody looks up, and I try to sit still and look impressive but I can't, so I bounce my leg on the floor while I explain. "He said I could come visit the gormling, right? So they'll let me in. And while I'm visiting I can tell him everything that's happened. He's, like, one down from the top muckety-muck in the city. So he *must* have some pull with the police. And if I can get him to help, maybe he can unstick things for us. Maybe he can overrule whoever Silvermask has in the police force."

Thom crosses his arms. "It's too risky, Nadya. We need to keep you here. Silvermask will be waiting to capture you."

I bounce faster. "I know, but what if we go by glider? We can just go roof to front door, no time on the streets, no sliding on the zip lines, no way for them to nab us."

Nic rubs his temples a few times, then looks at Rash, who sucks his teeth. "I could show her the way," Rash says. "It's not too hard a flight to City Hall from here. Just two thermals, and they're easy to ride. Goss?"

Gossner takes a deep breath and rolls the golden liquid in her glass around. "Up to you all," she says. "I'll lift my ban on guests using the gliders for this, but it's still your risk to take. I can't promise you it'll work."

"I want to come too," Tam says.

"No, me!" Pep chimes in.

"I'm the one who found the place!" Tian Li says.

"*We* found it," Salyeh says, raising an eyebrow at her. "And I want to go too."

Gossner shakes her head and holds up a finger. "Just one. Rash, you can take Nadya and somebody from the *Orion*'s crew. I'm still not letting you drag anybody else from the workshop into this. And Alé, before you even start, you're not flying a glider with that bad ankle." She looks apologetically at Nic and Thom. "Sorry, but my duty's to the kids who live here first, and others second."

Alé crosses her arms and glares daggers at Gossner. I bet she's trying to think of a way to sneak out with us anyway, but I doubt it'll work. I'm sure Gossner will be up watching when we launch tomorrow.

"One person," Gossner repeats, and she walks off toward her private workshop. "You can tell me who in the morning. Now I'm off to check on Raj and then go to bed."

That leaves us with Thom and Nic to convince. Nic scratches his head, then looks at me seriously. "Nadya," he says. "I won't try to stop you. I think it's pretty clear that Gossner's approach to protecting her kids isn't going to work with my crew. But I want you to think very carefully about this. You'll be putting Rashid at risk, and possibly somebody else as well. Is it worth it? Do you really think Alan will help us? He's not always reliable."

I take a deep breath and remember his smile, his handshake. He seemed so concerned about the pirates, and he promised to give us a bonus, plus he said he wished he could do more.

"It's our best shot, Nic." I look over at Rash. "City Hall's guarded like a fortress, right?"

Rash nods.

"So as long as we get there in one piece, we'll be totally safe. And I'm sure I can handle one of these gliders."

Nic sighs. "Then I suppose you have my blessing. Thom?"

Thom scowls. The fire under the boilers behind him flickers and flares. "I want to be there when you talk to Alan. I'll head out before you in the morning and we can rendezvous at the building entrance."

Nic nods. "Excellent idea, Thom. Are we agreed, then?"

Thom gives me a long, hard look. Little muscles under his eyes and around his mouth twitch. "I guess." Everybody's watching him, and he taps his foot softly a few times, then clears his throat. "I want to apologize to all of you," he says. "We never meant to involve you in this struggle so soon. Nic has always waited to tell his crews about the Roof of the World and the mission of the Diaspora until they're grown. I didn't find out till I was eighteen and leaving the *Orion* for

223

my first posting on another cloudship. 'Go see the world,' Nic said, 'and if what you see convinces you that this is a threat worth fighting, come back and I'll find a way for you to help.'" He shakes his head. "You all never got that option. The fight came to you. And I'm damn sorry for it."

I nearly topple over. Thom almost never curses, and when he does, it's usually at an inanimate object when he thinks nobody can hear him. It's really weird to hear him do it in front of us, on purpose.

"Well said," Nic echoes. He looks toward Gossner's private workshop, where we can see her chatting with a morose-looking Raj. "So I'll offer that choice now. If any of you wants to leave, then you may do so with my blessing. I can find you a place on a safer ship. Or," he says, nodding at Rash and Alé, "I can find you an apprenticeship in a different city, since it may no longer be safe for you here. Think on it. The door is always open."

He looks around at us. Everybody's sitting quietly. "Now," he says, "I think Thom and I should retire as well. I hope you'll all get some sleep tonight. I suspect tomorrow will be a big day."

Nobody wants to leave. Salyeh says the world is Goshend's jewel, and worth defending. Tian Li says her plans to fix T'an Gaban don't mean much if it's full of Shadowmen. Tam says he's not running away because he's scared anymore. Only Pep seems a little unsure, staring at the floor and kicking her feet, but she tells us we're her family and she'll never abandon us. Rash and Alé just laugh and say we're stuck with them. They've been fighting Silvermask longer than we have.

It takes a while to make our beds. Tam lays his down first, farthest from the boilers. Pep puts hers next to his, and then come Tian Li and Salyeh. I take the longest to set up—since hopping around with a pile of blankets is the kind of delicate balancing act that makes you move slow so you don't fall—so I end up at the far end of the line, closest to the boilers. The flames make me a little nervous, but if I close my eyes they're warm and comforting.

As everybody else leaves to wash up, I linger. Thom, who came back to say good night, stays too, standing by the boilers and staring at the long tongues of flame snaking up under them. The light flickers on his face like a signal lamp flashing out at sea. Occasionally his mouth moves silently. I wonder if he's talking to Far Agondy's giant fire spirit.

I know he's busy, but everybody else is off using the bathrooms, and this might be my best chance to get an answer I've been wanting for a few days now.

"Thom?" I say. "Can I ask you a question?"

He turns toward me, and flames disappear from his eyes. "Sure, Nadya," he mumbles. He rubs his face tiredly. "What's up?"

I clear my throat. My heart pounds. "What happened to Brittany Brikowski?"

Thom stops rubbing. He stares at me like he's mulling over whether to say anything, then sighs. "We let her down." He flops onto one of the couches near the boilers and stares at

225

the flames again. "She was a good friend. Bright and brave and very capable. About ten years ago, just after my crew all left the *Orion*, she got in touch with us. She'd heard from Alan, and he wanted to go to the Roof of the World, see what was there. He asked her to come with him." He shakes his head. "We tried to talk her out of it, but she wouldn't give up. She wanted us to come too, said we'd be safer together on the *Orion* than just her and Alan alone. Nic refused, so she focused on the rest of us."

A few kids cross over us on a catwalk, and Thom waits a few seconds before continuing. "The night before she left, she visited me on the cloudship *Rainbow's Flight*, where I was working. She and Alan were going to take a little cloudship he'd won in a high-stakes bet. She asked me to be their fire-minder. I turned her down." He clears his throat and rubs his leg. "The next I heard from her, it was by letter. They never got farther than the ruins of a fishing village on the edge of the continent. When they landed, she got on the Panpathia to look around, and the Malumbra wormed its shadow into her mind. They left right away, but it didn't matter. She said she was terrified of spreading the shadow, and she went into hiding somewhere far, far from other people." He gets up and scowls. "Alan came out just fine though. He always does."

I get a sinking feeling in my stomach. Thom raises his eyebrows. "So you promise me—when you're talking to him tomorrow, you be extra careful, okay, Nadya?"

Mouth dry, I nod.

226

Thom heads to the platform he's sharing with Nic as everybody else comes back. I'm about to turn in when Rash brings me a big bundle of cloth. "Here," he says. "You left this on the roof today."

It's the big black coat from the Shadowman, the one that got wrapped around my ankle as Rash rescued me. Remembering the chase makes me sick to my stomach. "Just throw it away," I grunt. "I don't want to see it." I can't believe that's all I got in return for making Raj sick. "Thanks for saving my life, by the way." I roll over and stare at the flames again. I'm feeling pretty down. The Lady's aching, I'm now doubting my plan to get help from Alan Salawag, and every few minutes it hits me again that Raj would be fine if I'd just held my nerve instead of chickening out.

Rash doesn't leave. "Look," he says, "I know you feel bad. It's written all over your face."

I huff. I wish he'd take the hint.

"But I'm impressed. It's not just anybody who'd go up against the Shadowmen to help some kid they've only known a month. The Dawnrunners? This is personal for us. We've lost siblings, cousins, kids we've been friends with for years."

I hunch my shoulders and he finally gets up, but I do start to feel better. Just a little, mind you, like the ice chest my heart's been marinating in is starting to thaw.

There's a rustle of paper as Rash stands. "Hey," he says. He sounds surprised. "What's this?"

I roll over. He's picking up a slip of paper from the floor. "Looks like a flyer," he says, and he turns it over so I can read it.

NEED WORK?
GET PAID TODAY! EASY HOURS, GOOD WAGES!
NEED STRONG, HEALTHY MEN AND WOMEN
FOR MANUAL LABOR AND ASSORTED TASKS.
START THIS MORNING, GET PAID THIS EVENING!
INTERESTED PARTIES SHOULD REPORT TO

**ARACHNYA HOUSE,
52ND AND TIMBERLINE,
BLEAK FOREST.**

I shudder when I see that address. Tian Li and Salyeh said the house there was like a big, dead grub—that its outside used to be white but it's covered now in gray-and-black mold, with broken windows and missing doors on one of the wings, but everything locked up tight as a bank on the other. "That must be how he recruits," I say. "'Manual labor and assorted tasks.'" I snort. "Like kidnapping!"

Rash sucks his teeth. "So many people would fall for this," he says. "Good people."

A little unease squiggles into my guts. I never thought of the Shadowmen as people. I just thought they were the enemy, the bad guys, the Malumbra's shadow made solid.

Rash rubs his shoulder. It must be sore from wearing that

heavy prosthetic arm all day. "I bet they never even knew what hit them. Just showed up looking for a job, and then he does whatever he does and they lose their minds." He shivers. "What a monster."

I think of his taunts on the Panpathia, the spider form he takes. "You've got that right," I whisper.

Rash flips the paper over. "It's got something written on the back," he says. "'Miller Square, Second and Olivine, the Forge.'" He looks up at me. "That's just a few streets from here. I bet he wrote down the address where his goons were supposed to meet, in case they got lost. You said some of the Shadowmen are controlled by him more tightly than others, right? Maybe they have trouble with directions."

I look blearily at the address, but it doesn't mean anything to me. "It's got a signature below it," I say, "or part of one."

Rash brings it closer to his face. "Huh. It just says '—S.' Think that stands for 'Silvermask'?"

Salyeh, who must have been listening for a while, props himself up on one elbow behind Rash. "Can I see that?"

Rash hands the flyer to him, and Sal squints at it. "This handwriting looks real familiar. I swear I've seen it somewhere." He scoots around and sits up. "Can I keep this? I wanna take it back to the *Orion* and compare it with some things. We have contracts, notes, letters from people in Far Agondy. I bet that's where I know it from. Maybe I can figure out who Silvermask really is."

Rash shrugs. "Suits me. It's hers, anyway."

He looks at me, and I look at Sal. His eyes are gleaming

like he's got a good puzzle to solve and he's not gonna let it go till it's licked. "Sure," I say. "Thanks, Sal."

He nods, and even after Rash leaves and I lie down to get some sleep, he's still up staring at that note, putting pieces together in his head. Maybe things are going to be okay. Sal will figure out who Silvermask is. Alan Salawag will get the police to help us. Before long, we'll have Aaron and everybody else back too.

And then we'll make Raj better again, somehow. I'm sure of it.

CHAPTER 18

IN WHICH NADYA MAKES A FOOLISH PROMISE.

The flight to City Hall is a blast. Rash spends about an hour showing me and Tam, who won a four-way contest of rock versus garden hoe versus cloud tree with the rest of the gang, how to use the gliders. The mechanisms are pretty simple. There are two switches up by your face, one to bank the glider left and one to bank it right. Then you use your feet, or foot in my case, to tug the tail up or down and change the direction the nose of the glider is pointed in. As long as you stay moving fast enough for the wings to work, or you hit a thermal, you're in business. We experiment around Gossner's tower, and by mid-morning I've got the knack of it, swooshing around and making tight left-and-right cuts across the street, riding thermals high and then plunging back down. It's totally awesome—even better than the Flightwing.

"Thanks," I say to Rash when we land to say goodbye to everybody. "That was amazing!"

He grins. "You're a natural!" He slaps me on the back. "You're pretty good too, Tam."

Tam stares at the controls on his glider, then at his hands, pantomiming how they work to himself. He struggled a bit—not so bad he's in danger of crashing or anything, but enough that Rash and I will have to take it slow so he doesn't get left behind.

We say quick goodbyes. Pep crosses her arms and sulks in the doorway. I wanted to finagle a way to bring her along, but the contest was her idea so I didn't step on her toes about it. Sal and Tian Li wish us good luck. Thom pulls me aside real quick and tells me to be safe on the flight and that he feels a duty to Mrs. T to keep me safe until we get her back. I feel a little guilty because the look on his face says he's been worrying about me a lot lately, and I sure haven't been helping with all the risks I'm taking.

So I promise him I'll be careful, and he heads downstairs to take a cab to City Hall. We wait about fifteen minutes to give him a head start, Nic reminds us not to go inside without Thom, and then we're off.

Like I said, it's a ball. The morning's bright and cheery, the sky blue, the air warm. Below us, crowds of people look like streams of bees buzzing around a garden full of flowers. Rash takes the lead, I follow, and Tam brings up the rear. He gets better as we go, and by the time Rash takes us up our last thermal and out over the Doubleflow River, we're flying in formation, like geese headed south for the fall.

I grin. For a few minutes I revel in the wind in my face,

the sun on my skin, my hair flapping this way and that. I'm free, able to be anything I want in all the world. I could fly anywhere, do anything.

Then Rash dives toward the tallest buildings in the city, right at the heart of Doubleflow Island, and reality comes crashing back down. I've got a job to do, and a lot of people are counting on me. By the time we flare to gentle landings outside City Hall, with a crowd of gawkers staring at us and Thom running up from the doors to meet us, using his walking stick like a crowbar to move people out of the way, I'm focused on the job again and ready to meet with Alan Salawag.

City Hall is filthy stinkin' rich. The floors are made of marble. The ceilings have murals of factories, saw mills, and mines. The walls are paneled in polished wood that looks cut from trees a thousand years old. Big windows everywhere let you see all over the city, people scurry constantly, and there are enough elevators to move an army.

We move with the crowd, and other than some dirty looks from people we bump with our folded-up glider wings when we get into an elevator, we don't hit our first major obstacle until the reception desk outside Lord Salawag's office. The desk's the size of a big couch, taller than I am, and made of deep brown wood that has rich, hypnotizing swirls in it. Physically it blocks our way. But worse than that, Markus—Mr. Beardy Tattoo Arms from the dock—perches like a vulture on a stool behind it, scribbling in a leather-bound book as big as Goshend's Ledger of Souls. His beard seems to have grown an inch, or maybe he's just fluffed it or something. Behind it, he's still as burly as ever, as tall as ever, as grumpy as ever, and all about stopping us from seeing his boss.

"I'm sorry," he says briskly, while frowning in a way that seems designed especially to let us know he's not, "but only the girl is approved for a short-notice meeting. The rest of you will have to wait."

"Listen," Thom says, planting his elbows on the desk. "People are trying to kidnap her. Tell Alan we can't just leave her alone, even with him, okay?"

Markus blinks twice, then clears his throat and nods pointedly at the policeman stationed near the elevators at the end of the hall. "Sir," he says beardily, "you're inside City Hall, in the office of the Lord Secretary of Far Agondy. Who, exactly, do you think is going to kidnap this little girl from here?"

I bristle at the words *little girl*, but this guy's our only way in, and I probably shouldn't make him mad at us. "I'll be fine, Thom," I say.

"Nadya—" Thom starts, but I just crutch away from Markus toward the waiting area.

"Fifteen minutes, right?" I call over my shoulder.

"I will call your name when the Lord Secretary is ready for you," Markus says back. He seems unsure whether to be upset with me for walking away or happy that he won his argument with Thom, so he settles on a general-purpose scowl and starts scribbling in his book again, peering up to glare at us every once in a while.

"Nadya," Thom says once we've gotten settled on a couch, "I don't appreciate being cut off like that."

"You were just gonna make him mad, Thom," I say. "And then maybe he wouldn't have let me in to see Lord Salawag at all!"

Thom sighs, and we look to Tam and Rash for support at the same time. They take a sudden interest in the white streaks meandering through the bloodred marble on the floor tiles and the silver trim on the ceiling.

"Look, if anything goes wrong, I'll scream bloody murder and you guys can run in and help me, okay? I'll be right through those doors." I point to the doors I assume lead into Salawag's office. They're enormous, made of some kind of wood that looks heavier than stone, and painted black with shining door handles I think are probably real silver.

"Fine," Thom says. He plonks down on the couch next to me and rubs his face. "Just be careful, Nadya. Alan has a way of persuading people to do things that serve his interests more than theirs."

I think about rolling my eyes, but then I remember he's trying to protect me, and I decide not to. "Right."

The doors open. The guy who opened them—another secretary? an undersecretary?—bows his head as six people walk out. It's obvious that one of them is a pretty high mucketymuck. She's dressed in a suit that probably cost as much as a month's worth of provisions for the *Orion*, all slickly tailored black silk with silver pinstripes down it, and she wears black spats. Her hair's dark black, her skin's a deep tan that's pretty similar to Gossner's, and she's wearing a long silver pendant that looks like a feather quill. She glances at us as she walks past, and then she's gone in a flurry of footsteps and paperwork.

I wonder briefly who she is, and then Markus's beardy voice calls from behind me: "Nadya Skylung. You have fifteen minutes."

I hop off the couch, ignore Thom's worried look, and crutch into Alan Salawag's office.

It's even more done up than the waiting area was. The floors are black marble, each tile placed inside a square of real silver. The walls are lush brown wood so dark it almost looks purple. There's a little kitchen on one side of the office, a sofa and several chairs around a coffee table, some big flowering plants that look like they come from very far away, and a desk roughly the size of an oilcar.

The doors boom shut behind me. The undersecretary takes a seat facing them, as though not to eavesdrop on the meeting his boss is about to have.

"Nadya! Come in, come in!" Lord Salawag says. He stands up and comes around that enormous desk. "Would you like any refreshments? We have coffee, tea, a bit of sherbet . . ."

I'm awfully tempted by the sherbet, but my time's already ticking down and I can't let myself get distracted. "No thanks," I say. "I came here to see the gormling. And . . . um . . . to ask for your help with something."

"Of course, of course," Salawag says. He sits in one of the plush armchairs near the coffee table and beckons me over

236

to the couch. "Unfortunately, as I'm sure you've noticed, the gormling isn't here."

My stomach crunches up. I'd just assumed it was hidden somewhere I couldn't see, like in a tank behind one of these wooden panels. "I . . . What? Where is he?"

Lord Salawag frowns, and the undersecretary appears with a cup of coffee for him. He stirs it twice, then takes a sip. "He didn't seem comfortable here, took a little ill, so I had him taken to my home instead. He's much happier there. You're welcome to come and visit sometime. With your guardians and friends, of course."

I almost let him know that my guardians and friends were just stopped from coming in here, but judging by the silver grandfather clock in the corner, I'm down a minute already. *Focus, Nadya.* "Sure," I say. "That'd be swell. But look, you said you wished you could do more to help us than just give us a bonus . . ."

He nods, blowing on his coffee. "Yes, of course. Go on."

"Well, maybe you can. One of us got kidnapped."

He nearly drops his cup. "What? No! Who?"

"Aaron," I say. "He's—"

"The cloudling who helps you in the garden." Salawag's expression darkens. "Silvermask. It must've been."

I blink. "You know about Silvermask?"

Lord Salawag stands up and starts pacing. "Everyone knows about him. He's the scourge of the city! We look like idiots not being able to bring him down. I was just speaking with the mayor about it."

My heart thumps. He cares. Maybe he can help. "We know where he lives."

He stops pacing. He seems like a pretty steady guy, but his jaw drops a little. "How in the world did you manage that?" he asks. "The police have been searching for months."

I tell him about the ambush and how it went wrong, and how Salyeh and Tian Li followed Silvermask's goons back to Arachnya House. He listens intently, nodding and asking questions, but I start to sweat because the clock in the corner is ticking down and he still hasn't promised to help yet.

"But how do you know it's the right house?" he asks.

"What?" I sputter. "They *saw* those goons go in there!"

Salawag nods. "Of course, of course. But what if that was just where they stash their vehicles? Or worse, someplace they were going to rob?"

Now it's my turn to stand there with my mouth open. I hadn't thought of that. None of us had. We were so sure.

"I want to believe you." Lord Salawag frowns. "I really do. There's nothing I'd love better than to find Silvermask and put him away for good. But I can't ask the police to go that deep into Bleak Forest without definitive proof. You have to understand, they'd be risking their lives. There would undoubtedly be violence." He taps his finger on his lips. "Hmm. Hmm, hmm. And Silvermask does seem to always be one step ahead of you. How can we be sure this wasn't all a trick?"

My mouth goes dry. The clock keeps ticking. I've got less than two minutes left to convince him, and this might be my only shot. "I can show you," I croak.

"Hmm?" he asks.

I nod toward his gills. "You're a skylung, right? Can you use the Panpathia?"

He coughs. "A little, I admit. But not very well. I never liked it much."

That seems like somebody not liking bacon or chocolate to me, but I guess there's all types in the world. "Well, what if I could get in there and find the kids? If I contacted you over the Panpathia, would you be able to see what's around me? Would you be able to see Aaron?" My hands start sweating just thinking about it, but that clock keeps ticking, and it's all I can come up with.

"Yes," he says. He taps his lips some more. "Yes, yes. I believe I could. But you'd be in terrible danger. Would you really do that?"

I nod, still sweating. "I would. I will, I promise. Are you usually in your office? It'll be easier to find you if I know where to look."

He snorts and finishes his coffee, setting his cup down on the table. The undersecretary sweeps it up in seconds. "Yes. Most days I'm here from morningdove to evening star." He laughs. "I work longer than the sun this time of year!"

The undersecretary coughs quietly, and I realize the clock has just about ticked my time away. Lord Salawag gets up, and I do the same. He walks to the door with me as I crutch out. "Remarkable. You are truly a remarkable person, Nadya Skylung." He waves to Thom and the others as the undersecretary closes the doors behind me. "Good luck!" he calls out. "Be careful! I hope to see you again very soon, triumphant!"

The doors boom shut. Markus fastens his glare on me right away, as though now that my business is concluded, me and my party should kindly get on the elevators and shove off, thank you very much.

Thom, Tam, and Rash stare at me suspiciously. My gills burn. They're not going to like what I did. Except Rash, maybe. He seems to enjoy adventure.

"'Good luck'?" Thom asks. "What did he mean by that?"

Markus clears his throat meaningfully, and I crutch toward the elevators, my heart sinking into my shoes. "C'mon," I say. "I'll tell you on the way up to the roof."

CHAPTER 19

IN WHICH NADYA MAKES A FATEFUL DECISION, AND HAS AN UNEXPECTED ENCOUNTER.

I'm wrong about Rash liking the plan. Even he thinks it's too dangerous.

"Look, Nadya," he says when I ask him for help. We're putting away the gliders after getting back to Gossner's workshop. Thom already told me he thinks the plan is terrible, and Tam, who's now disappearing inside, was worryingly quiet about it. "It's not that I don't want to help, but this is too big a risk. You're talking about flying *into the hideout* of the guy who's trying to kidnap you, finding the kids, getting on the Panpathia—which if I understand it is like shining a big old searchlight around and yelling 'Here I am!' to Silvermask—convincing the Lord Secretary to help you, and then sneaking out without getting caught." Rash folds up the wings on my glider and leans it against another, then pulls a tarp over the whole set. "I've seen you do some incredible things, but I don't think even you are capable of this. And I *know* me and the Dawnrunners aren't."

My mouth dries out as we head toward the stairs to the workshop. Somewhere down there, Raj is pacing, worrying, self-quarantined. "There's no *time* to come up with a better plan," I protest. "We don't know what's happening to Aaron and the kids, and we don't know how long it'll be before Raj loses himself to the shadow. I know it's a big risk, but we have to take it!"

Rash wipes the sweat off his face, then takes off his prosthesis and stretches his shoulder out. "Sorry," he says. "But there's got to be a better way."

The reception I get downstairs is pretty much the same. Pepper, who's working on some kind of boiler gadget, tells me it's too dangerous. Alé, supervising Pep while propping her hurt ankle up on a table with an ice pack under it, shrugs, as if to say, *Sorry, but I'm not going anywhere.* Tian Li and Salyeh are back at the *Orion* with Nic, which I count as pretty even, since they might help, but Nic would definitely be against the plan. I don't bother trying Gossner. Instead I keep wheedling and needling people all morning, until when we're all at lunch, Thom finally loses his patience after I accuse him of giving up.

"We're not giving up, Nadya!" He rubs his forehead and tosses the crust of his sandwich down. "We're just not going to do things the way you want." He raises an eyebrow at me. "I thought you'd learned by now that's important sometimes."

I did learn that, last month when we were fighting the

pirates. And Pep's been trying to teach it to me again. But . . .

"This is different," I say. "This isn't about the best way to do something. This is life and death, and we have to move fast."

"What about Sal and Tian Li?" Tam asks around a mouthful of noodle soup. It's the first thing he's said since we started. He slurps down his noodles and peers into the workshop, where Gossner's kids are working and laughing like everything's normal. "Maybe they've got something cooking. Sal said he thought he could figure out who Silver-mask is, right?"

My stomach shrivels. Tam was my last hope, and it sounds like he's going to come down on Thom's side.

"So why don't we get in touch with them and see what they think?" Tam clears his throat and taps his spoon on his bowl. "Sorry, Nadya. But it kinda *is* like last time, you know? We need everybody working together or we'll never pull this off."

Everybody watches me hopefully, except for Pep. She looks away, like she doesn't even want to see me right now. The fire in my heart cools. I almost give up. I almost give in.

I'm scared too, y'know? I don't want to go into Silver-mask's mansion. I don't *want* to risk facing him. I want Nic and Thom and Gossner and the adults to solve this problem for me, the way things are supposed to work.

Down below, I hear Raj crying softly. The last time I let my fears stop me, it was a disaster. I'm not gonna do it again.

"Sure," I mumble. I look down at my crutches and the Lady, wiggle my leg a bit because it's falling asleep. "We can wait a little longer, I guess. Maybe Sal and Tian Li will have a better idea."

Everybody but Pep smiles. Everybody but Pep looks relieved. Pep, on the other hand, looks up for the first time in ten minutes and frowns.

My heart tumbles toward my ankles like a flightless bird rolling down a hill. Because I know what I have to do now, and even *I* don't really think I can pull this off alone.

We send a message to the *Orion*, but Sal and Tian Li don't respond before bed. So I wait until everybody's asleep to make my move. It's a little hard to extricate myself from the big nest of blankets by the boilers, but I manage it eventually. I almost trip over Pep, and my heart twangs. Her face is scrunched up like she's having a bad dream, and she twitches every few seconds, sending her curls fluttering. We were so close just a few weeks ago. I want to burrow up against her and cry my heart out because this is so darn *hard* and I want my best friend.

But if I do that, I'll never get out of here, and we'll never rescue Aaron and never save Raj, and I'm pretty sure I'll feel like I'm responsible for that the whole rest of my life.

I know this is a big risk. I know I could end up like Brittany Brikowski. But there's a risk to *me* of doing nothing. If I just sit here safe in Gossner's tower while Aaron and Raj suffer, it'll be like I'm drinking poison, and that poison will sit in my soul the rest of my life. Eventually it'll do what the pirates and Silvermask and even the Malumbra haven't been able to: It'll eat my heart, and I won't be Nadya Skylung anymore.

I don't blame them for not wanting to risk their lives on this rescue mission. They're taking care of themselves and each other, and in a way I'm glad. But if I don't do this, I'll lose myself as surely as I would if Silvermask got hold of me. At least if I go, there's a chance I won't.

I leave Pepper behind and start the long, painful crutch up the stairs to the roof where the gliders are. The lifts are too loud and there's nobody to help me use the swings so I'm on my own, starting now. I take it slow, place the crutches carefully. I've got a long way to go and a lot to do, and I've gotta stay stealthy. I can't get caught now, and I can't burn my arms out like I did on the bicycle. Like Rash said, getting in is only half the battle—once I'm there, I have to get *out* again.

Gossner's workshop after dark is kinda eerie. The electric lights of the city cast strange shadows through the window, even on a clear, moonlit night like this one. Kids cough and groan in their sleep, and the platforms they're on squeak and pop as they move. Every once in a while somebody gets up to use the bathroom, and their footsteps make my heart race until a door closes and I hear a flush a little later.

But eventually I reach the door to the roof. I pause to rest, looking back at the stairs I climbed and all the sleeping kids below, searching for my friends, my allies, the people trying to keep me safe, who I lied to and am running away from.

"Kinda hard, isn't it?" says a voice by the door.

245

My heart leaps into my mouth, which is good because if it wasn't there blocking the sound I'd probably scream, and then I'd be in even worse trouble than I am already. I turn around, and Tam moves into the moonlight coming through a window to our left. He shakes his head. "I knew you'd try this, Nadya." He sighs, then looks down at all the stairs I climbed. "I was sorta hoping you'd change your mind partway up though."

My heart slows down, but I'm still breathless from the climb, my hands are sweating, and my wrists are sore. "Well, I didn't," I say. "What're you gonna do about it?"

Tam jerks his head up like I smacked him. "I'm gonna come with you, of course." My jaw drops, and he frowns. "Goshend's teeth, Nadya." He rubs the back of his head. "Did you think I'd rat you out or something?"

I wince. "Kinda. I mean, you were on everybody else's side this afternoon."

Tam rolls his eyes. "I knew you wouldn't give up. I was *trying* to help you roll the wool over Thom's eyes."

My guts feel like a cloud frog diving for the bottom of the pond. "Sorry," I say. "I should've known I could trust you."

Tam sighs. But after a second, he shakes his head and shrugs. "Heck, at least you know now." He holds up a key and twirls it around his finger. "The door's locked, but I got the key from Alé." He grins. "She says, 'Good luck. Wish I could join you.' She's down keeping a lookout. And she wanted to pass this on too." He tosses me her rod, the one she used to beat up the Shadowmen who attacked us on the zip lines.

My stomach warms back up. "I gotta find a good way to thank her when all this is over," I say, hitting the button that telescopes the rod and swishing it through the air a couple times. "She's been a huge help."

Tam nods. "Yeah. We'll think of something though. *Together*, right?" He raises an eyebrow.

I smile. "Yeah. Together."

Then Tam unlocks the door to Gossner's roof, and together we walk through it.

CHAPTER 20

IN WHICH A PERILOUS NIGHTTIME FLIGHT IS UNDERTAKEN.

Tam and I get everything set up together, just like he said. I check the straps on his glider, and he checks the straps on mine. We map out the route in our heads, remembering the thermals we used this morning. Thermals are different at night, Rash said, but a couple of these should be permanent. One's the exhaust from a power station by the river, and another's the hot air coming off the decomposing garbage at an enormous landfill. They should get us enough altitude to glide all the way into Bleak Forest.

We decide Tam should go first, since we won't be able to see each other very well or communicate much, and he's slower. I wouldn't want to leave him behind. Our plan is to land on the roof of Silvermask's mansion and find a way in from there. Tam's brought some lock picks, which I'm glad for. Breaking in with a hammer or something might be too noisy. Silvermask's compound is probably pretty quiet.

Once we're strapped in and my crutches are cinched tight to my harness, Tam pulls a blue button about as big as my palm out of his pocket. "Here," he says. He hands it to me.

"What's this?" I ask, turning it over. It's a glass bead with some kind of metal on the back. Steel, maybe, or brass.

"It's a locator," Tam says. "I made it today while you were bugging everybody. It's in case we get separated." He pulls another one out. "Listen." He presses his button, and the one he handed to me chirps. He shakes it, then walks halfway around me and presses it again, and it chirps a little differently. "Gossner showed me how to make machines talk to each other. I don't understand it all the way yet, but if you put an electric charge through the right kind of metal, you can send out some kind of wave. Other pieces of metal get hit by the wave and react."

He takes a deep breath. He sounds excited. "There's a couple electromagnets and a copper wire inside the button. When you press the button, the wire moves by the electromagnets, which creates a charge and makes some of these waves." He pulls the back off one of the buttons. There's a whole mess of stuff in there. "See these little glass tubes? They've got metal dust in them. When the waves hit the dust, it sticks together. This little nub here stores electrical charge, and when the metal dust sticks together it completes a circuit and makes this little brass foot rub the back of the case, which makes the chirp and shakes the dust loose in the glass tubes, resetting the locator. So if the locators are close enough when you hit the button, they make each other chirp, and if you listen real careful, you can tell which direction the other locator is in by how the chirp sounds, because the wave hits one glass tube before the other."

I stare at Tam, dumbfounded. "You just . . . whipped this up?"

He scratches the back of his head. "I'm kinda surprised it works, actually," he mumbles.

He's a genius. There's no doubt about it. I lunge forward and give him a hug. It's awkward in the gliders, but it works.

"Wait!" a voice shouts behind us.

Pepper runs toward us from the door to the workshop. "I'm coming with you," she says as I let go of Tam. I feel like dirt. She's totally going to get the wrong idea about that hug.

She's puffing real hard, like she ran the last few flights of steps, and she starts strapping herself into one of the gliders. "I watched you guys learn to use these things, and I'm sure I can fly one."

Tam stares at her for a second, then shrugs, looking relieved. When Pep finally turns to me, all I get's a scowl.

"Um . . . ," I say. My stomach twists. She's still mad at me, and I'm kinda worried about her coming along. Tam and I work real well together, and I know I can count on him. Up until last week, I'd have said I could count on Pep too. But I feel like me and Pep need to get back on the same page before we do anything as serious as flying into Silvermask's mansion.

Unfortunately, we don't have time for that.

"Nadya!" Thom bellows from the door to the workshop. "What in Goshend's holy name do you think—"

I don't hear him finish. He rushes toward us, and then Pep, Tam, and me are bumping into each other and all three of us half jump, half fall off the balcony together.

The initial drop is terrifying. You're supposed to launch real careful with one of these gliders, but we had to get out so fast we didn't have time to take a gentle step. I end up between Pep and Tam, my back to the ground and my face toward the sky, looking at Thom's stricken face in the faint glow of the streetlamps.

Luckily, Rash taught us what to do if we ever got caught in a bad position and the gliders stopped flying.

Nose down, he said, *and once you're moving fast, level out again.*

Tam noses down above me, and I don't see what Pep does because I have to roll over to get myself oriented. Once I'm facing down, I push up with my foot on the tail of the glider, which tilts the nose down, and dive straight toward the street. The wall of Gossner's tower rushes past beneath me, all windows and electric lights. On the ground, the cars race by like mice scuttling after crumbs. The wind's a sharp, cold bite in my ears. I count to two, then tug down on the tail loop and straighten out. Goshend be good, I'm moving fast enough that the wings fill with air and I glide toward the river, following the street.

I'm breathing so hard I might pass out, so I focus on taking normal breaths and look around for Tam and Pep. I see two bat-wing shadows up ahead and figure that must be them, and I angle off behind them.

Whoever's in the lead—Tam, I hope, since we didn't get to talk over the route with Pep—takes us along the avenue for a few blocks. He checks over his shoulder to see we're both following, then turns left down an alley. We're losing altitude fast, and this isn't the route he and I picked out, but I'm not sure we've got enough altitude to get all the way to the first thermal we planned on, so hopefully he knows another one and that's where he's taking us.

Sure enough, a block later we coast into a rising wall of hot air. I look down at a big grate in the street with fiery orange light leaking up through it and shudder. I try not to think about how Far Agondy's perched on top of a giant fire creature unless I have to.

I hit the thermal last, and by the time I start wheeling upward, Tam and Pep are a hundred feet high already, soaring like the buzzards outside Vash Abandi do on hot days when they're looking for carcasses. I follow them up and up and up, until the thermal loses its potency as it gets over the rooftops, and then I take off toward the river behind them.

Far Agondy at night, from the sky, is as pretty as anything in the world. The river glitters like a ribbon of liquid silver in the moonlight, and the skyscrapers look like knife-edge mountain peaks of diamond and gold.

It's a cool night, which helps

us with the thermals, and the salty breeze off the ocean feels like a climbing line, connecting me to the Cloud Sea and all those ships out on it, all that water running between the Six Cities and all the way up to the Roof of the World, where my parents lived. I can feel the Panpathia stretching out in front of me, golden and warm—and then cold, directly ahead.

I shiver, even though we're rising in a column of warm air off that power plant we planned to hit earlier. The Panpathia's icy and dead ahead of us, more like a tangled, twisted spiderweb than its usual bird's nest of spun gold. And Silvermask's at the heart of that web, waiting while I fly straight to him with Pepper and Tam alongside me.

The fear-octopus peeks out for the first time in a while and nips my stomach. Maybe we shouldn't do this. It's one thing to risk my life. It's another to risk theirs. But last time I chickened out, it ruined everything. We can do this. Everything will be fine. We just have to be perfect.

Right as I'm getting my confidence back, we sail past City Hall looming like a silent guardian, over the river, and into Bleak Forest.

I can *feel* the change. The air gets drier and colder. The buildings aren't lit up as much here. Even the streetlamps seem dimmer. What I can see in the light of the moon seems old and dead: dirty stone buildings, stained and peeling facades, broken windows, roofs with gaping holes in them. I realize how desperate people here must be to trust someone like Silvermask, and I swallow. There's something evil about this, and it's not the buildings—it's the *unfairness* of it all. Just across the river there's so much extra money that people put marble tiles in offices and have huge windows and light up skyscrapers all night long. Here there's so much poverty that somebody would risk their life to work for a crook just to put food on their table, or patch their roof to keep the rain out. And the worst of it, the part that really hits me in the gut, is that I don't think Silvermask caused it. I think the people of Far Agondy just let it happen, and Silvermask only took advantage of the evil that was already here, waiting for a creep like him to come and build a web in it.

We sail over those cold-bone buildings for a long time. The lights become less and less frequent. The people below us dart fearfully from shadow to shadow or stroll awkwardly like the guys who've been chasing me all over the city. My heart pounds, and I'm really, really glad for Rash's gliders, because I have no idea how we'd ever have gotten in without them. It's amazing that Tian Li and Sal pulled it off, even during the day.

Up ahead, a white mansion looms in the darkness. It's got a front yard bigger than the *Orion*, walled off by a fence topped with long iron spikes. In the garden in front of the house there's two huge dead trees, reaching toward the sky like a skeleton's bony fingers. The house itself looks like that skeleton's head and shoulders. The central portion of it has a rounded room where I bet they used to welcome visitors, and there's a grassy, overgrown path leading to it from a gate in the fence. The main building is four stories tall, full of windows, and topped with a pyramid-shaped skylight. The house turns ninety degrees at either end of the skylight and moves toward the front gates of the estate, with more skylights dotting its roof like jagged teeth. There's probably a hundred rooms in there, easy. My stomach sinks. How in the world are we gonna search something so big?

Tam angles hard for the closest part of the roof, and I realize we're so low that landing's gonna be pretty dicey. I grit my teeth and urge my glider to stay just a little higher, a little higher, but all it does is creak in the wind and sink inch by inch. I'm twenty feet above the lip of the roof. Fifteen. Ten. Tam and Pepper clear it and land, but I'm lower than them and still losing altitude. I'm terrified I'm gonna smack right into the side of the mansion.

At the last second, I roll onto my back to keep my legs from hitting the wall, and I just barely clear the lip of the rooftop and land hard on my shoulder. The glider scrapes and bumps along beneath me, and I bowl into somebody and knock them over, and then both of us and our gliders crash into a skylight. I hear an awfully ominous *snap*.

"Get *off*," hisses Pepper. I try to, but it takes a few seconds to untangle our arms and legs and gliders. She tugs one way and I tug another, and there's another *snap* before we finally get separated.

"Sorry," I whisper, sitting with my legs in front of me, my shoulder scraped and smarting.

Pep stares back at me, mouth open, squatting with her

glider wings above her like some kind of gargoyle. Her eyes are wide as engine dials. "It's busted," she whispers.

She points at my glider, and I look over my shoulder and realize my left wing is totally broken. The crash shredded the fabric on top of the metal, and the two main struts snapped right in half.

I let out a long, careful breath and start undoing my straps. My crutches, thankfully, survived the crash. "It's okay," I say numbly. "We'll just, ah . . . we'll just find another way out." On feet and crutches. Through a neighborhood so scary that even the people who live here don't want to be out at night.

Pep looks like she wants to slug me, then sighs. "There weren't any good thermals for the way back anyway," she mutters, "so I guess it doesn't matter much." She starts looking around for Tam.

"Wait," I say, "was that *you* leading us?"

Pep tosses her curls and glares at me. "What, you didn't think I could?"

My gills burn. I want us to be friends again, but I keep mucking it up. "I just, I mean . . . you hadn't . . ."

She rolls her eyes, and she looks like she's gonna say something else, but Tam trots up behind us and motions for us to crouch down and be quiet. A second later, a flashlight beam sweeps across the rooftop. All three of us shuffle behind a big chimney, where we ditch our gliders in the blackest shadows we can find. Peeking out from behind it, I watch two Shadowmen search the roof.

"They must've heard us," Tam whispers.

I nod. Pepper closes her eyes. She's breathing real hard and fast. I feel bad for bringing her here. I feel bad for bringing both of them here.

But that won't get us in, or back out again.

"Let's go while they're distracted," I say, nodding at the trapdoor they came up through.

"What if there's more of them in there?" Pep asks.

I open my mouth, then close it again. I know Pep wants me to stop disagreeing with her, but I've got some pretty strong feelings here. "There might be, but it's our best shot. Otherwise we have to keep dodging them out here and try to find another way in, and we have no idea where the other doors are, or how they're locked, or . . . where's Tam?"

He's not at my shoulder anymore. I slink back around the chimney and realize the Shadowmen have gotten to the part of the roof where we landed, and they're sweeping the flashlight around more slowly now. One of them picks something up, and in the beam of his friend's light I recognize it as a shiny piece of my glider.

Pep looks like I clobbered her from behind with a wrench. "I thought you were watching him!" she whispers. "What if he got caught? What if—"

A shadow wriggles toward us from the skylight a few feet over, and I just about kick it in the face before I realize it's Tam, on his belly. "I'm fine," he whispers when he gets to us. "And I found us another way in. C'mon."

CHAPTER 21

IN WHICH NADYA, TAM, AND PEPPER ARE SEPARATED, AND NADYA DISCOVERS SOMETHING AWFUL.

Five minutes later, I'm dangling from my fingertips over a narrow balcony, trying to avoid falling or cutting my hands on broken glass. Tam found a busted spot in the skylight, and all three of us are sneaking through it.

Below us, this part of Silvermask's estate is a big open atrium. There's nothing but air under the balcony all the way to a greenhouse that takes up the whole bottom floor, where a bunch of sun-in-a-jars hang in air all misty and thick. The ground's covered in rows of big plants. I wonder for a second if it's a cloud garden, like the one Rash and Alé built inside Gossner's workshop.

Then I cut my finger, and I decide I'll worry about that later.

I drop onto the balcony, wincing at the thump and the way my ankle barks from taking all my weight. We're trying to stay as quiet as possible because we keep seeing people move through the greenhouse. Every once in a while a Shadowman ambles past, or a kid rushes by carrying a tray or a message or something.

Every time I see those kids, my heart flips. I want to call out to them. I want to jump on the Panpathia and see whether they're okay. I want to know whether Silvermask is controlling them like he does the Shadowmen, and whether they've seen Aaron. But I have to be silent, and I can't touch the Panpathia or I'll risk letting Silvermask know exactly where I am.

I wipe the blood off my finger and discover the cut's not bad. Tam hands me my crutches and drops down beside me, and Pep thumps after him. We wait a second, peeking over the balcony edge to be sure nobody noticed us, then duck off the balcony into a dark room full of dusty old pool tables and dartboards.

"Did you see the kids?" Tam asks as we sit down to rest. "Is that good enough? Can you tell the Lord Secretary where we are now?"

I wish. "No," I say, remembering our conversation in City Hall. "He wants to see them for himself. We have to be right in front of at least one kid, and preferably a whole bunch. We need to find where Silvermask *keeps* them."

Tam curses and starts to fidget. "Nadya, I dunno if we can do this. This is way harder than I was expecting, and we're just getting started." He looks nervously back toward the balcony.

"We've already *done* the dangerous part though," I protest. "We're in. Now we just have to find the kids and get out again. We're so close!"

"Remember what happened last time you were 'so close'?" Pepper asks stonily.

I rub the Lady. My gills burn. "Yes," I mutter. "This is *different*. No improvising. No fancy rescues. Just find the kids, tell the grown-ups, and go. Nobody's going to get hurt."

Tam sighs. "Where do you think they are?"

"The ground floor," I say, thinking about those kids running messages. "That's where we saw them, so that's where we start. Maybe we can find one of those messengers and ask them a question, or maybe we can follow them back to the others."

Pep and Tam are both quiet for a few seconds. I rub my leg, think about how I lost my foot and shin. It's real easy to get afraid, sitting around like this, waiting for Tam and Pepper to make up their minds. What it's like for Aaron and the other kids? How long have they been locked up in the darkness with their fears for company?

Tam takes a deep breath. It seems to steady him, because he gets up again. "Okay," he says. "Let's go."

We never make it to the kids.

We sneak all the way down to the ground floor, dodging a pair of Shadowmen with flashlights on the way. The greenhouse turns out not to be a cloud garden after all, which

261

is good because Tam and Pep can breathe the air inside. Listening for footsteps and hoping to find a kid, we creep between the plants, mist in our eyes, dew on our cheeks.

When we're so far in I can't see the walls anymore, I hear someone coming and wave at the others to hide. We sneak behind a big black fern. The footsteps sound small, and they're moving fast. As they reach us, a kid-shaped blur appears in the mist.

"Now's our chance!" Pep whispers. The kid's moving too fast to catch, but she takes off after him. Tam follows.

Presumably, they've forgotten I can't run.

They disappear into the mist, and all I can do is I try to follow them because I'm afraid to risk calling out. Anything loud enough to get their attention might be heard by a Shadowman. My heart pounds. My eyes play tricks on me. Every shadow looks like a person trying to grab me. The old mansion creaks as the wind blows. Footsteps echo everywhere. I have no idea where Pep and Tam are. I have no idea where *I* am. I'm all alone.

"Pep," I whisper. "Tam!"

I can't help it. They must've realized they lost me. They must've turned around by now to come back and look. Another shadow looms in the mist, and I hop back and raise a crutch up to smack it before I realize it's just a tree in a pot.

I take a deep breath. I'm not gonna help anyone by panicking at shadows and trees, or if I get caught whispering Tam's and Pepper's names louder and louder. I feel a lump in my pocket and remember Tam's locator. Carefully, I take it out and press it, but nothing happens. I shake it, then press it again, but there's still no chirp. Maybe it's busted after my crash landing.

Still, I know the direction they went in. I just have to keep moving, footstep by crutchstep, until I catch them or they come back to find me.

So that's what I do. Plant my foot, plant my crutches. Pause, listen. Plant my foot, plant my crutches. Pause, listen. I see a light up ahead. As I get closer, the mist thins around a black lantern hanging over a door. I stop there for a second, wondering what I should do. This is probably where Pepper and Tam went. But it might not be. That kid they were following could have swerved, or I could've gotten lost in the mist.

Still, I'm here to explore, and I've seen more Shadowmen in this greenhouse than anywhere else in the mansion. Wherever this door leads, it's gotta be safer than it is in here.

Carefully, I try the handle. It's unlocked. I try Tam's locator one more time just in case, but nothing happens, so I slip through the door and close it gently behind me, and then I try to see where I am.

The room's enormous, and it's got no lights. It was pretty dim in the greenhouse, but the lamp over the door messed up my night vision, and it takes my eyes a few seconds to adjust. First I make out a little illumination on the floor to my left. I crutch that way and figure out there are huge windows all along the left wall, with big black curtains over them. A little light squeezes underneath those curtains onto a polished wood floor. Maybe I'm in some kind of ballroom. Mrs. T told me once about a ball she went to at the Roof of the World, in a room lit by a hundred sun-in-a-jars. Everybody in the city was entered in a lottery to attend, and she only won once, but she said it was amazing, all bright lights and beautiful dresses and suits and live music and swirling color.

As my eyes adjust, I see *this* ballroom more clearly. Lined up along the inner wall across from the windows, there's bed after bed after bed. And on those beds are shadows, lying perfectly still, that look an awful lot like children.

My skin crawls. There's something wrong about those kids. There's forty, fifty beds easy, and most of them look occupied, but I don't hear a thing. No snoring. Nobody tossing and turning. No whispers or thumps or moans. None of the sounds that kids usually make when they're sleeping. I can see they're alive—their chests rise and fall as they breathe—but it's like they're in a trance.

Like they're Shadowmen.

As quietly as I can, I crutch over to them. This is what I came here for. I guess I should be contacting Lord Salawag on the Panpathia and hightailing it out.

But I can't do that yet. For one thing, I don't know how to get out from here. For another, I don't know where Tam and Pep are, and I can't leave without them.

And for a third, I really, really don't want to get on the Panpathia in here. I feel like there's a spider on the ceiling the size of a bus, just waiting for me to make the wrong move before it pounces. The sensation's so strong I can barely look up.

My heart feels squeezed like a sponge. My veins burn. But all that's up there is shadows. No spiders, no nothing.

I stand next to one of the beds, watching the rising and falling chest of a boy about my age with dark skin and black hair. I'm not sure what to do next, so I decide to look for Aaron. Maybe if I can break him free, he'll know how to help me.

I work my way down the line of beds, looking at the kids. Every fifth bed or so is empty, but I see a lot of people. There's little kids, big kids, teenagers who almost look like adults. But I can't find Aaron. I get all the way to the last bed without seeing him.

I'm trying to figure out the safest way to go look for Tam and Pepper when I realize there's more light in the room than I thought. Most of the illumination comes in through the windows, but there's also some from a big glass tank just beyond the last of the beds, pushed up against the wall. The light in there shimmers and shakes, like the tank has water in it.

I keep looking at it, wondering what it is, and then something moves at the bottom. Slowly, a shadow unfurls, and I see a very familiar pattern of glowing dots.

You ever see something so completely out of place, so totally unexpected, that your head says, *No, that can't possibly be right, look again.* But you keep looking and it's still definitely that thing, and for a few seconds your brain and eyes argue until one of them wins?

Seeing those dots is like that.

I crutch closer while my eyes and my brain are fighting, and the closer I get, the more my eyes have the advantage, until eventually my brain gives up and admits that those glowing dots definitely, undeniably, one hundred percent totally belong to the gormling.

I touch its tank. "Why are you here?" I whisper. "How did Silvermask get you?"

The gormling turns its head toward me sadly. I can't see its eyes in the shadows, just those glowing dots and the rainbow scales. Slowly, as though it's sick, it floats up until our heads are level. It looks like somebody splashed a bucket of ink over it. Most of the places it was light before are dark, either glowing sickly purple or jet-black. It turns so I can see its eyes, and I find shadow there, thick as molasses, just like in the eye of the leviathan I saw before we got to Far Agondy.

My conversation with Lord Salawag flashes back through my mind. *He didn't seem comfortable here, took a little ill, so I had him brought to my home.*

My heart turns to ice, falls into my legs, and shatters on the floor. "Oh no," I whisper, crutching away from the tank. "Oh no. Oh no. Oh no."

"Oh *yes*," says a voice from the shadows, and I turn around and there's Alan Salawag, walking toward me from the line of beds, grinning like a spider that just caught its dinner.

CHAPTER 22

IN WHICH EVERYTHING GOES TO PIECES.

My heart drums like an army full of ants on tambourines. My mouth tastes like sour candy and bitter bread. Alan Salawag walks toward me gleefully, his cape trailing behind him.

"Oh, Nadya," he says. "I couldn't believe it when you walked into my office and proposed to actually *come* here yourself." He laughs. "The luck of it! Here I've been trying to get my hands on you ever since you came to town—I freed the pirates from the *Orion* so I could question them, sent my Shadowmen to the ship, boxed you up with Gossner, chased you down on the streets. Every time you eluded me. And then you waltzed through my door and asked for my *help* tracking down Silvermask." He laughs again. His eyes still look friendly, like it's all a big joke, and that makes me so cold I shiver.

"You wanted to find him? Well . . ." He stops halfway between the beds and the gormling tank and reaches into his pocket. Slowly, like he's loving every second of it, he pulls out a glittering silver mask with a terrifying, sharp-toothed face carved on it, then puts it over his head.

"Here I am!" he shouts. The light shimmers over that silver mask, running up and down it with a life of its own. The rest of him seems dimmer, as though his whole body's wrapped in the shadows of his mansion.

My hands feel weak. "I . . . you . . . But you used to be on the *Orion*," I croak. "You used to crew for Nic."

He snorts. "You crew for him now, and you don't understand? He's a weak-willed, spineless old goat. No ambition. No respect for the gifted. Always rattling on about his mission this, help the downtrodden that. The strong make the world go round, Nadya. Everyone else is just a bloodsucking insect."

I think over everything he said and everything he did, trying to spot the clues I missed and understand how I didn't see who he was. He didn't come back from the Roof of the World untouched after all. He came back as a servant of the Malumbra.

"Oh, don't ask so much of yourself," he says. He tilts his head to the side, and the mask glitters. "You're just a child still. Maybe you could've been one of the strong one day, but you crossed the Malumbra. Now it wants you. And what the Malumbra wants, I deliver."

That jolts me into action. It doesn't matter whether I could've spotted him before. It doesn't matter that this is the worst screwup of my whole life, that I'm in danger and Tam and Pep are in danger and Silvermask was right in front of me and I never saw him.

All that matters is that he's ten feet away, and if I don't get out of here I'm doomed, and Aaron is doomed, and Raj is doomed, and everybody else is probably doomed too.

I've still got Alé's rod tucked inside my jacket. He won't know about it. He'll think I'm beaten and broken, just a kid on crutches, separated from her friends, terrified and alone. I am all those things. But I'm not *just* those things. I'm Nadya Skylung, and I beat the Malumbra on the pirate ship *Remora*, and I'll beat it here too, somehow.

I cook up a plan. I'll wait for Silvermask to come close to me. He's gotta touch me to get the Malumbra's shadow into my head, since I'm not on the Panpathia and I'm sure not gonna get on it with him right in front of me. When he's close enough, I'll jab him in the crotch with a crutch, then get out Alé's rod and whack him in the leg, and then I'll crutch for the door as fast as I can while he's down, find Tam and Pepper, and we'll get outta here.

I watch him. I tense my leg. I wait.

Silvermask crooks his head to the other side. "You have a plan, don't you?" His voice is muffled through the mask, but it doesn't sound like it did on the Panpathia. I wonder if that nails-on-a-saw screech is just the way he wishes his voice sounded, a reflection of who he'd like to be. He snorts. "Of course you do. Nadya Skylung *always* has a plan, doesn't she?"

My guts freeze. I don't like the sound of that. "Maybe," I say. "You should probably let me go, just in case."

"Oh goodness," he says with a laugh. "You really think highly of yourself, don't you?" He pulls up the mask and smirks at me. "Well. I'm not sure I want to get whacked in the leg or whatever you've got in mind, so I think I'll show you just how far out of your league you are."

My stomach sinks, because clearly my plan wasn't as clever as I thought and I don't really have another one. He puts the mask back down, and for a few seconds nothing happens. Then the Panpathia *shifts*. It feels like standing on a sand dune as it gives way. Things are changing beneath me, falling, sliding.

Don't you want to see what's here? Silvermask says over the Panpathia, his voice the old screeching metal wail. *Don't you want to know what's coming?*

I crutch toward the door I came in through as fast as I can. If he's distracted doing something on the Panpathia, maybe he won't notice. And this is definitely a trick. He wants me to go onto the Panpathia so he can get me easier, and I'm not gonna do it, no way.

Ah, he says with a sigh. *You disappoint me, Nadya. The Malumbra is truly something to behold up close. It's eaten dozens of worlds, you know. Worlds of ice, worlds of jungle, worlds of sand, worlds of sea. But you'll see it soon, I promise. Can't you feel it?*

A shiver runs down my spine. That feeling of sand giving way gets as icy cold as the metal on the *Orion*'s rails in the dead of winter. I feel something enormous lurching up from beneath me like a leviathan, jaws open.

Its senses don't work very well in our world. It was born in the freezing darkness of the space between, and it needs a guide to glimpse more than hazy silhouettes here. That's me. Can you imagine it, Nadya? All that power at my fingertips, following my every direction, bearing down wherever I say.

My heart pounds. I keep crutching as hard as I can. I don't want to be here when the Malumbra shows up. I really, really don't.

If you won't come to the Panpathia to see what you're up against, I suppose I'll have to bring it to you, Silvermask says. *The space between is always close by, like the open sky around a cloudship. And with enough willpower, sometimes you can just* punch—he grunts as he says it—*right on through.*

I'm halfway across the room now. Silvermask's far behind me. I can see the door. Maybe there's safety outside it, maybe not, but I still want to get far, far from here as fast as possible, because that feeling of cold is getting worse, like I'm not just touching the *Orion*'s rails but I've gone outside on the coldest, windiest night of the year, soaking wet, wearing a thin shirt and shorts.

The shadows move in front of me, swimming like oil slicks on top of those faded wooden squares. I don't like that. For a few more feet I dodge between them, but then two shadows close up and there's a pool of darkness between me and the door. I don't know what it is, but I don't want to touch it.

Oh, come on, Nadya, Silvermask urges behind me. *Don't be shy. The darkness feels fine. Your friend is here already, waiting. Turn around and look, why don't you?*

This is probably a trick too. My scalp's crawling, but I can't help it. I look back, and there's Aaron, standing with his head down right next to Silvermask, his feet in one of those pools of shadow.

My heart just about snaps in two. I was supposed to protect him. He was counting on me to help him find his sister.

My crutch starts to feel real cold, and I whip around and see the shadow at my feet licking the bottom of it. I jump back, but I slip as I land and lose the crutch. As I fall, the shadow touches the other one and races up it, and I kick the crutch away so it won't get to me.

The shadows keep coming. I scoot away from them, but there's more behind me too, and to the side. They move in from all directions, building, not just oil slicks but waves, not just waves but towers. They look like teeth, and I realize this whole room is a trap. Out between the worlds, the Malumbra must have its mouth around this space. Somehow Silvermask is letting it in, and now its mouth is closing.

It's here, Silvermask breathes. *It wants you. And the Malumbra* always *gets what it wants.*

My heart pounds. My gills burn. There's nowhere to go, no way to run. All that's left is to jump on the Panpathia and try to fight somehow. I close my eyes, take a deep breath, and get ready . . .

My pocket chirps.

I open my eyes again. Tam's standing in the door, holding the locator in one hand and a giant length of carpet from somewhere in the mansion in the other. Pepper's right behind him, eyes closed, mumbling to herself.

"No!" I shout. "Just run! He's *here* and it's a trap—"

They don't listen. Tam drops the carpet at his feet, then kicks the bundle, and it rolls toward me. The shadows pool around it, then start to build on top of it.

Pepper opens her eyes. They glow bright orange, like they do when she's calling fire.

She kneels and touches the top of the carpet, and flame spreads along it, blue at first, then violet and orange and bright, shining yellow. The shadows shrink back from the light and the heat—Thom said the only thing the Malumbra hates is fire—and suddenly there's an open path between me and the door.

The only problem is, it's in flames.

But that doesn't seem to bother Tam. He takes off over the flaming carpet, sprinting like a beetle running from a bird. The flames lick the bottoms of his shoes and his pants, but they don't catch. Maybe Pep figured out how to keep the fire spirits from burning us.

Tam reaches me quick. He scoops me up and starts running again, and then we're both passing through the flames. They feel strangely cool, and a second later we've reached Pep on the other side of the shadows. Tam keeps running and Pep turns to go with him, and I think for one wonderful second that we're actually going to make it.

The door slams in front of us. A bar thunks down on the other side to lock it.

Silvermask laughs, so loud it hurts my ears and so long it echoes. "Did you think I'd just let you get away? *Really?* You kids . . . Oh, you have no idea who you're dealing with. Before I met Nic, I outsmarted a hundred like you to earn a spot in school in Deepwater. After I left the *Orion*, I outsmarted a hundred more kids to get into the civil service academy, then a hundred adults to become the undersecretary of the old Lord Secretary. Then I set *him* up to take the fall for embezzling money and assumed his position. In another six months I could've been mayor, but it got so *boring* tricking people in Far Agondy. I wanted more, and the Malumbra gave it to me."

My throat dries up. The flames on the carpet start to die as whatever fire creature Pepper summoned works its way through the fuel. Once those flames die, the shadows are going to move back in on us, I'm sure of it.

"More?" I ask. "You call this more?"

Silvermask stops laughing. I swear he's glaring at me under that mask. I shiver, but I keep talking. I want to distract him, and I think I'm starting to get what drives him. "I mean, we're just kids. How much glory is there in outsmarting us?"

"None," Silvermask growls. "But in outsmarting your parents, your guardians, the whole adult world of the Cloud Sea? In stealing their children out from under their noses, in opening the way for the Malumbra by getting everyone in the world to turn against one another? That's a puzzle worthy of my time."

I don't get what he means, but I don't think we have time to figure it out, either. "The fire's dying," Pepper says behind me.

I swallow. "Any other ideas?" The shadows are starting to

stack and look like teeth again. The Malumbra's mouth must be closing.

"Um," Tam says. "That was kinda it. The locator wasn't working right and it took us forever to find you. We didn't have much time to plan." He's looking around at the walls and the door, but he doesn't seem very hopeful.

The shadow teeth keep growing. The light from the burning carpet's almost gone now. The fire spirit must be about to head back to the World Beyond. "Can you burn the walls or the door or something?" I ask.

Pep puts her hand on the door. "I could try. But I think the spirit would probably break its contract. It might burn the whole house down. I don't think we'd make it out. Those kids in the beds sure wouldn't."

I gulp, trying to think of something else to do.

Then one of the windows shatters.

I flinch. There's flying glass and suddenly one of the curtains is on fire and snaking toward us over the shadows. A tall, skinny man crouches on the sill of the broken window. Calmly, he touches the curtain on his other side, speaking to himself in a low, rumbling voice. The curtain catches fire, and the man whips it toward Silvermask.

It's Thom. Somehow, he followed us here.

"Over the fire!" he shouts, stepping into the room and snapping the flaming curtain toward Silvermask. "Hurry!"

The first curtain he lit lies in front of us in an S-shape, curving through the shadows. It's a long jump to the edge of it, too far for me to hop on one leg. Tam takes a deep breath, then scoops me up again.

"Tam, you can't," I say. "It's too far."

"I can," he says. "I gotta."

"No," Pep says. "I'll go first, then you hand her to me."

"Just go, you guys!" I shout. "I'll find another way!" Thom's still snapping the curtain at Silvermask, but Silvermask's snarling and shouting and I can hear the Shadowmen hurrying to unlatch the door behind us. "There isn't time for this!"

Pep jumps from the guttering edge of the flaming carpet to the brightly lit end of the curtain, and then Tam hands me to her. For a second I'm suspended over a pool of shadow. One of those teeth starts to form under me, but Pep throws me over her shoulder and starts moving. Tam jumps over the shadows behind us, and then we're all running through the flames and I'm bouncing along on Pep's shoulder.

Silvermask shouts, "Really, Thom? Fire spirits? How *predictable*. How utterly *uninspired*! You always were an unimaginative slug!"

If Thom's surprised to recognize Silvermask's voice as Alan Salawag's, he doesn't show it. He whips his flaming curtain forward again, but Silvermask, already running toward him, catches it and yanks. Thom has to let go, and when he does, Silvermask tosses down the curtain. Before the rest of us can get there, Silvermask tackles Thom.

Thom and Silvermask wrestle on the floor under the window, and Thom's head gets closer and closer to the

Malumbra's teeth. "Ready, Thom?" Silvermask shouts. "Ready to face what Brick did?"

We hit the end of the flaming curtain where there's a little bit of open space, but another shadow forms in front of us, cutting us off. Thom chokes and sputters angrily. Pepper screams. Tam shouts, "No!"

"Wait!" I yell.

Silvermask, still pushing Thom toward the shadows, looks up at me.

"You wanted a challenge?" I ask, my mind racing. "I've got one for you. You and me, on the Panpathia. Shadow versus light, right where the Malumbra can see us."

"What?" Tam sputters.

"What?" Pep echoes.

Silvermask just stares. The door we came in through opens up. A crowd of Shadowmen pours in and charges around the shadowy teeth, surrounding us. Silvermask takes long, heavy breaths. I can almost *feel* him thinking.

The Shadowmen pounce on Thom, and Silvermask lets him go and stands up. "I accept," he says. "You versus me, Nadya Skylung. On the Panpathia." He takes off his mask and shakes his hair out. Two Shadowmen come up behind us and grab Pep and Tam.

"Shadow, as you say"—Silvermask grins—"versus light."

CHAPTER 23

IN WHICH NADYA FACES SILVERMASK.

A few minutes later I'm holding Tam's shoulder for balance, staring hard at Silvermask and trying to remember everything Aaron taught me.

"Nadya," Thom murmurs behind me. The Shadowmen have stood him up, but they still have his arms pinned behind his back. "I've got another plan. Just let me know when he's distracted, okay?"

I nod absentmindedly, but I'm not really listening. I'm trying to think of something I can be that's big and strong enough to beat Silvermask. My leg shakes. My hands tremble. I can't do this. I'm not good enough. Everything I try gets messed up and I get hurt, or someone else gets hurt, and it's gonna be the same this time, I know it!

I'm waiting, he says in my mind. *But I won't wait forever. You have ten seconds to get on here and face me, or I start throwing your friends to the Malumbra.*

The fear-octopus swims circles around my head. I can't think. Can't breathe. I'm gonna screw everything up.

One . . .

When I was a little kid, I used to be so scared of the dark it would paralyze me. If I woke up in the middle of the night and had to pee, sometimes I'd wet the bed rather than risk getting up. Mostly Mrs. T took care of me in those days, but sometimes Nic would visit us when the *Orion* was in port. He'd keep a lamp lit for me, even if it kept him awake, and if I was scared he'd sit next to my bed and sing. Sometimes, when he thought I was asleep, he'd whisper that he was so glad they found me, and the world was brighter because I was in it.

Two . . .

The fears and hopes and dreams tumbling around in my head all click into place. I'll never screw up. Not in the eyes of the people who matter most, like Nic and Mrs. T and my parents—wherever they are. I'll never be like Alan Salawag. Other people love me for who I am and what I've already done, and I love them back, and nothing will ever change that.

Three . . .

I can do this. I look across the room, where Aaron's slumped against the wall, staring blankly at his feet. His lion didn't work in the end. Couldn't beat that huge spider.

Four . . .

What eats a spider? What in the world could take on a spider the size of a house?

Five . . .

Centipedes eat spiders, but I don't think I could be a centipede. Spiders eat other spiders, but I definitely couldn't be a spider.

Six . . .

Tam shifts his weight, and his pocket bumps into mine. My locator chirps. And then I've got it.

I close my eyes and reach for the Panpathia.

It's like shaking the hand of a corpse. The web's dead, covered in that sticky purple stuff the Malumbra makes. I look for the little glowing dots that should be my friends and I can sort of see them, but everything's drowned out by the presence of two enormous wrongs.

First, there's the Malumbra. Silvermask called it glorious, but that's not what it looks like to me. All I see is the inside of a mouth, enormous dark ridges and huge black teeth the size of the statues of Far Agondy's city founders in the center of town. That mouth is frozen now, not closing anymore, but I can see down its throat and there's nothing there. Not darkness, not shadow, just a vast and stomach-wrenching void, like a hole ripped in the world.

Second, on one of the cold, dark lines he's poisoned, there's Silvermask.

You ever see a big spider unfurl its legs? Like it's sleeping or something and you can see it's pretty big, and then you spook it or a fly lands on its web, and all those legs uncurl and spread out and suddenly it's five times the size it was before?

Imagine that happening with a spider whose body is as big as a city block, and you should have a pretty good idea of what Silvermask does when I get on the Panpathia.

For a second, I lose my confidence. My heart skips. He's so huge, so powerful. There's nothing in the world that could beat a spider that size. Nothing.

Except, I tell myself, *a bird the size of the* Orion.

Because birds eat spiders, and the *Orion*'s the sturdiest thing I know. If I have to bet my life on anything, I'm betting it on her.

I wrap myself in the Panpathia's light and fire and let my mind become a huge bird, with wings the size of cloud balloons, a tail like a waterfall, and claws as big as the launches in Far Agondy's harbor. The Panpathia shrinks as I get bigger. Silvermask shrinks too. He doesn't get as small as I'd like, but that's okay, because I can fly, and he's just a spider. I flap my wings and take off, up away from his web, and then I float there, watching him.

Inspired, he hisses. *Truly. But ultimately a poor choice. On some islands, spiders eat birds too, Nadya Skylung.*

I glare at him, flapping wings of brilliant flame.

Not this one, I say, and I dive toward him like a hawk. He has to scramble out of the way, and still I swipe a chunk out of his leg with a talon. Birds are *fast,* when they need to be.

But so are spiders. All of sudden there's a leg whipping toward me and I have to take off again, and then the duel is really on, and I'm flying and scrambling and slashing and biting, and he's jumping back and forth, leaping between

281

strands of web, trying to get above me or trick me into flying in front of his two huge fangs, glistening with venom.

Round and round we swirl. I bite his back. He scrapes my wing. I scratch his face. He bruises my leg. Every time I hit him, a little of the Malumbra's shadow bleeds away. Every time he hits me, the fire cools and the light dims. At first I think we're evenly matched, but the hits I'm landing on him don't seem to make much difference, and all the bruises and whacks and scrapes really add up for me. I start to worry whether I can beat him.

Free us, someone whispers.

I'm pinwheeling around, trying to avoid two strands of web and get to his abdomen, and it takes me a second to realize someone's talking to me. *What?* I ask.

Over here . . . free us . . .

Listening to the voice distracts me, and Silvermask almost pins my wing with two of his legs. I have to push really hard to tear free from him and flap away. But when I do, I spot what the voice was talking about.

On the beds, where the children are, there are other shapes in the darkness.

I see a bear three times the size of the largest grizzly I've ever heard of. I see a shark with a head so huge it could swallow a good-sized anchor. I see a cobra and an eagle and a crocodile and a tiger.

And brighter than all of them, at the edge of the beds, I see a lion.

They're cocooned, wrapped up in the same sticky purple stuff that's all over the web. It muffles their glow and keeps them from moving. They must be the cloudling kids from Aaron's town, able to do the same thing he can. And that lion must be Aaron.

Silvermask jumps onto another strand of the web. He's scrambling real fast now, coming straight toward me, and the kids are under him. Getting there would take me right below his belly. If I'm not fast enough, he'll jump on my back and pin me. It seems like a big risk.

But I'm tiring out. My wings aren't so big anymore. My

fire's not as bright, and my mind's starting to feel cold. If I don't do this now, I might not get another chance.

So I tuck my wings and dive as fast as I can. No time to hesitate. No time to think. Just fly, like Butterbeak protecting her chicks or Wormgobbler hunting for food or Bluebelly when she's happy in the morning and stretching out her wings. Fly like the *Orion*. Fly like the Flightwing. Fly like Rash.

Fly like me.

I beat my wings hard and sail in an arc along that line of kids, breathing fire into my talons and slicing through the cocoons that bind them. Too late, Silvermask sees what I'm doing. He shrieks and drops toward me, but by then I've finished my arc and I'm pounding my wings again, trying to get out from under him.

It doesn't work. His spider shape crashes into my bird shape, and my head reels. The Panpathia snaps in and out of focus. For a second I'm looking at Silvermask with two sets of eyes, one staring up at an enormous spider's fangs and the other watching a man crow triumphantly.

There's a roar.

And a growl, and a snap.

I refocus on being the bird, and all those kids come to help me, piling into Silvermask and pushing his enormous body off mine before he can bite me or poison me or wrap me up or whatever he was going to do. Aaron sinks his lion fangs into one of the spider's legs and tries to wrench it off. The shark grabs another leg, and the bear charges and the cobra strikes.

Silvermask squeals. Shadows spill off him like water, and he shrinks and shrinks.

"Thom!" I call out, "we've got him!"

And as my awareness shifts off the Panpathia, I hear Thom mumbling and grunting in the language he and Pepper use when they're calling fire, and then there's a sudden, painful burst of light.

CHAPTER 24

IN WHICH A VICTORY IS WON, AND A FRIEND IS LOST.

I leave the Panpathia and look at the real world. The light's coming from Thom, shining out of his eyes and glowing beneath his skin like he's a giant lantern. The floor rumbles ominously, and the Shadowmen holding him let go as an arm of fire the size of a subway car bursts through it. The shadows shrink. Silvermask howls. The flame grows until it's as bright as the sun. I hold my hand over my face and shut my eyes, and there's a rush of heat. Silvermask screams again. The Shadowmen echo him all over the mansion.

The heat fades from instant sunburn to comfortably warm. The light dims from staring-at-the-sun to the-sun-just-came-up. I open my eyes.

The tongue of fire has dimmed. It's just dancing and flickering under the ceiling, like the flames that heat the boilers in Gossner's workshop. And Thom's still glowing.

His eyes are bright white, like the hottest part of a fire, and his whole body swirls with orange light. When he opens his mouth to breathe, fire licks the edges of his lips. He mumbles something in the fire-spirit language, and the flame leans forward and touches Silvermask, who's huddled on the floor, shaking. For a second he glows like Thom, and then the light dims and he goes limp.

Thom looks back at us, takes a deep breath, and blows a cloud of light and sparks our way. As it hits the Malumbra's teeth, they burn up like dry paper. I can feel the Malumbra retreating, opening its mouth and jerking back just like you would if something in your mouth caught fire.

The sparks pop and fizz, but they don't hurt. Being touched by them's sort of like being wrapped in a big warm blanket. The Shadowmen holding Pep and Tam groan and collapse, unconscious, and that wave of sparks and light continues through the rest of the mansion.

"What is this?" I ask.

Thom smiles. "This is the spirit that lives under the city. It's the biggest, baddest thing from the World Beyond, and it *hates* the Malumbra."

Pepper's jaw drops. "How'd you get it to talk to you? You said it doesn't talk to anybody these days."

Thom walks to the gormling's tank and touches it. The shadow burns off, and in a second the gormling's glowing like it used to, floating sleepily toward the bottom of the tank. "Gossner had a book that pointed me in the right direction." He returns to the flame. "I just needed the right thing to talk about, and the Malumbra was that thing."

"What'd you promise it?" Pepper frowns. "What's the contract?"

Thom doesn't answer right away. He squats next to Silvermask, putting a hand on his neck. "Alan's still alive," he says softly. "I want to believe he's not as bad as he made himself out to be. We were friends, once."

"Thom," Pepper says, "what'd you promise?"

Thom stands up. "Turns out I'm leaving the ship after all. I'm going to the World Beyond to study with the fire spirits. I want to learn how to beat the Malumbra for good, and they want to teach me."

My stomach churns. I look at that fire burning under Thom's skin, and I have a horrible feeling. Tam must be thinking the same thing, because he looks like somebody just whacked him in the head with a wrench.

"What's it burning?" I ask.

Thom looks down at his hand. "Me," he says. "My lifespan. But there should be enough of that to last a few minutes without costing me much."

Pep's eyes swim. "How long will you be gone?"

Thom shrugs. "I don't know. Could be six years, could be sixty. The fire spirits don't really reckon time in the same way we do."

"Sixty years?" I swallow a lump and try to wrap my head around that. "We'll be ancient."

Thom laughs. "And I'll be the young one. Humans don't age in the World Beyond. Won't that be a change?" He ruffles my hair, then gestures for us to come in for a hug. He's all fire and warmth, strong and bright. He squeezes us gently. "You three, and Salyeh and Tian Li, make an amazing team," he says softly. "Do me a favor and stick together, all right? It's easy for a crew to drift apart. I don't want it to happen to you."

I swallow, trying to think of something I can do to stop this. It's my fault. Thom was protecting me, again. If I'd just listened . . .

Tam sobs, pressed up against Thom's chest next to me. "Don't go," he whispers. "Thom, I'm not ready."

"We're never ready till we have to be," Thom says. He pulls out of the hug and looks Tam in the eyes. "There's no machine on the *Orion* you can't handle. You know that, right?"

Tam trembles. "Yeah, but what if there's a problem I've never seen, and I don't know what to do about it? Who do I ask? Where do I get help?"

"You won't need it," Thom says. "I promise." He turns to Pepper. "That goes for you and your fireminding too."

Pep shakes her head. "I can't handle the big ones," she cries. "Not alone. They still hate me. Thom, we won't even get out of port!"

"You'll find a way," Thom says. He puts a hand on her shoulder. "You're so much stronger than you realize, Pepper. They know your name in the World Beyond already."

Pepper sniffs and hugs herself, still shaking her head.

"And you, Nadya," Thom says. He puts his hand on my shoulder. "You keep learning, okay? You listen to Nic, listen to Raj. You have so much potential. I . . ." He quiets. The flame from the fire spirit brightens, then fades. Thom's face falls. "Darn. I thought we'd have more time."

My stomach flips again. Pepper flinches. Tam looks around in panic.

"The deal was that the spirit and I would stay here until you were safe," Thom says.

"We're not!" all three of us say at the same time.

"There could be more Shadowmen!" Tam shouts.

"We don't know how to get home!" Pepper says.

"We still need you!" I finish.

Thom shakes his head. "Listen."

I hear sirens, far away but getting closer.

"That's good enough for the spirit," he says. He holds his hands up and smiles sadly. "And I'm not in a position to argue." He pulls us in close again. "Remember what I told you. Be brave. Stick together. Whatever life throws at you, you can handle it, as long as you stay a team."

He squeezes us again. I close my eyes. I don't want him to go. He's one of us.

His skin gets warmer.

And then I'm just hugging air, and Pepper cries. Tam flops down and stares at the floor where Thom used to be, because he's gone, along with that enormous tongue of flame, and there's nothing left but the lingering warmth of his touch and our memories.

The police get there a few minutes later. We meet them at the gate of the mansion, tearstained and bruised and exhausted.

Aaron and the other kids were all asleep, just like Silvermask and the Shadowmen, so we left them inside on their beds. Whatever Thom burned out of them, it must've made them pretty tired.

I'm tired too. My head aches like I worked a whole day in the sun with no water, my mouth's dry, and my eyes sting. My crutches were all blackened and twisted after being touched by the shadow and Thom's fire, so I left them in the mansion. I'm leaning on Tam instead. He makes a pretty decent crutch, in a pinch.

Outside the fence, we see bright headlights. There's gotta be a dozen cars and vans out there. Two men in police uniforms are cutting the chains that hold the gate closed.

"Hey!" one of them shouts. "You kids! C'mere!"

I look at Pep and Tam. Tam shrugs. Pep still seems so distraught over losing Thom that she's hardly paying attention. We limp over to the policemen just as they get the gate unlocked.

"What're you doing in there?" one of them says. "Were you kidnapped?"

"Nadya!" someone shouts from the vans, and two silhouettes run toward us in the headlights. I recognize one as Salyeh's and the other as Tian Li's. "Tam! Pep!"

The policeman rolls his eyes. "Unbelievable," he grunts. "You two know these kids?"

"Detective," says a third person flatly. "Leave them here for now. Just get in there and find me Silvermask."

The policeman looks at someone in the bright lights where Tian Li and Salyeh came from, then clears his throat. "Yes, ma'am, Lord Mayor."

He whistles, and a bunch more policemen trot into the yard and start forming up.

I look into the Lord Mayor's face. She's got a grim stare and her hair pulled back in a ponytail, and she's chewing on something. It takes me a second to figure out it's gum.

"Silvermask's in the ballroom in the left wing of the house," I tell her. "He was unconscious when we left."

The Lord Mayor nods, without taking her eyes off the policemen now charging into the house with pistols drawn and flashlights out. "They'll find him. These cops are the best." She chews for a few seconds. "You kids . . . I look forward to hearing your story, but not now. We still have work to do, and you look exhausted."

She gestures toward the back of one of the police vans, where there's benches we can sit on. I blink in the light as Salyeh and Tian Li lead us that direction. I've got so many questions to ask, but I can't get them all straight.

Tam beats me to it. "How in the world did you guys get the police to come?"

Tian Li slips under my arm so I can lean on her and Tam doesn't have to take my weight anymore. "It was Sal, mostly. He spent all day and all night digging through correspondence and records in Nic's office, and eventually he found out who that flyer came from."

Sal looks pretty proud of himself. "It was the Lord Secretary's handwriting. The address was on the same street as a cafe in the Forge he wanted to meet Nic at one time, and the way he formed the letters matched up perfectly. I showed it to Nic, and he took us to one of the detectives he'd been working with, and she called up the Lord Mayor's office, and half an hour later we were all on our way here to bust down Silvermask's door."

"Where's Nic now?" I ask.

Tian Li adjusts my arm on her neck. "On his way to Gossner's to tell you guys what was happening. What are you doing here, anyway?"

"I sorta took things into my own hands," I mumble. "Pep and Tam came along to help."

"And we lost Thom," Pep says, throwing her arms up and glaring at me. She kicks the ground. "Nadya, we coulda just *waited*! You *always* do this! And now Thom's got sixty years in the World Beyond!"

Sal's jaw drops. Tian Li coughs. "What?" they ask in unison.

My gills burn. "I . . . I thought . . ."

"It might not be that long," Tam says softly, "and I think it had to be this way." He points at the mansion, where the police are moving through in teams. We can see their lights in the darkened windows, hear them call out from time to time. "How bad do you think this would've gotten if the police had come in here without Thom taking out Silvermask and his gang first? How many people woulda got hurt, or died?" A thick stew of emotions passes over his face—fear,

294

pride, sadness, and a whole lot else I can't quite catch. "Maybe Silvermask woulda won. He definitely woulda gotten away. I think maybe Thom was planning this all along."

Pep takes deep breaths. She looks at Tam. She looks at me. And then she stomps off. She walks right past the police van we were headed toward and picks a different one to sit in, then puts her feet up on the bench across from her and stares at the wall.

I want to go after her, but I'm so tired I can't see straight. And so's she.

So instead I climb into the other van with everyone's help and stretch out on one of the benches. We're long past due for some rest.

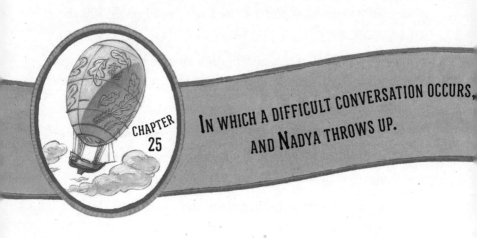

CHAPTER 25

IN WHICH A DIFFICULT CONVERSATION OCCURS, AND NADYA THROWS UP.

I don't get to talk to Pepper till the next day.

The rest of the night's too hectic. The police come out with all the kids, who are starting to wake up scared and groggy, and we help Aaron get them settled down. They seem to trust me pretty well, since I freed them from Silvermask. Aaron finds his sister, and sure enough she's the girl I saw on the Panpathia all those weeks ago out on the Cloud Sea. In all the hubbub of kids wailing and adults trying to calm them down and corral them into the vans, he flies to her like a rocket. The two of them don't leave each other the whole rest of the night. Not at the police station where serious officers write down our stories one by one. Not on the trip back to the *Orion* over the bay on a police launch. Not on the long lift ride up the spire to our docking slip. And not once we're back on the ship, trudging off to bed as dawn turns the sky gray. Sal sleeps on the floor in Tam's room and lets the two of them have his.

I nab a little sleep, but it's not very good. I keep remembering that fight with Silvermask on the Panpathia, and Thom with the fire spirit of Far Agondy burning him up from the inside. I wake up pretty often. The fourth time I open my eyes, the mid-morning sun's creeping across the *Orion*'s deck and I figure it's not worth trying to get back to sleep again.

So I pick up my old crutch, the same one I used right after my leg got hurt, and head for Pepper's cabin.

I hesitate outside her door. I don't want to wake her up if she's sleeping. But she's probably not. She was more upset than any of us last night. Gently, I knock.

For a few seconds, there's no response, and I figure she's still asleep. I'm about to head for the galley to make breakfast when her floorboards creak. A second later, the door opens.

Pep looks like she's been up all night. Her eyes are puffy, her hair's a rat's nest, and her cheeks are red. She stares at me blankly, then sighs, "Come in."

She closes the door behind me, then slumps toward her bed and waves at the chair by her desk. Her room's still pretty dim, and the morning air is cool and damp. The sun won't hit her side of the *Orion* for a while yet.

I sit in her chair and lean my crutch against her desk. My stomach churns and swirls, and my arms tingle. I've had all night to think about what I'm gonna say, but I'm still not sure it's right. "I'm sorry, Pep," I say. "For everything. I'm sorry for Tam and I'm sorry for Thom and I'm sorry for being a jerk." My eyes tear up. My jaw aches. "I wish I was a better friend," I whisper.

There's silence. A long silence. The tears break free and run down my face. I was so sure she was gonna forgive me.

But she doesn't.

"Yeah, well . . . ," Pepper says. "Me too."

I look up. Her eyes are bloodshot. Her chin quivers. She's holding her arms so hard her fingers are going white.

"Why are we fighting like this?" I ask. It shouldn't be this way. Not between us.

Pep looks at her feet, then up at the net full of stuffed animals on her ceiling. "It didn't used to bother me that everybody thought you were so great. I did too." Did. I feel like puking. "But, Nadya, you're taking everything I want. Tam. Thom. What would you do if I told you *I* wanted to be captain?"

I blink. "You were gonna be the engineer . . ." On the ship we'd run together someday, I mean. The one we've always dreamed about.

Pep snorts. "Well, maybe I don't wanna be anymore. You move so fast, you talk about everything, you think about everything, and you act before I even get a chance to open my mouth. Everybody just stares right past me at you, and then you do stupid stuff and people get hurt, but nobody cares. They just go, 'Oh, poor Nadya,' and help you out and then you do the same thing over and over again!"

I look down at my leg. "That's not true," I say automatically. "They . . . I mean . . ." But the more I think about it, the more I think maybe it *is* true. I do think and act fast, and people have gotten hurt because of me. Thom's gone, and that feels like a boot stomp to the stomach. My head spins.

"I'll be better," I say miserably.

Silence again. Pep sits on her bed and starts to cry. I look up, and she's got her head in her hands.

"Pep . . ."

"Just go," she says. "I want to be alone."

"Pep, I—"

"Go!" she screams. "Why don't you ever *listen*?" She picks up a shoe and throws it at the wall above my head.

My fingers shake. My leg shakes. But I get up and crutch my way out, because what else am I going to do? I have to lean against the wall in the hallway to pull her door shut. I feel like I might throw up any second, so I slide to the floor and sit there, shivering, my hands and foot cold, my missing leg aching, thinking about everything Pepper said. I wonder if it's true, whether I'm really that bad a friend, that bad a crewmate, that bad at everything. And as my head goes farther and farther down that path, my stomach finally does lose it, and I barf all over the hallway.

I'm still sitting there, waiting for my head to stop spinning long enough to crutch into the galley for a mop and some rags, when I hear footsteps. My gills burn, and I look up.

Alé's standing next to me, hands on her hips. She looks a lot less surprised than I'd be if our situations were reversed. "Hey," she says. "Need a hand?"

Shakily, I nod. She helps me into the galley and sits me down on one of the benches. "This is the kitchen, right?" she asks, nodding at the door that leads there.

"Yeah," I mumble.

She limps in—I guess she's off crutches now—and comes back a second later with a wet cloth for my face. "I'm making tea," she says decisively. "What kind you like?"

"Chamomile," I mumble. Alé disappears into the galley, and a second later I hear the kettle heating up. She takes a bucket and some rags into the hallway and spends a few minutes there while I try to make my hands stop shaking. We don't talk again until she plunks two cups of tea down in front of me. Hers smells like chai.

"Fighting with your best friend?" she asks.

I nod.

"I figured," she says. "Her window was open. We could hear you guys as we came on the ship."

My gills burn even hotter, and I thump my forehead against the table. "Who's 'we'?"

"Me, Gossner, Rash, and Raj. Raj is here for help from Aaron and his sister, and the Goss brought your prosthesis. It's finished."

I stare at my tea, blinking. I should be excited about that. Raj is going to be okay. The prosthesis means walking again, maybe running.

But all I can think about is the look on Pepper's face when she was screaming at me to get out, and her talking about how people get hurt because of me.

Alé nudges my tea toward me. "Drink," she says. "You're not gonna feel any better just staring at it."

I do like she says. It's warm and sweet. It reminds me of Mrs. T, but she's gone too, just like Thom, and it's all I can do to hold my heart together because it feels like everything's cracking in half right now.

Alé takes a deep breath. "Look," she says. "I don't know you that well. I don't know your crew that well either. But the Goss told us some things about Thom, and I don't think you should be beating yourself up like this."

I look up. Alé stares at me across her tea, sipping it slowly.

"You're not giving him any credit. You're not giving Tam any credit. And you're not giving anybody else any credit either."

I thump my skull on the table again. "That's what Pep was accusing me of," I mutter.

Alé shakes her head. "No, it's not. She's not giving them any credit either. Look," she says. "How do you think Thom knew what to do in that mansion? How'd he know he needed to summon that particular fire creature in order to beat Silvermask?"

I never really thought about that.

"Because he'd been *preparing* for it. Because he knew he might have to and he thought it was the right thing to do. He and the Goss spent hours reading through her library, trying to find information on the Malumbra and how to beat it." She leans back. "He didn't do that because he wanted no part of fighting Silvermask. He did it because he wanted to be ready. You ask me, he did it because he wanted to be the hero. When he left the Goss's tower last night, he didn't look surprised, didn't look upset. She was with Rash and me, asking what was going on, and he just came in and said, 'They're gone.

301

I'm ready. I'm going,' like they'd discussed the whole thing already."

I wipe some tears from my eyes. That sounds like Thom, I guess. Maybe that's what he was doing when I saw him staring at the boilers. Getting ready. "I never thought about him wanting to be a hero," I mumble. "I never thought about him wanting anything. He was just . . . a grown-up, you know?"

Alé nods. "Believe me, I know. I made the same mistake about the Goss once, and she gave me a lecture that just about burned my hair off. So lemme tell you something: Grown-ups have dreams. They want things. And mostly when they do something it's because of what *they* want, not because of what *we* do."

I think of Thom as he hugged us all and got ready to head to the World Beyond. Maybe he does have dreams I don't know about. Maybe he's making some of them come true.

"As for Tam," Alé says, and I want to crawl under the table and hide because I really don't want to think about Pep liking Tam and Tam only paying attention to me, and I still feel terrible about that hug at Gossner's tower. "Tam's gonna like who he likes, or not. He's his own boss. And if Pepper really wants his attention, she should be talking to him, not to you."

"It's not that easy," I say. "She—"

Alé waves me off. "I know it's not easy. You think with all those kids crammed together at the Goss's we don't have fights over who likes who? It happens all the time, and the Goss has some strict rules about it to keep things from get-

302

ting out of hand." She counts down on her fingers. "Rule number one: If you like somebody, you talk to *that person* about it, not to their friends or your friends or the person you think they like or whatever. Rule two's that everybody gets to make up their own mind about who they like, no begging or arguing or manipulating. Rule three's not really a rule, but it's still important. The Goss says crushes come and go, but the best friendships last forever." She pauses, then shrugs. "The rest of the rules are all just, like, logistics and who sleeps where and stuff."

I was kinda wondering about that. "So," I say delicately. "Are you and Rash . . . ?"

Alé snorts. "Ha! Not even. He's not into anybody and I like girls. We're just best friends, like I said before."

"Oh," I mumble, and my gills burn again. I'm not exactly at my sharpest lately.

Alé slurps down her tea, then listens to someone stomping around above our heads. "And that's it for your pep talk." She grins, then rolls her eyes. "Get it? 'Pep talk'?" She shakes her head and offers me her arm. "The Goss is probably done talking with Nic by now, so let's go get your prosthesis, okay?"

CHAPTER 26

IN WHICH NADYA GETS A PROSTHETIC LEG, AND A RECONCILIATION OCCURS.

A few minutes later, Alé leads me into Nic's cabin. It looks a little different than usual—the table and most of its chairs have been pushed against the couch by the windows, so there's a big open space in the middle. Gossner, Nic, Tam, and Rash are there. They've set up two metal bars at waist height with a little path between them and a chair at one end.

"Is that for me?" I ask.

"Yes," Gossner says. "Are you ready?"

I nod, but I also swallow. I still feel queasy after what happened with Pep, and I'm kinda nervous about trying out my prosthetic leg. I'm just getting used to my crutches, and now I'm gonna have to learn something completely new. I know eventually it'll let me do a lot of my favorite things again, but now that the moment to start using it's here, I'm having second thoughts.

Gossner clears her throat. "How much or how little you

use the prosthesis is completely up to you, Nadya," she says. "In fact, I'd suggest taking it slow for a while. Just an hour at a time, maybe less if you feel uncomfortable or sore." Slowly, she takes the prosthesis out of a bag at her feet.

My heart thumps. The leg is still stainless steel and iron, a big cylinder for my residual limb up top with a rod leaving it and going down to that ankle mechanism of springs and hinges, then a little scoop for a foot. I can't really tell what Gossner changed—the length, something in the ankle maybe?—except for a molded piece of plasticose that she fits around the scoop so it looks even more like a foot. "For socks and shoes," she explains, "in case you want them."

Once it's all together, she beckons me over to the chair at the end of the metal bars. "Here," she says. "Sit down and get to know it for a few minutes."

I crutch over and sit, my heart fluttering. Rash, Tam, and Alé beam at me though, and their enthusiasm's kinda catching. I turn the leg in my hands, feel its weight, check out all the springs and gears in the ankle.

"Push on the foot," Gossner suggests. "Watch it flex. See how it moves."

I wiggle the foot around a little, watch the mechanism. I don't think just looking at it's gonna help me that much, but it does make it feel more real.

When I'm done with the foot, Gossner walks over. "Ready to put it on?" she asks, and I nod.

Again, she shows me how to roll the sleeve on, fit the metal leg to my residual limb, and use the little valve to let air out. It feels really good today—I dunno if she just got the measurements that much better or whether my leg's healed up or is just the right size at this moment or maybe all three, but it's real comfortable, like putting on a perfectly broken-in shoe.

"Ready to stand?" Gossner asks. I nod, and she beckons to Tam and Alé, who stand on either side of me and hold my hands. Slowly I get up and let the leg take my weight.

Gossner steps away. "How's it feel?"

"Good," I say. It's not like having my old leg back, but it is like having the world's best crutch—one made just for me, that takes my weight exactly where I need it. Just being able to use the muscles in my thigh and back and knee to hold my weight again brings up a whole flood of memories I'd forgotten—of running, of jumping, of climbing. I grin.

"Start off by grabbing the bars," Gossner says, "and just rock back and forth on the foot."

I spend the next hour practicing walking. It takes a little bit of doing, and Gossner stops and adjusts the length of the sleeve and the gears and springs in the ankle. I feel like a bird who's just gotten out of the nest. I can imagine my whole life opening up, all the stuff I needed so much help to do after losing my leg getting easier again. The world's not built for people with crutches, although now that I've spent so long

on them I think maybe it should be. But it is built for people with legs, and while this thing's not quite the same as my old leg, it's close enough that it's gonna make a lot of stuff a whole lot more convenient.

Just before she goes, Gossner shows me a little lever on the ankle. "This," she says, "is for running. It changes the way the ankle mechanism works. With the lever up, like it is now, it's set for walking. If you try to run, you'll probably fall, because the ankle won't flex right. Flick it down"—she demonstrates—"and you'll be able to run, but walking will feel very awkward." She puts it back in the walking position. "Don't try running anytime soon. You've got to master walking first."

She turns to Nic. "You catch all that?"

"I did, yes," he says. He's been watching the operation like a hawk.

"And you'll be in port for a while?"

He frowns, and I notice for the first time how worried he looks. As bad as Pep did, or worse. His hair's ruffled and unkempt. His jacket's stained. His shirt's untucked. "Yes. We have to ensure Captain Varma's recovery, plus we need a new set of officers." He lowers his head. "I don't know how we'll go on without Thom."

The mood in his cabin changes instantly, like somebody sucked all the warmth out. My skin pricks up in goose bumps. *Still my fault,* I think, no matter what Alé said.

"You'll find good people," Gossner says. "This is a big port, and your name's like gold here. Give it a few weeks, and chin up. Thom got almost a hundred kids back to their parents, and got the rest into better care. Nobody here's gonna forget this, Nic. Not for a long time. And Thom'll be back someday to hear how his own legend's changed. I think he'll like that."

Nic nods, but he doesn't look any happier. "I suppose you're right, Machinist Gossner. Thank you." He shakes her hand as she walks toward the door. "If you ever need anything . . ."

Gossner laughs on her way out. "Oh, I'll call, that's for sure. Rash, Alé, let's head home. We've got a better tank to build for that gormling."

Rash waves goodbye and heads out with Gossner, but Alé hangs back. She claps me on the shoulder and grins. "Thanks for a heck of an adventure, Nadya. I hope I see you again real soon."

I smile. "Me too. You're a lifesaver, Alé. Literally. I owe you big."

Alé tugs her cuffs. "Guess you do, huh? I'll have to think of a good favor you can do me." She flips me a two-finger salute and runs off, and I grin as she bowls into Rash and he pulls her jacket over her head and sticks his tongue out at her.

I nap through the afternoon, then spend a little while before dinner walking around the deck, getting used to my prosthesis. As I'm doing it, Nic brings Raj up from below with Aaron and his sister. I bet they're coming from the infirmary, and I wobble over to them. "Well?" I ask. "Did it work?"

Raj looks like he's just recovered from the flu. "I think so. I can't feel the shadow anymore."

I throw my arms around his waist and hug him. "Thank you," I mutter into his shirt. "I'm so sorry all this happened."

Raj pats my shoulder gently. "Thank *you*, Nadya," he says. "For saving me. And for stopping Silvermask."

I pull back and nearly lose my balance, but Raj catches me. "Why do you think he was doing it?" I ask. "Kidnapping kids, I mean."

Raj tugs at his beard. "My best guess is that he was hoping to weaken resistance to the Malumbra by making people fear one another. Everyone wants to help a child in trouble. It's one of the deepest caring instincts in the human heart. But if you can get someone to ignore that instinct—perhaps because they're afraid a child might pass the Malumbra's shadow to them—then you can crush the heart right out of them. And without heart the world will divide and fall." He coughs. "I can't be sure, of course, because the plan never progressed that far. But perhaps we can ask Mr. Salawag once he recovers."

"Nadya," Nic says gently, "I think it's time we let Captain Varma return to his ship. He's been through a lot."

My gills burn a little, but Raj smiles at me as he turns to go and I don't feel so bad. He and Nic head up the gangplank, and I watch them, enjoying the cool seawater breeze on my neck as the sun goes down.

"H-h-hey, Nadya," Aaron says sheepishly behind me. I turn around. He's standing next to his sister, who nudges him forward. His hug hits me so hard it nearly knocks me over. "Th-th-thank you," he says. "For everyth-thing."

I squeeze him back, feeling warmer than I have since Pep

laid into me this morning. I still wish Thom hadn't gone away and we'd done things different somehow. But when I think about all those kids free, I feel a whole lot better.

Aaron's sister follows him. Her cheeks have little divots in them, like from acne, and she tucks her hair behind her ears before she speaks. She doesn't look much like Aaron, but I think I've figured that out. One of them must've been adopted. People don't have to be born to the same parents to be a family.

"My name's Jaya," she says. "I wanted to say thanks too. For taking care of my little brother." She hugs him around the shoulders. "I thought I'd lost everybody when the Shadow-men came, but now at least I've got him back."

I swallow. "Glad I could help. It's tough to lose your parents."

She frowns, and then her eyes soften. "Yeah," she says. "It is." We stand there a little longer, and it hits me just how much *she's* been through, and how lucky I am to have the *Orion* and everyone on it.

Then the irresistible scent of dinner hits us, and Aaron runs toward the stairs, pulling his sister behind him and telling her how great the food we make is. All I can do is smile and follow.

We all dine together. Sal and Tian Li have made a spicy yellow curry and bean curd dish, along with Nic's rice pudding and a spinach-and-cheese thing that I go back for seconds and thirds of because it's so good. Everybody's in a great mood except for Pepper, who excuses herself as soon as she finishes

311

her plate, and Nic, who still looks upset over losing Thom. Sal and Tian Li tell Aaron and his sister how they cracked the mystery and brought the police to Silvermask's mansion. Tam doesn't speak much, but he keeps staring out the window and crossing his arms over his chest, like he's got big things on his mind.

I snarf down sweetened rice pudding and make a plan to get my best friend back.

I've been thinking about what Alé said, and after the meal's over and I've helped with dishes, I head to Pepper's room. I take the prosthesis, because the Lady's feeling pretty good and I'm excited to test it out. The stairs are a challenge, and I have to go real slow and hold the rail and the wall, but I don't mind. It feels great to be learning how to do all this.

Lamplight shines under the bottom of Pep's door, and I knock in our old *rap-a-tap-tap-tap-rap* pattern.

"Yeah?" Pep says.

My heart races. I'm scared of having her blow up at me again, but I want to take one more stab at this. Our friendship's worth it. "Can we talk again?" I ask.

Pep's quiet for a few seconds. Her chair scrapes, and then she lets me in. "Sure," she says, crossing her arms and closing the door behind me. "Congratulations on your leg, by the way."

It sounds like she means it. "Thanks," I say, and I launch straight into what I came here to do. "Look, I'm sorry."

She sighs. "I know, Nadya."

"Really, I am," I continue. "I've been thinking a lot about what you said, and I'll try to stay off your toes." I swallow. "I *care* about you, Pep. You're my best friend, even when you don't like me anymore, and I'm gonna start acting like it again. I'm gonna ask how you're doing, ask what you wanna do, let you take the lead on things. I'm gonna listen when you disagree with me, and—"

Pep walks away, and I can't keep going. I can't breathe. This was all I had. If she never forgives me, I don't know what I'll do. I can't just not be friends with her. It would leave a hole in my heart the size of a leviathan.

Pep sniffs. She wraps her arms around herself and squeezes. "I'm sorry too, Nadya," she says. "I . . . I . . ."

But she's sobbing too hard to finish. She just walks over and hugs me. For a whole minute we stand there, crying. I smile, and she smiles, and then we both start sobbing again, and eventually we end up sitting next to each other on her bed, holding hands. "I shouldn't have yelled at you like that this morning," Pep says. "I'm scared, Nadya. I never wanted to be in a fight against the Malumbra. I never wanted to lose anybody to pirates. I thought we'd spend our whole lives running around the Cloud Sea having fun. I think I've been blaming you for everything that's happened lately, even the things that weren't your fault." She looks at her feet. "I still want to be your best friend. I miss you."

I sniffle again. "Me too," I say. "I—"

"I know I shoulda just kept talking to you until you understood what was wrong, but you kept cutting me off and it was driving me nuts and then you were always with Tam and people were ignoring me and I got in trouble and Aaron was missing and . . . ugh." Pep presses her fists against her temples and flops back on her bed. "Let's never do this again, okay?"

I laugh and wipe my eyes. "Okay."

Pep holds up her hand. "Swear it on a pinky?"

I grab her pinky with mine and shake. "Swear it on a pinky."

We sit there into the night, long after everyone else has gone to bed and the *Orion*'s quiet. We catch up and make new plans to co-captain our cloudship. I feel like a chain around my heart's been taken off. I've lost so much over the last couple months—Mrs. T, my leg, and now Thom. It would've been so hard if I lost Pepper too.

By the time I head up to my cabin, the Lady's real sore from having the prosthesis on for so long, but I think maybe I oughta make one more stop before bed.

Nic's light is on, and I knock on his door, real careful. A few seconds go by, and he opens it. "Something wrong, Nadya?"

He seems so scared. The lines on his face are tighter and deeper than I've ever seen them. His eyes are as red as Pepper's were this morning. He's bathed and dressed, but he's still so far from being all right again.

I pick up his hand and hum. I don't remember the words of the song he used to sing me, but I'll never forget the tune.

He stiffens, and I stop humming.

"You're how I beat Silvermask," I tell him.

His caterpillar eyebrows knit together.

"You used to tell me I made the world brighter," I explain. I press his hand against my forehead. "Thank you."

Nic coughs. When I look up again, he's crying. He pinches his eyes shut with the fingers of his free hand. It's shaking.

"You've still got us, Nic," I say. I lean into him. "And we still think you're great."

He crumples. He folds up like adults aren't supposed to, but I guess he really is a lot older than I thought, and maybe even adults aren't supposed to fight as long and as hard as he has. He sits down against the doorjamb and cries, and I put my arms around him. After a few seconds, I hear footsteps and feel Salyeh's arms over mine. He whistles, and a little later Tian Li joins us, then Tam, then Pep.

"Thank you," Nic says eventually, patting my arm, then everyone else's. "Thank you all." He wipes his eyes and stands up, and when he smiles, it looks real for the first time in days. "Now, please. Everybody get some sleep."

But I can't sleep. Instead, I climb into the catwalks around the *Orion*'s cloud balloon and hang there, just thinking, drumming my fingers on the metal and looking at the faded design on the fabric, listening on the Panpathia to the happy chatter of the plants and animals in the cloud garden. To my right, the electric lights of Far Agondy blink in the darkness. To my left, lightning flashes under a storm cloud out to sea. Beneath me, the *Orion*'s deck lamps glitter warmly. My best friends are down there, sleeping. So's Nic. The people I care most about in the world. My family.

I don't know what's coming next. Maybe we'll be off to a new port with new officers, doing the same old thing. Maybe we'll take the fight to the Malumbra and find out what happened to my parents. Maybe Thom and Mrs. T will be back in a few months, or maybe I won't see them till I'm an old lady.

But whatever happens, we'll handle it, together. I'm Nadya Skylung, and I keep the cloudship *Orion* afloat. I fought the Malumbra, defeated Silvermask, and broke up a kidnapping ring that spanned the Cloud Sea. I have the best friends in the whole world, and I'm still only twelve years old. My whole life's ahead of me.

I can't wait to live it.

ACKNOWLEDGMENTS

All the usual suspects helped make this book a reality. Cass contributed an astounding number of critical late-night sounding-board and brainstorming sessions. Oren gamely tolerated my near disappearance for days at a time when deadlines had to be met. The extended Seymour clan and all my friends and early readers were invaluable. Everyone who babysat, everyone who understood when a deadline slipped or a get-together was missed or I was buried in my office instead of spending time with you, thank you. This could not have happened without your forbearance. Thanks as well to Danielle, Katherine, and Stephanie for the editing; Marikka and Brett for the art and design; Anne for the copy editing; Lizzie for the PR wrangling; and the whole team at Putnam for all their support. Jeremy and Geoff were back for characterization help, aided this time by Alejandra and Silanur. Thank you all from the bottom of my heart.

But the real stars of the show are the many amputees whose kindness, openness, and direct or indirect assistance helped me do this book right. The YouTubers KarinaAmelia and AmputeeOT are astonishingly open and marvelously informative on their channels—if you want to know what it's like to lose a limb, you might want to watch their videos. The authors of a whole trove of blog posts, articles, books, and book reviews helped as well—you can find links to most of them on my website. Most importantly, author Kati Gardner rode shotgun on this whole journey for me, reviewing the manuscript, answering questions, sharing stories, and helping me be accurate. Where I've done well, it was with her help, and where I screwed up, the blame lies entirely with me.

Photo credit: Vanessa Isenbarger

Jeff Seymour is the author of *Nadya Skylung and the Cloudship Rescue*. In addition to writing speculative fiction, he works as a freelance editor. Jeff lives an unexpectedly hectic life with his wife, their son, and two energetic cats.

Visit him online at jeff-seymour.com.

Brett Helquist has illustrated many books for children, including the bestselling A Series of Unfortunate Events by Lemony Snicket. He lives with his family in Brooklyn, New York.

Learn more at bretthelquist.com.